PRAISE FOR CHRISTINE NOLFI

The Passing Storm

A WOMAN.COM MOST ANTICIPATED BOOKS OF FALL SELECTION

A POPSUGAR INCREDIBLE BOOKS OF NOVEMBER SELECTION

A WOMEN WRITERS WOMEN'S BOOKS FALL MUST-READS SELECTION

"Tautly plotted, expertly characterized, and genuinely riveting, Nolfi's emotional tour de force will capture readers' hearts."

—*Publishers Weekly*

"Nolfi has a gift for drawing out her character's secrets slowly, and crafts interesting depictions that feel real, complicated, flawed, and compelling."

—*Booklist*

"Nolfi dives deep into the well of human emotions as her characters fight to right their journeys after life's storms have blown them off course, showing us that sometimes the bravest thing of all is facing our own truth."

—Barbara Davis, bestselling author of *The Keeper of Happy Endings*

The Road She Left Behind

"At the very heart of *The Road She Left Behind* are the powerful lessons of humanity: forgiveness, healing, and letting go, all woven together with the threads that bind family and friends. You will laugh, you will cry, you will root these characters on and miss them profusely when they're gone. I know I do."

—Rochelle Weinstein, *USA Today* bestselling author

"Secrets have a way of seeping out, and when they do, they will shatter relationships or bring about healing. In *The Road She Left Behind*, Nolfi has penned a moving story of family, betrayal, and healing."

—Kay Bratt, bestselling author of *Wish Me Home*

Sweet Lake

"[This book] has such a charming small-town vibe and endearing characters that readers will find themselves falling in love with quirky Sweet Lake and hoping for a series."

—*Booklist*

"In this uplifting and charming story, each room of the inn is filled with friendship, forgiveness, and love."

—*Kirkus Reviews*

The Comfort of Secrets

GOLD MEDAL WINNER, READERS' FAVORITE AWARDS

"Welcome back to the Wayfair Inn, where discovering secrets and overcoming human frailty are the ingredients for finding love and happiness. Reading Nolfi's *The Comfort of Secrets* feels like coming home."

—Kay Bratt, bestselling author of *Wish Me Home*

The Season of Silver Linings

GOLD MEDAL WINNER, READERS' FAVORITE AWARDS

FINALIST, INTERNATIONAL BOOK AWARDS

"In *The Season of Silver Linings*, we see love on every page. Each novel in the Sweet Lake series offers a special experience for the reader, and the third book may be your favorite yet."

—Grace Greene, *USA Today* bestselling author

Second Chance Grill

The Tree of Everlasting Knowledge

A
BRIGHTER
FLAME

A BRIGHTER FLAME

A NOVEL

Christine Nolfi

LAKE UNION
PUBLISHING

Published by Lake Union Publishing, Seattle

www.apub.com

Amazon, the Amazon logo, and Lake Union Publishing are trademarks of Amazon.com, Inc., or its affiliates.

ISBN-13: 9781542038843
ISBN-10: 1542038847

Cover design by Caroline Teagle Johnson

Printed in the United States of America

For Barry, with love

Chapter 1

Vale awoke to the scream of sirens.

Two police cruisers sped by the apartment building, one after the other. The repeated blare of an air horn followed. A fire truck stopped somewhere nearby in Pittsburgh's strip district. Just down the street, Vale guessed, dragging her eyes open.

A dank odor spiked the air. Coughing, Vale lifted her head from the pillow. Dawn light streamed across the floor. Shaking off the remnants of sleep, she recalled last night's argument with her father. Lately it seemed they argued every Saturday night. Now the memory blended with the acrid scent filling her nose and the commotion down on the street. It took on the significance of a warning.

Vale scrambled from the bed. In some small part of her heart, she feared her greatest worry had come to pass. As if the scent of smoke, seeping into the apartment, signaled the folly of her dreams.

After dressing quickly, she rushed out the door. She raced down the staircase to the ground floor. A second fire truck rumbled past. The din of its air horns lifted Vale's shoulders to her ears.

Popular restaurants and bars lined the strip district. The vibrant assortment of nightlife rimmed the Allegheny River's sparkling waters. This early on a Sunday, the area was usually quiet. Today was frighteningly out of the ordinary. Heavy wisps of smoke curled through the air. Sleepy-eyed apartment dwellers stumbled out of buildings. They joined the worried business owners and their employees, most of whom were craning their necks at the fire trucks farther down the street. Vale did the same, looking past the sea of faces in an unsuccessful attempt to get a fix on the unfolding calamity.

Firefighters spilled onto the sidewalk. A heavyset woman in a baker's apron shouted encouragement. A young man with dreadlocks steered his open-mouthed girlfriend off the curb, away from the danger. Stepping around them, Vale approached the chaotic scene with her heart in her throat.

Another police cruiser flew past. It screeched to a halt behind fire trucks.

Vale's stomach lurched. She spotted a crowd gathering across the street from the bar she owned with her father.

Snapping and sparking, flames rippled across the northern end of the Crafty Cocktail's roofline. Tongues of fire raced down the side of the building. The blaze hadn't yet reached the adjacent buildings, an Indian restaurant and a French bakery. In a daze, Vale joined the crowd eyeing the smoke billowing from the one-story bar. A sob threatened to burst forth, and she covered her mouth. The conflagration's intense heat had shattered all the windows, including the signature stained-glass window she'd commissioned a local artist to create. The river of broken glass crunched underfoot as firefighters sprinted around the side of the building.

The fire captain appeared beside the second truck. Vale's heart pounded in her ears as she approached him.

"The bar is empty, isn't it?" she asked, desperate for confirmation.

"There's no one inside, ma'am."

"You're sure?"

"I am." She was about to inform him that she was one of the bar's owners when he glanced back toward the building. "Excuse me."

A female officer climbed out of the last cruiser. She eyed the growing crowd.

"Get back, everyone." She marched into the street. "You're too close."

Vale and most of the onlookers readily obeyed. They walked several storefronts down to congregate before Fresh Fix Smoothies.

A man with arms covered in tats ignored the order. He sauntered into the street with his smartphone held aloft to film the scene. As if the demise of Vale's hard work—all her dreams, gone to ash—were entertainment.

Vale withered the man with a look. Then she flinched as a torrent of water rocketed skyward. A team of firefighters appeared on the roof's southern end. They were barely visible behind the wall of smoke colliding with the fearsome torrent of water combating the flames.

We'll lose everything. She watched, transfixed. *There won't be anything left but a hollow shell.*

The prospect sent a kaleidoscope of images shuttling through her. The tense set of her mother's jaw when Vale informed her that she was leaving Philadelphia. The flawless summer day when she and her father purchased the building that would become the Crafty Cocktail, cementing their business partnership. Bo working in the bar's long galley kitchen on Monday afternoons, experimenting with house-made infusions and rare liquors to create his unique cocktail blends. After a lifetime of feeling like second best, Vale latched on to the belief that, in Pittsburgh, she'd find happiness and a true sense of belonging.

An illusion.

Two more officers walked into the street; they stopped new arrivals from venturing too close. The tattooed man continued filming from a safer distance, his expression brimming with sick fascination. Her lungs burning, Vale ducked through the crowd. She felt seasick, unable to stand by helplessly while flames consumed the business that represented her first real success. Her *only* success after years of minor fumbles and larger disappointments.

Eyes blurring, she walked all the way to the corner of Twenty-Third Street. The air was cleaner here, carrying only a small trace of smoke. There was no one nearby. The isolation came as a relief.

Vale sank onto the curb and sobbed.

How late had Bo stayed at the Crafty Cocktail last night with his so-called friends? Six people had been hanging around with him at closing time. He'd been pouring himself a drink and flirting with a brunette embarrassingly close to Vale's age. When the cook and the last of the waiters clocked out, Vale stopped arguing with her father. Whenever Bo was in party mode, reasoning with him met with defeat. She'd trudged out of the bar with her feet aching, disappointment slowing her pace.

Had one of the late-night revelers dumped a smoldering ashtray into the garbage? Or made a snack in the bar's kitchen and left the gas stove on? It was doubtful Bo, playing host and pouring free drinks, would've noticed.

In the last four years, she'd discovered some upsetting truths about the father who'd drifted in and out of her childhood. Normally Bo's good traits outweighed the bad, and she tried to overlook his worst habits. But now the Crafty Cocktail was aflame. All due to a fire that might have been avoidable.

Anger and sorrow vied for prominence in her heart. Pulling out her phone, she swiped Bo's number. The call went to voice mail.

Hurried footfalls came from behind her.

"Vale!" Marci Dilonga halted abruptly at the curb. "Good grief, I've been looking everywhere for you."

Marci lived in the apartment next door to Vale's with her twelve-year-old son. An RN at West Penn Hospital, she worked many night shifts, freeing up daytime hours to ferry her son to his after-school and weekend activities. Sometimes she invited Vale over for an early dinner before they left for their respective jobs. With their nontraditional work schedules, they were both glad for the company.

Vale glanced up at her. "Has the fire spread to the other buildings?" She prayed that it hadn't.

"I don't think so. It looks like the other businesses will be spared."

"Well, that's something."

"I can't believe the Crafty Cocktail is burning down. It's awful." Marci peered down at her with concern. "Are you all right? You look shell-shocked."

Swiping the moisture from her cheeks, Vale attempted a smile. "That's putting it mildly."

"You left the door to your apartment hanging open. I closed it on my way downstairs. Do you have your keys?"

Do I? Unsure, Vale patted the pocket of her jeans. "No worries. You didn't lock me out."

"Where's your dad?" Offering a hand, Marci helped her to her feet. "I didn't see him in the crowd."

"Probably still asleep." Bo lived on the eastern side of the city, near Schenley Park. "It doesn't matter. There's nothing he can do to fix the situation."

"Are you hungry? There's a diner on the next block if you don't mind the walk."

"I should go back and speak to the fire captain first. Let him know I'm one of the building's owners. I didn't get the chance to tell him when I saw him a few minutes ago."

"He isn't going anywhere, Vale. Talk to him after you've had coffee and something to eat." Gently Marci hooked a length of Vale's long hair behind her ear. "The walk will do you good."

The suggestion lifted Vale's flagging spirits. She detected a slight tremor in her arms and the threat of more tears collecting in her eyes. Falling apart wouldn't solve anything. She appreciated Marci's company.

This early in the day, the diner was nearly empty. At a table close to the door, a silver-haired gent in a fedora bent over the Sunday crossword puzzle, his plate of waffles untouched. The waitress led them past, to a booth near the kitchen.

Vale slid into the booth. "Just coffee for me," she told the waitress.

"Ignore her," Marci said, handing over the menus. "We'll each have the veggie omelet and coffee. Oh, and please bring my friend a glass of orange juice."

The waitress left. "I'm not sure I can eat," Vale admitted.

"You can give it a try."

"I feel queasy."

"Try breathing in and out . . . slowly. Besides, it'll help to get something nutritious in your tummy, and the orange juice will settle the shock." The coffee appeared, and Marci slid a cup before her. She nodded with satisfaction when Vale took a sip. "Do you want to come back to my place after you talk to the fire captain? You shouldn't be alone."

"I appreciate your concern, Marci, but I'm fine." A lie, but she couldn't impose on her friend. Last night Marci had worked the graveyard shift at the hospital. "You need to get some shut-eye this morning."

"I'll manage."

"Yes—without me underfoot. Once my dad gets in touch, I'll need to put my game face on. We'll have to file the insurance claim and contact our staff. I hate the thought of ruining their weekend with the news that their jobs are gone." Cradling her cup, Vale hesitated. Then she couldn't help adding, "This will sound odd . . . When I woke up and smelled the smoke, I had the strangest feeling the Crafty Cocktail was burning down. So many buildings on the street, but I felt like my luck had run out."

"You had a premonition," Marci suggested.

"It was just a bad feeling, that's all."

"Maybe it was your intuition. I've heard stranger things."

"Marci, if I had anything like intuition, I wouldn't be in this mess." Pinpricks of despair scattered through Vale. "How can someone lose their best dream like this? It's not fair. All the hours spent making the bar profitable—years I'll never get back. And I'm worried my father or one of his friends inadvertently caused the fire. They were all getting pretty drunk last night when I left."

Marci offered a sympathetic smile. "I'll give you credit. If my business partner put my financial stability at risk, I'd be livid."

A temptation, which Vale quickly discarded. Yes, she quarreled with her father about his late-night parties at the Crafty Cocktail. The rest of the time, they got along great. She was grateful he'd given her a new start in Pittsburgh, away from her mother and stepfather. Away from her half sister, Blythe. For too many years, Vale had allowed anger to rule her emotions—and her relationships. With the catalysts for her worst impulses living separate lives in Philadelphia, she was learning to tame her temper.

Her sole regret about leaving Philadelphia? Her only grandparent—her beloved Nana—lived outside the city in the Media borough. Bo's parents had died in a car accident when he was nineteen, and Nana had lost her husband when Vale was just a baby.

When she remained silent, Marci said, "Did I ever tell you about my parents' house? Century home in Erie—a real beaut. They bought it for a song when I was in college. They spent years fixing it up. The same year I got divorced, the place burned down. There was a problem with the old wiring, something my parents overlooked during the renovations."

The disclosure lifted Vale's brows. "Please tell me your parents weren't injured."

"No, thankfully. They'd gone out to the movies. They came home to find the Erie fire department battling a blaze of epic proportions. There was nothing left of the house but the foundation."

Like the Crafty Cocktail. Vale's stomach knotted. She doubted they'd salvage anything from the bar.

"Furniture, mementos, the stamp collection my father had been working on most of his life—it all went up in smoke," Marci added.

The waitress returned with the omelets and the glass of orange juice. Murmuring her thanks, Vale took a sip of the juice.

Picking up her fork, she poked tentatively at the omelet. "How did your parents deal with the loss?" she asked when the waitress left.

"My father handled it reasonably well. Mom was heartbroken about their belongings *and* the house. She'd always wanted to own a century home and spend her golden years fixing it up. I'm sure my parents would've been happy if the fire had never occurred and they'd grown old inside those musty walls." Marci took a bite of her omelet, chewed thoughtfully. "When they received the insurance check, I suggested they consider pulling up roots and heading to Sarasota. Both of Mom's sisters moved to Florida eons ago."

"Your parents live there now?"

"And they're happy as clams, winding out their retirement on the beach. Which is why I can't help but wonder . . ."

The queasy sensation returning, Vale pushed her plate away. "What, exactly?" she demanded, certain she didn't want to know.

"Is the fire at the Crafty Cocktail a blessing in disguise?"

"Of course not!"

"Are you sure? Perhaps the universe interceded to offer you a different path." With a look of apology, Marci lifted her palms. "Listen, how you live your life is none of my business. All I'm saying is that I'm not sure you *are* living your best life. The one that fits your hopes and dreams."

"I hardly saw my father when I was a kid. I wouldn't trade the last four years for anything."

"Vale, I get that you like owning a business with your father. Who doesn't love Bo? He has more energy than a toddler and puts everyone into a celebratory mood the minute he starts pouring drinks. It's like he's a mad pixie. But the Crafty Cocktail was his grand vision, not yours."

"I'm not looking for an exit plan. We'll use the insurance money to rebuild. We'll stay in business."

"Or you could split the insurance money and start a *different* business—on your own. Something with normal hours and weekends off to afford you a private life. You hate working nights. You live and breathe your job 24-7. More importantly, a woman your age should be available for the occasional Saturday night date."

There was no refuting the observation. In a perfect world, Vale would own a small business with normal hours. She'd rise with the birds and give up the night-owl routine. She'd fall in love with a stable guy, someone who liked books, eating in, and experimenting with different cuisines. Simple dreams, surely. But her life had always been complicated—and often disappointing. Why wouldn't she cherish secret wishes most people took for granted?

Her phone vibrated. Reading the panel, she frowned.

"It's one of my employees," she told Marci, glad to drop the conversation. "I should take this."

Chapter 2

Throughout the day, Vale's repeated calls to her father went unanswered. It seemed a minor inconvenience compared to more pressing concerns. Within hours, news of the fire reached every one of their employees, all of whom subsequently called.

Slumped on the couch in her apartment, Vale fielded calls while nursing a temple-throbbing headache. When would the Crafty Cocktail reopen? Would they find their jobs waiting when it did? The answers were elusive—like her still-missing father.

Even a fire lacked the power to alter Bo's habits. On a normal Sunday, Vale managed the bar with a small crew; her father was predictably absent, sleeping in late, then spending the day glued to the sports channel. If motivation struck, Bo headed to the gym for a workout. If he took a new girlfriend home on Saturday night, they spent Sunday together.

Since he wasn't picking up, there was no telling when he'd learn of the fire. Drive over to his apartment to share the grim news? Vale quickly discarded the notion. Given last night's after-hours party, Bo probably wasn't alone. Vale loved her father with defensive, rosy-eyed devotion, but his overactive sex life was a secret embarrassment. Thrice divorced, he'd stopped dating women his own age. Recently he'd dated a girl two years younger than Vale. The chirpy paralegal had taken it hard when his affections waned.

Once her phone stopped ringing, Vale hazarded a glance out the window. She looked down the street at the Crafty Cocktail. The fire department had put out the flames by late morning, and a crowd no longer milled around the bar. Only the occasional passerby stopped to gawk at the charred brick-and-wood building. The fire had destroyed the north wall, leaving the blackened studs visible. Inside, the intense heat had reduced most of the furnishings to heaps of ash.

Vale pulled her attention from the pitiful sight. Despair trailed her into the apartment's small kitchen. It was nearly six o'clock. With disinterest she surveyed the fridge's meager contents.

A series of familiar raps sounded on the door. She drew in a steadying breath. *Finally.*

Leaning against the doorjamb, Bo flashed a boyish grin. "Hey, blue eyes. Sorry I didn't pick up." When she frowned, he doused the merriment. "Don't look so glum—the world hasn't ended. Granted, the situation is bad. We'll think of something. We always do."

A blindly optimistic remark. Typical fare for a man who viewed life sunny-side up. Normally Vale found his optimism endearing. Now it merely added to a bad case of the blues.

She folded her arms. "How did you find out?"

"Dennis told me," he supplied, referring to the Crafty Cocktail's lead cook. "He showed up at my apartment. I would've called you immediately, but I went to the fire department after I drove by the bar . . . or what's left of it."

"There's nothing left, Dad. We've lost everything."

"C'mon, Vale—we still have each other. We're the best father-daughter team in Pittsburgh's nightlife scene. You're acting like this is our first speed bump. We've been through hard times before."

"Get serious." She added sarcasm to the displeasure in her tone. "In four years of operation, we've never encountered a disaster this big."

"Not true. Remember when the pipes burst during the January from hell? The bar was a sheet of ice. We could've rented a Zamboni and turned the place into a skating rink. We were closed for days."

"*That* was a speed bump." They'd dealt with the plumbing fiasco two winters ago, during a record-breaking freeze. "We spent a large chunk of cash fixing the plumbing, but we had the funds to make the repairs. This is a full-blown crisis. For once, will you please ditch the happy talk? I'm really not in the mood."

"All right, all right." Bo held up a bag of takeout. "Can we eat while discussing next moves? I brought sushi. Three rolls, just the way you like them."

Taking the peace offering, she led him inside. "How do we handle this?" she asked.

"Short-term? Find jobs to tide us over."

"I'd hoped for a better solution."

During their first year of business, they'd both held down part-time jobs. A grueling necessity on top of long hours at the Crafty Cocktail. After the first year, Bo quit his other bartending gig. Vale continued stocking merchandise on a wholesale club's morning shift for another two years. In the process, she forfeited anything resembling a private life.

A sacrifice willingly made. Steering the bar to success—while forging a close relationship with her father—had meant everything to her.

"Here's an idea," Bo said. "Why not tap the well? One more time for luck."

The suggestion struck Vale like ice water. "Don't even go there."

"What's the harm in asking? She cares about your welfare."

"Totally *not* the point."

"Yes, it is. Let your grandmother show her love with one more donation to the Vale and Bo Lightner opportunity fund."

"*No.* It didn't feel right accepting Nana's help when we opened the bar. Other than you, she's the only relative with whom I'm on good terms." An understatement. Long before the move to Pittsburgh, Vale had secured her position as the family disappointment. Only her grand-mother, Iris, believed she'd eventually get her act together. "Besides, Nana can't afford to fix a mess this large. What do you think she'll do, give us enough cash to rent somewhere else while we rebuild? You're talking thousands."

Bo fired up his dazzling smile. "We'll never know unless you ask."

"Forget it." Escaping the charm offensive, Vale strode into the kitchen. From over her shoulder, she added, "I don't want to give Nana the impression I've become a . . . mooch. She's helped me enough in the past—more than you know. I'm twenty-nine now, too old to request assistance just because my life has taken another nosedive."

"Fine. We don't beg Iris for help. But we can't reopen any time soon. There's not much left of the building. We'll need to demolish. Start over."

"How long will *that* take?" Pulling down dishes, Vale grimaced. Even if their insurance policy covered the entire cost, rebuilding from the ground up seemed a daunting task. She didn't know the first thing about construction. She doubted Bo did either. "It's April, and spring fever is in the air. The bar has been packed most nights. Business has been great. Until this morning's tragedy, I assumed we'd enjoy nothing but blue skies ahead."

Bo expelled a frustrated sigh. "Me too."

Seventy percent of the bar's income rolled in with the first heat wave. College kids and other young adults flocked to the Crafty Cocktail for Bo's inspired concoctions and the live bands they booked nightly, May through September. If construction took months to complete, it would seriously threaten their finances. Even if they reopened by autumn, they'd barely make it through winter. Not without the funds that Vale, ever careful, would've insisted on tucking away during the fat months.

Vale asked, "Will we lose the summer—our most profitable months?"

Dodging the query, Bo kicked off his shoes and sat on the couch. For an instant, he resembled a teenage boy with his tousled golden hair and tall, well-toned physique. The expression on his face cinched the impression, the confusion darkening his vibrant blue eyes. He threw his feet up on the battered coffee table Vale had purchased at a garage sale. His toes wiggled and his ankles popped as he rotated his feet in circles, then up and down.

Bo couldn't face the smallest dilemma with his shoes on. Thornier issues kept him barefoot for long minutes. It was one of the first things she'd discovered after moving to Pittsburgh and beginning a full-on relationship with her absentee father.

Affection for him carried Vale back into the living room. Bo Lightner wasn't a bad person. He skated by on his looks—dating too many women and breaking too many hearts. He didn't like to plan ahead. He treated Vale more like a buddy than a daughter.

Yet she never doubted his love.

The proof was readily evident. Unlike her mother—who'd always made Vale feel like a failure—her father never criticized her. If she altered her hairstyle or bought a new blouse from Lulu's Luxury Consignment, he showered her with compliments. Nor was his kindness reserved only for her. Bo insisted on paying their employees well. Whenever they needed to talk, he offered a sympathetic ear and encouraging words— even if his ability to offer sensible advice was dicey at best.

Last August, when someone dumped a box of mewling kittens in the parking lot behind the Crafty Cocktail, Bo ferried the starving litter back to his apartment. He spent the following days showing the bar's customers adorable pics on his smartphone. Every kitten found a home.

Vale set a plate of sushi before him. "Promise me one thing," she said, joining him on the couch.

"Name it."

"Once we do rebuild, you'll leave at closing time. No exceptions on Saturday nights. I'm your number one fan, but I'm also your business partner. I'm entitled to a guarantee."

"C'mon, Vale. How was I supposed to know the building would burn down?"

"Great question, since you may have accidentally started the fire. You or one of your friends."

"Stop jumping to conclusions. We don't know the fire's cause. It might take days to find out. Weeks, even."

"Yeah, and that doesn't change the facts. You shouldn't have parties at the Crafty Cocktail. How many times have I told you it's incredibly stupid to stay after hours?" Vale reached for the spicy tuna roll. Hesitating, she thought of something else. "Will it matter to our insurer *how* the fire started? If it was preventable, will they still honor the policy?"

A reply wasn't forthcoming, and a swishing sound caught her attention.

Beneath the coffee table, her father's anxious feet carved grooves in the rug. His tongue, however, remained still. The tension creeping into the room sent her thoughts back to Marci's advice this morning at the diner. As if a benevolent universe had shut one door in preparation of opening another, lending Vale a better path.

A notion she immediately rejected. *I don't need a better path.* With misgivings, she studied her father. *I need to kick the rocks out of the road I've chosen.* To begin, she'd take charge. A first, since her father usually took the lead.

"Let's go online, download the contract," she said, breaking the silence. "Unless you have a copy of the policy in your apartment."

Abruptly Bo's feet stopped moving. "Vale . . ."

He left her name floating in the air like an untethered balloon. Bouncing across the ceiling in search of escape. The sudden buzzing in Vale's ears warned she'd need to flee, and soon.

Thwarting the emotion, she rested her palm on her father's wrist. "What's wrong now?" she asked.

"It's about the insurance . . ."

Another silence, and a sensation like drowning caught her unawares. *This is not happening.* With effort, Vale pulled in a lungful of air. It didn't allay the anxiety swooping into her belly.

Bo palmed his forehead. "We'll both need to get on payroll somewhere else. And I mean pronto. This week I'll put out feelers, see what's available. Don't worry. We'll get back on our feet. It'll just take some time."

Dizzy, she closed her eyes. "What are you saying?" She covered her face with her hands.

"Vale, I'm sorry about this. Truly. You see . . . well, I let the insurance policy lapse. In December, when we were having trouble making ends meet. I never mentioned it because I didn't want you to worry. I'd planned to get the policy reinstated this summer, once we were flush with cash. We really *are* starting over. Do you understand?"

Disbelief prevented Vale from responding. Opening her eyes, she glimpsed doom.

Chapter 3

On the hiking trail beside the Allegheny River, Vale stared, unseeing, at the waters.

For three days running she emotionally checked out, abandoning her normal habits to sink into gloom. Vale left her father to handhold the employees through the steps of filing for unemployment. She didn't help Bo contact the Crafty Cocktail's vendors to cancel the upcoming deliveries. She declined to accompany him to the Bureau of Fire, which hadn't yet made a final determination on the cause of the blaze. The conclusion didn't matter. Without the safety net of business insurance, there wasn't a path forward. Bo's talk of starting over was little more than fantasy.

Walking Pittsburgh's streets, Vale covered miles of self-reproach. Why had she assumed the bar's insurance policy was in force? She took care of the day-to-day operations, scheduling the staff and ordering supplies. Bo liked handing out the weekly paychecks, but he left the rest of the paperwork to her. She'd set up their insurance in automated bill pay—when had Bo gone in and messed it up? At minimum, she could've logged in to their bank account and skimmed through the transactions to check that the premiums were paid.

A foolish oversight. Not once had it occurred to her that he might let the policy lapse.

In between chastising herself, Vale suffered pangs of guilt regarding her grandmother. She left her phone powered down to avoid reading more texts from Iris—embellished with floral and kissy-face emojis—inquiring why she was too busy for their weekly chat. Like the rest of Vale's family, Iris lived in the Philadelphia area. She owned Green Iris, a plant shop, with her friend Detta Green.

I didn't forget to call, Nana. I've just flamed out—again.

Heartache swept through Vale. She'd begun screwing up in childhood, as if the acts of disobedience could punish her mother for divorcing Bo. She couldn't recall a time when she *wasn't* angry with Audrey. For remarrying quickly and having another child. At the sudden, overwhelming changes that shunted Vale into the background. Life became a confusing puzzle, with the pieces swiftly rearranged.

Vale didn't fit in.

In preschool, when the teacher asked if she liked helping Mommy care for her baby sister, Vale winged a Lego minifigure across the classroom. With impressive aim, she cracked a lens in the teacher's eyeglasses. At four, Vale popped her stepfather over the head with a hard-plastic baby doll on the one and only time he attempted to tuck her into bed. Grant Wittman wasn't her father. With a child's imperfect logic, Vale had believed that if she could drive him off, her real father would miraculously reappear.

With her glossy mane of golden hair and attractive features, Vale was a mini replica of Bo, who'd vanished from her daily life. Yet she'd inherited none of his people-pleasing skills. In kindergarten she earned so many time-outs, the other kids scattered when she marched onto the playground.

Puberty ushered in bigger acts of defiance. Vale, flunking sixth grade. Sneaking off to the girls' lavatory in middle school to slather the stalls with Silly String and earning a week's worth of detention. By high school, she was a sullen teenager convinced she didn't fit in anywhere. Two of the popular girls wrote LOSER on her locker with

Magic Marker, and she clocked them both. During her junior year her stepfather, Grant—pointing out that her half sister, Blythe, consistently earned high marks—threatened to ground her if she didn't pull her grades up. Soon after, Vale lifted the keys to his BMW convertible. She drove to Philadelphia's Franklin Square for a night of unsanctioned revelry and left the keys swinging in the ignition.

The sweet ride was never seen again.

Oddly enough, college wasn't a complete disaster, though it *did* take Vale three attempts and six years to graduate with a lackluster GPA. A series of unrewarding jobs followed: receptionist at a law firm, general gofer at the Philadelphia Water Department, a stint as a dog walker at an eldercare facility. Finally, an acquaintance of her grandmother's took pity, hiring Vale as a salesclerk at a boutique in Queen Village. Despite her admittedly short fuse, Vale possessed a tall, lithe build that showed off the shop's dresses and jewelry to perfection.

Yet in predictable fashion, she flamed out by getting into an argument with a customer. The woman—one of the boutique's regulars—insisted on returning a cocktail dress weeks after its purchase, the collar smudged with lipstick.

Vale hit rock bottom when her job prospects dried up. Who wanted to hire a twenty-five-year-old with a checkered employment history and no references? She no longer saw much of her mother and Grant. She couldn't bring herself to ask her grandmother for more help. For weeks, Vale relied on a local food pantry to get by and waited for an eviction notice to slide under the door of her ratty apartment.

The humiliating experience made her resolve to get a handle on her anger.

That, and the lifeline Bo tossed her way: after years of infrequent contact, she'd begun initiating the calls just to see how he was doing. When Bo hatched the scheme of going into business together, she quickly agreed.

A dream now gone.

Absently, Vale withdrew her phone from her purse. The urge to power up and call her grandmother for advice was strong. But then what? Admitting to another defeat was an unbearable humiliation. She'd invested the latter part of her twenties in an enterprise that had disappeared in a flash of heat and flame. A risky venture that her kind-hearted grandmother had generously helped to bankroll. She couldn't foist her problems on Iris.

Which left only Marci's advice from Sunday to latch on to. Was the fire—and Bo's reckless decision to cancel the insurance policy—a blessing in disguise? *If the universe has opened a door, where is it? I need GPS.*

Returning to Philadelphia wasn't an option, even though Vale missed her grandmother. Compared to the grand Colonial Vale's mother and stepfather owned in Mount Airy, with its Ethan Allen furnishings and overbearing silence, Nana's home was a sanctuary brimming with love. Vale missed Nana's garden and the wafer-thin almond cookies she sweetened with advice whenever Vale—normally stubborn—overrode her defensive nature and sought her grandmother's counsel. She missed lolling away the afternoon on the front porch of her grandmother's Victorian house in the charming Media borough where all the neighbors seemed like family.

Yet no matter how much Vale regretted the distance she'd placed between them by moving to Pittsburgh, she couldn't go back. Not if she wanted to avoid her hypercritical mother and stepfather. They both excelled at eroding her confidence.

There was also the matter of her younger half sister. Blythe was married to the Phillies' star pitcher, but Vale hadn't rated an invitation to the lavish wedding three years ago. The relationship between sisters was in worse condition than the charred remains of the Crafty Cocktail.

Meaning Vale needed to stay put and reinvent herself in Pittsburgh. Find a job with decent wages to replenish her skinny bank account.

Regret slowed her pace as she left the hiking trail. Would she ever have another chance to be her own boss? It seemed unlikely. She'd no longer work beside her father—the original reason for moving to Pittsburgh. *I'd rather eat glass than work with Bo again.* Thanks to his lack of foresight, she was heading into another do-over with limited means. And with a résumé that wasn't much better than when she'd lived in Philly. Unless, of course, she wanted to apply for a management position at one of Pittsburgh's bars.

I'd rather eat worms. A whole squirmy bucket of them.

Vale's feet carried her into the busy streets surrounding her apartment. Restaurants were opening their doors, sending mouthwatering scents into the air to lure customers inside. Spending the night alone with her dismal thoughts didn't appeal. As dusk retreated beneath the approaching night, she walked to Penn Avenue. Buzz Bar & Grill teemed with customers, thanks to a live rock band. On impulse, Vale went inside.

For a woman who earned her living working the nightlife scene, Vale rarely went out. She drank infrequently—booze often gave her a headache or made her nose stuffy. But the dance floor was packed with gyrating couples, and the long bar was filled from end to end. The thrum of conversation and the thumping beat of the music steered her to a table in back. She'd barely taken a seat when a man in a beautifully tailored sports coat and a loosened silk tie materialized before her.

"Drinking alone?" When she nodded, he seated himself in the chair opposite. He motioned to the waitress. "Let me buy the first round."

In defiance of her gloom, Vale smiled. She liked his thick, dark hair; the first hint of crow's-feet crinkled his eyes. Pain arrowed through her. She couldn't recall the last time she'd had the leisure to flirt with a man. The drunks who'd hit on her at the Crafty Cocktail didn't count.

"Feel free to buy all the rounds." She felt desperately sad and surprisingly upbeat all in the same instant, as if losing the Crafty Cocktail were somehow liberating. To the waitress, she added, "A tequila manhattan, please. Go heavy with the tequila."

The man grinned. "Make that two."

Chapter 4

The rumble of gale-force winds shook Vale awake.

With confusion she cast her bleary attention on the partially open and unfamiliar brown drapes. Sunlit clouds scuttled past. Yawning, she blinked at them.

Her temples sang with agony. Despite her inexperience with hangovers, this one seemed deserving of the record books. It dawned on Vale that she was naked, in a strange bed. Not only naked: a muscled and enticingly scented arm was flung across her waist.

Eyes rounding, she gasped.

Beside her, the man she'd met last night snored loudly. To her chagrin, she couldn't dredge up his name from the murky depths of her booze-addled brain. Many of last night's events were fuzzy. *How much tequila did I knock back?* Too much, obviously.

Extracting herself from his hold, Vale slipped out of the bed. Clothing littered the floor. Her bra hung from a lampshade as if flung off in a moment of revelry. Embarrassment climbed her cheeks. What woman with an ounce of self-respect slept with a stranger? A nice enough man, but that was no excuse. With horror, Vale recalled throwing back her fourth tequila manhattan, then offering to spend the night at his place.

Scooping up her clothing, she fled the memory and the bedroom. She dressed in the living room with her self-respect in tatters. Her purse lay on its side on the couch, its contents spilled onto the plush carpeting. In a mad dash, she scooped up her wallet, lip gloss, and phone.

This is not my best week.

Sneaking out of the apartment, Vale got her bearings and ran to the elevator. She leaped inside with the uncomfortable sensation that her life was unraveling at breakneck speed. How could she fall so far, so fast? Losing the Crafty Cocktail didn't justify becoming a boozehound. Or spending the night with a stranger. *Did I have unprotected sex?* She'd stopped using birth control after moving to Pittsburgh. Why risk the pill's side effects when she was married to her job? Now she wondered if her mystery date had brought condoms to the party.

As the elevator descended to the ground floor, she *did* suddenly recall the sex. It had been good. A low bar to jump, considering her barren social life.

Stick with the shame and stop thinking about sex. What if he'd been a psycho in Brooks Brothers attire?

Cars moved bumper-to-bumper in the morning traffic. Powering up her phone for the first time in days, Vale scheduled a ride. The driver, in a red Ford Escape, would arrive in four minutes. Relief pooled in Vale's belly. One night of foolish behavior didn't seal a woman's fate. She'd go home, take a shower, then scroll through employment postings on her laptop.

Wasting more time mired in self-pity was *not* happening.

Her phone rang—her grandmother, Iris.

"Nana, hi." Shielding her eyes, Vale searched the traffic for her ride.

"Pumpkin, I've been trying to reach you for days! Why haven't you been picking up?"

"Can I call you back in twenty minutes? I'm, uh, running errands this morning before heading in to work." A cringeworthy lie, but this wasn't the time to mention the Crafty Cocktail's sudden demise. *Or my risky night with a mystery date.* "I'll call you once I'm back at my apartment."

"Is everything all right? I've been worried about you." A hint of displeasure colored Iris's voice. "You could've at least answered my texts. How long does it take to peck out a reply?"

"It's been a hectic week, Nana."

"You sound stressed. What's going on?"

The Ford Escape appeared at the curb. "Nothing. I'm just busy." Vale jumped inside. She nodded at the driver, a woman with a shock of pink hair. "Can I call you back?"

"No."

"Nana—"

"If I hang up, you'll turn your phone back off. I'll never get to the bottom of this."

"Maybe I've been too busy to chat." Vale winced at the guilt rimming the hasty rebuttal. Keeping secrets from her grandmother was harder than escaping a heat-seeking missile. On the emotional battlefield, Nana held the tactical advantage.

"Vale Lightner, you can't hide from your troubles. It's a wonder you haven't learned that by now. Or don't you remember the garden-shed fiasco?"

The Ford Escape turned onto Twenty-Fourth Street as the memory rushed over Vale. How she'd been doodling in a notebook during tenth-grade world history. The teacher, Mr. Hastings, shouting her name. Embarrassing her in front of the entire class. Vale, her pencil skittering across the floor, released a shocking torrent of profanity in response. The trip to the principal's office, where she received a week of detention.

Later that night—after sitting through her mother's scorching tirade about how foul language reflected poorly on the family—Vale darted out of the house. She took the bus to Media, where her grandmother lived. Second thoughts intruded when she arrived at Nana's house only to discover the lights were off. Inspiration struck—the foolish sort— and Vale crept through the backyard to camp out in the shed amid the bags of potting soil and birdseed. At daybreak, her grandmother caught her shimmying through the kitchen window to use the bathroom.

"Your mother was beside herself when you disappeared," Iris was saying. "The point being, you didn't solve your problems by avoiding them. You were still grounded for weeks. Longer, I suspect, than if you hadn't pulled the disappearing act. Skulking around my garden shed only made matters worse."

"I was fifteen. It seemed like a smart move at the time."

"Well, you're older now. Have you acquired better coping skills? Because I'd like to know why you haven't been taking my calls."

The car glided to the curb before Vale's apartment building. Thanking the driver, she got out.

"Pumpkin? Are you there?"

Miserable, Vale trudged into the building. "Nana, would you ease off? There's nothing earth-shattering I need to discuss." *Nothing,* she mused, *except the utter shambles of my life.* A situation she needed to fix on her own, *after* popping some aspirin to subdue the vicious hangover. "If anything major comes up, you'll be the first to know. And I promise not to miss any more of your calls. Day or night, I swear I'll pick up."

A stony silence descended. Muffled coughing followed.

The sound put Vale on alert. "Nana, why are you coughing?"

"I'm not. You're hearing things."

"There's nothing wrong with my hearing." Worry brought Vale to a standstill. "Are you ill?"

"Don't be ridiculous. I'm in tip-top shape."

Another bout of coughing, and Vale's stomach clenched. It was a nice complement to the teeny jackhammers she imagined pounding at her temples.

For decades, her grandparents were heavy smokers. The photographic evidence was readily available in Nana's house, the snaps of the attractive couple during their long marriage with cigarettes dangling from their fingertips or a blue haze of smoke encircling their smiling faces as they played bridge with friends. Losing her husband to lung cancer peeled Iris off the habit. But Nana *did* have slipups. Occasionally Vale caught her sneaking a smoke during stressful moments.

"If you're not sick, then why are you coughing?"

"Because I'm allergic to your evasions. Not that I'm optimistic you're prepared to confide in me." Another silence, and then she added, "If you're interested, I *do* have tests next week at the hospital. Well, the first round anyway."

"What do you mean, 'the first round'? How many tests are you having?"

"That depends on the results. There might be a second round the following week." A wheezing breath came across the line. Then Iris put sugar in her voice, adding, "It's no biggie."

Anxiety skipped through Vale's blood. "What is your doctor looking for?"

"Redemption, if you ask me. She lured her husband to Atlantic City recently, and they lost big at blackjack. He'd wanted to book a spa weekend."

"Stop joking. I really want to know."

"For Pete's sake, don't worry yourself into a tizzy. At my age, one doesn't visit the doctor without receiving a battery of tests in the bargain. Poor Detta," Iris added, referring to her business partner. "The shop has been incredibly busy, and I'll need days off. Spring always brings customers out in droves. I don't know how she'll manage alone at the helm."

Coming to a decision was easy. "Don't worry about it," Vale said. "I'll help Detta."

"You will?"

"What, you thought I'd leave you in the lurch?"

"I don't know what to think. Your visits to Philadelphia are more infrequent than monsoon rains in Cairo. If I didn't make time to fly to Pittsburgh, I'd forget what you look like."

"We Zoom most weekends," Vale pointed out, letting herself into the apartment. "I wish you'd mentioned the tests right away. A better conversation starter than grousing about the calls I didn't return. I'll drive to Philadelphia in the morning."

"Who will cover for you at the Crafty Cocktail?"

An unwelcome question, and Vale bit her lower lip. She hated adding to the lies. The only alternative at the moment.

"We have a staff, you know. Dad will have all the help he needs—"

Startled, Vale broke off. *Speak of the devil.* Lying prone on the couch, her father stared dejectedly at the ceiling.

On the other end, Iris said, "Then it's settled. I'll see you tomorrow, pumpkin. I love you."

"I love you too, Nana."

Pocketing the phone, Vale approached the couch. She arched a disapproving brow.

Her father pulled his attention from the ceiling. "Your grandmother is having tests?"

"Don't ask for the details—she wouldn't share them." Vale tossed her purse on the coffee table. "Just because we've swapped keys doesn't mean you can show up at my place uninvited."

"Like you gave me a choice. FYI, blue eyes: dodging my calls is a crappy way to treat your business partner."

"So is dropping the bar's insurance policy without giving me a heads-up. And don't call me 'blue eyes.'" Her father was inordinately proud that she resembled him. Usually this gave her an emotional boost. *Not today.* "You only do that when you're trying to butter me up."

"Or beg your forgiveness." Pulling himself into a sitting position, Bo caught her irritated gaze. "I never meant to let you down. If there were a simple way to fix everything, I'd do it. I'm a lousy businessman, Vale. If you hadn't come on board, the bar never would've gotten off the ground. It was too much work for one person. And it was wrong to drop the policy without talking to you first." The apology halted abruptly. "Where were you this morning?"

"That's privileged information."

His brows lifted. "There's a hickey on your neck."

Shame prickled Vale's skin. So did the warm oval of flesh her fingers located at the base of her neck.

"It's a long story. I'm not going into it."

Recognition broke across Bo's face. "You were with a guy? Who is he?"

"I wish I knew."

"What's that supposed to mean?"

"I don't remember his name. I blame the tequila."

"Since when do you drink?" When she shrugged, Bo shook his head with bemusement. Patting the sofa, he waited until she sat down before adding, "It's not like you to lie to Iris. Why didn't you tell her about the bar? You're not at fault. I'm the one who screwed up."

"We're partners, Dad. We screwed up together."

"Cut yourself some slack. You're not responsible for every mishap that comes your way. Bad stuff happens. You can't always get out of the way in time." Playfully he flicked her nose. "You sure like carrying the world's troubles on your back—like a pack mule. How's that working out for you?"

"Not great."

"Then stop." Something akin to regret flashed across his features. "I'm glad you're going to Philly to see Iris."

"I'd be less nervous if I had some idea about what's going on."

"She's not getting any younger. When you get to her age . . . stuff can happen." He nodded toward her bedroom. "Do you want help packing? If I were you, I'd bring enough clothes for a long visit. Just in case."

Chapter 5

A spring rain accompanied Vale on the drive to Philadelphia.

The patter of raindrops and the soft swishing of the windshield wipers helped allay her nerves regarding her grandmother's health. Until now, Iris had been fit and hale, even as an ex-smoker. Only the occasional cold slowed her down. She kept busy working part-time at the plant shop she owned with Detta, and she speed-walked the pretty neighborhood where she lived. In wintertime, Iris rode an exercise bike she'd placed in the smallest of the three spare bedrooms of her rambling Victorian house. The two perfectly arranged guest bedrooms were rarely used, now that Vale lived across the state and Blythe was married.

Vale frowned. She preferred to believe her grandmother was invincible. What if the situation had changed? The possibility sent fear leaping through her.

It was Friday. The series of mysterious tests wouldn't begin until after the weekend. The results probably wouldn't be available right away. At minimum, Vale planned to stay for two weeks. Should the results prove worrisome, she'd stay longer. Letting Iris down was out of the question.

The bigger conundrum: how to manage the visit without running into the rest of her family.

Since moving across the state, she'd returned to Philadelphia only twice to see Iris. Short visits both, and her mother and stepfather were none the wiser. Vale wouldn't describe her relationship with Audrey and Grant Wittman as irreparably damaged, but it was distant.

Every holiday season, they extended an invitation to join them. When Vale predictably declined, they feigned disappointment. They never forgot to send a card on her birthday. And the small, meaningless tokens of family devotion were reciprocated. On their anniversary, Vale dropped a card in the mail. On Mother's Day, she sent Audrey a bouquet of the shell-pink roses she loved.

Phone calls were infrequent and stilted. Audrey and Grant kept the conversation afloat with mundane news about their health or their jobs at Stern-Belkins, the accounting firm where they both worked. They avoided the topic of Bo. They never asked how the bar was faring.

Rarely did they even mention Vale's half sister. They seemed quietly thankful Vale lived too far away to disturb Blythe's successful life.

As Vale exited the turnpike and entered Media, she came to a depressing conclusion: neither her parents nor her stepfather viewed her as a daughter in a traditional sense. To Bo, she was a fun companion—a buddy who happened to be his business partner. Audrey treated her like an inconvenient relative, one who fortunately stayed out of sight. And her stepfather? Grant considered her a bad influence on Blythe, and a vivid reminder of her irresponsible father.

Tears collected on Vale's lashes. She'd always wondered who'd decided not to invite her to Blythe's gala wedding three years ago—her half sister or her stepfather. Iris, infuriated by the slight, had wanted to get to the bottom of it. Vale had begged her not to intervene. There seemed no point. A wedding invitation couldn't mend the broken relationship between sisters.

The rain tapered off, leaving the air fresh-smelling and clean. The sun came out, and Vale brushed the tears away. She resolved not to appear unhappy. Maybe her relationship with the rest of her family *was* irreparably damaged. But she still had Bo—and Iris. For her

grandmother's sake, she'd maintain her composure, even if circumstances forced her to see her mother and Grant.

Blythe was the greater concern. Vale knew she'd earned her contempt. If they ran into each other, an argument was sure to erupt.

Slowing the car in the afternoon traffic, Vale pushed aside those
thoughts. Instead, she focused on the upcoming visit. Nearly a year had
passed since her grandmother's last flight into Pittsburgh. She looked
forward to catching up.

Trees rustled leafy arms on Iris's street. Before a tidy brick ranch,
a group of women sat in lawn chairs watching their toddlers romp on
the grass. An older man in sweats and a Phillies T-shirt bicycled past.
Early-blooming lilac bushes perfumed the air.

The light-green Victorian—the largest house on the street—came
into view. The white paint trimming the windows and the curved front
porch looked fresh. The flower beds wore a new coat of mulch.

Near the garage, Iris's van was parked at an angle. Vale pulled in
beside a red Audi sedan she didn't recognize.

The screen door creaked open, then quickly slammed shut. Iris
breezed across the porch. At seventy-four, she still possessed the energy
of a younger woman. Ribbons of violet color streaked her silver hair,
which was cut in a pixie style. Pink-and-white-striped compression
stockings peeked out from beneath her long apple-green peasant skirt.
Sensible, thickly soled slip-ons encased her feet.

Vale assessed her grandmother for signs of illness. Her eyes were
bright. Her complexion, with its webwork of wrinkles and smile lines,
glowed with apparent good health.

"You made great time." Iris pulled her into a rocking hug. "How
was the drive?"

"Easy." Vale was several inches taller, and she brushed her nose
across the crown of her grandmother's head. Iris loved botanical prod-
ucts, and her hair smelled wonderfully of rosemary and mint. Drawing

back, Vale added, "Traffic was light on the turnpike. Mostly semis, but they stayed out of the passing lane."

"I thought the rain might delay you. I'm glad it didn't."

Vale nodded at the Audi. "Is that Mom's car?" Audrey preferred luxury sedans; Vale wasn't sure of the make and model of her current ride. "If she's inside, I'll stop somewhere for a snack. I'll come back after she leaves."

"Your mother and Grant are on a long vacation in Aruba. Their first real getaway in years. And before you ask, I didn't mention you were coming into town."

Relieved, she grabbed her luggage. "Thanks for that."

The less Audrey knew, the better. Once she learned of the Crafty Cocktail's demise, she'd pepper Vale with barbs about ill-timed ventures and foolish choices. From the outset, she'd predicted the father-daughter partnership would end in disaster.

Apprehension rose inside Vale. She was still on the fence about mentioning the fire to Iris. Given the upcoming tests at the hospital, it seemed unwise.

She started toward the house. "If Mom's not inside, who's visiting?"

Stepping before her, Iris blocked her path. She removed the suitcase from Vale's grasp and placed it by the steps.

"First things first." Iris wiggled impatient fingers. "Give me your car keys. Then I'll explain."

"Why? So I won't bolt?" *Meaning there's a reason I should.*

"I'm asking nicely."

The wrinkles comprising Iris's face deepened with crafty intent. If she was afflicted with an unknown malady, it didn't hamper her ability to get her way. In a family of stubborn women, she knew how to hold her own.

Wary, Vale handed the keys over.

Pocketing them, Iris said, "Now, I want you to remain calm. It isn't often the stars align. Not in our family at least. We're usually at

cross-purposes. Which is why you should view this as an opportunity—
one I hope you'll seize wholeheartedly."

The mystical advice increased Vale's discomfort. "What's going on?"

"Your sister is inside."

That was the stars aligning? It felt more like a prophecy of doom.

"All righty then. I'll stop somewhere for a bite. If you won't hand
back my keys, I'll walk." There were plenty of restaurants nearby. "Call
me when she leaves."

"You're not going anywhere. You'll dredge up your party man-
ners and treat Blythe civilly. If she fires a few salvos, take it in stride.
Considering how you've treated her, it's no less than you deserve."

Insulted, Vale rocked back on her heels. "Jeez, Nana—whose side
are you on?"

"At the moment? Blythe's. She'll have a big enough shock once I
explain that you're also staying with me."

Vale looked at her, aghast. "She's bunking at your house? We're
staying here *together*? Why didn't you tell her I was coming into town?"

"I've been waiting for the proper moment to break the news."

"You should've given her a heads-up!"

"Calm down, sweetheart."

Vale recalled her friend Marci's advice on the morning of the fire
about calamity bringing the possibility of new opportunity. *If this is the
door the universe has opened, a mad prankster rules the cosmos.*

A more pragmatic thought surfaced. "Hold on. Blythe has a fabulous place on Rittenhouse Square. Can't you suggest she vacate the
premises? She's a married woman. Tell her to go home to her husband."

Iris shushed her. Taking Vale by the arm, she led her around the
side of the house. A cardinal rocketed from the bird feeder as Iris pulled
her to a stop.

"Pumpkin, listen to me." She lowered her voice. "Your sister asked
to stay while she sorts herself out. She's considering a divorce, and
Booker hasn't a clue."

"If she's staying here, Booker must have some idea. Hasn't he noticed she's not around?"

"He assumes she's visiting to stay out of his hair."

"He considers Blythe a . . . nuisance? That doesn't speak well of his commitment to their marriage."

"You don't understand. Their marriage takes a back seat during the baseball season. Booker travels constantly for away games. The rest of the time, he's pitching a gold streak here in Philly and spending most of the day with the team. Even so, he'll be devastated if Blythe leaves him—you know how much he adores her. I've never seen a man so smitten."

The explanation didn't sit well. No, she wasn't familiar with Booker's adoration for her sister, outside of photos she'd glimpsed on the internet, of Blythe with Booker at Phillies charity functions or standing together at Citizens Bank Park. They looked happy together, but Vale had never met the talented pitcher.

Like every other fan, Vale avidly followed his career. From what she'd gleaned online, Booker Banks was uncorking some of the fastest pitches of his career. His violent fastballs were the stuff of legend. It made no sense for Blythe to leave a star athlete who apparently worshipped her. At minimum, she should let Booker lead the Phillies to this year's World Series before serving him with papers.

Tamping down her irritation, Vale focused on the more critical issue. "Does Blythe know about the tests?"

"What, dear?" Iris frowned with confusion.

"Your tests, Nana. The ones they'll administer at the hospital. I'm assuming you didn't tell Mom for fear of spoiling her vacation in Aruba. Does Blythe know?"

The muscles in Iris's throat worked. Her gaze skittered away.

Trepidation bounded through Vale. She'd been worried about her grandmother's past history as a heavy smoker. Now she wondered if the doctors were looking for something other than lung cancer. Were the upcoming tests of the neurological sort? Alzheimer's *did* run in the family. Nana's brother, now gone, had suffered from the malady. One of Vale's great-grandparents had too. She couldn't recall which one.

Her distress broke through her grandmother's fog. "I've only told you about the tests," Iris said. She reconsidered. "And Detta. She's my business partner and best friend. Naturally she'd want to know."

"We're keeping Blythe in the dark?"

"Let's not burden her. It's more important that I find the opportunity to advise her before she does something rash."

"*Why* is Blythe considering divorce?" None of her business, yet Vale's curiosity was piqued. "She's only been married for three years. That's hardly past the newlywed stage."

Iris stared absently at the house. "I wish I knew. She's being awfully tight-lipped. It's as if she's ashamed to discuss the matter."

The reasons couples broke up were varied. Disagreements over money, the kids, life-work balance, or just plain boredom—once Vale had served drinks to a man at the Crafty Cocktail who'd been dumped by his wife because he kept forgetting to pick up their schnauzer's stink bombs in the backyard. At least that was *his* story. You never knew how much to believe when a customer was getting trashed.

In a depressing number of cases, infidelity factored in.

"What if Booker stepped out of line with a sports groupie?" Vale suggested. "He *is* a hot commodity. Women must throw themselves at him all the time."

"Nonsense. His devotion to Blythe is absolute."

"Okay, then try this on for size. Blythe is embarrassed because she's burned through all their credit." Like their mother, Audrey, her sister *did* have expensive tastes. Back in high school, she'd purchased her first pair of Jimmy Choos with a season's worth of babysitting money. "What if she's heading for the exit out of shame for her shopping disorder? Ditching Booker is easier than fessing up."

The theory brought a snort of disbelief from Iris. "Now you're being silly. Whatever's bothering your sister, it's more serious than her credit score."

Vale gave up on unraveling the mystery. "Good luck getting to the bottom of it. If Blythe isn't talking, you'll never pry the details from her." They retraced their steps around the side of the house, and she asked, "Do you have any idea how long she's staying?"

"Until she patches things up with Booker, I suppose—or settles on divorce. I'm afraid she'll make a bad choice before your mother returns from Aruba. If she's going to disappoint Audrey, she'll do it after filing for divorce."

"Blythe's an adult. I doubt she'll make a life-altering decision based on how our mother will react."

Conceding the point, Iris shrugged. "It will be easier to reason with her while Audrey and Grant are vacationing. They mean well, but they can be too . . . demanding. It's the last thing your sister needs." Iris flashed a warning look. "Please don't argue with her. Do it for me, pumpkin. I'll never get her to confide in me if she's spending every minute fighting with you."

With resignation, Vale picked up her suitcase. "I won't start any fights."

The promise would prove difficult to keep. For her grandmother's sake, she'd try to remain on her best behavior.

Chapter 6

Sunlight cascaded through the foyer's leaded windows. New plants were scattered among the lacy ferns Vale remembered from her last visit. Pleasing hints of ginger and butter hung in the air, sharp and sweet. Given the rare circumstance of both her granddaughters staying at the same time, Iris had undoubtedly gone on a baking spree.

From the second floor, the soulful music of Diana Ross and the Supremes drifted down. "You Keep Me Hanging On." Apparently, Blythe had dug their grandmother's record player and vintage LPs from the attic.

Iris motioned toward the kitchen. "I've made a lovely batch of valerian and mint tea. Would you like a cup? I'll add a dollop of honey."

Valerian root possessed light sedative qualities. Mint helped with tummy upsets. Clearly Iris feared the meeting between the half sisters might not go swimmingly.

"Nana, stop pushing drugs," she joked. "I can handle this."

Grinning, Vale walked into the living room. New throw pillows graced the overstuffed couch. Houseplants festooned the curving bank of windows overlooking the front porch. A stack of books sat beside the tapestry chair where Vale had often snuggled during winter months. Despite her nerves about seeing Blythe, she savored a sense of well-being. The days spent under her grandmother's roof were always the happiest.

"Would you like a cookie?"

A reassuring offer befitting a child. "I'll sample your treats later." At the bank of windows, she watched a school bus trundle past. "Let's get this over with."

"I'll go upstairs and fetch your sister."

"Okay."

Indecision rooted Iris in the foyer. At her waist, her hands worked. "Nana, are you going or not?"

Iris joined her in the living room. "Maybe *I* need a cookie. A spoonful of sugar for courage." She hazarded a glance at the ceiling. "Oh, why didn't I bring this up at breakfast? I had a good ten minutes to break the news before your sister went back to her room to mope."

The opportunity to reply never came. Vale realized the Motown tune was no longer playing above their heads. Footfalls echoed on the staircase. As the sound grew louder, Iris pulled in a gulp of air. Vale found she couldn't breathe at all.

Time slowed as Blythe appeared in the foyer. Her attention stalled on the sunglasses she pulled from her purse. She was about to slip them on when her eyes found Vale.

The half sisters were both slightly taller than average. The similarities ended there. Blythe took after her father's side of the family with ebony curls tumbling around her shoulders. Dark brows framed her deeply set eyes. Unlike Vale, with her pale complexion and slender build, Blythe's skin was olive toned like Grant's. Her figure—athletic, curvy—was nearly voluptuous.

Vale searched for her voice. Like her confidence, it fled the room.

Blythe tottered on her three-inch heels. "What's Crazy-cakes doing here?" she blurted.

Crazy-cakes. It was the handy insult Blythe kept on standby during their teenage years. A hateful nickname that inevitably hit the mark. In fairness, she'd come up with the zinger to defend against Vale's taunts about her weight. It took until puberty's closing act for Blythe to peel off the last of her baby fat.

Crockadillapig. Self-reproach nicked Vale. Of the many cruelties she'd inflicted on her sister, the epithet had wounded Blythe the deepest.

"I'm waiting." Blythe's accusing gaze landed on Iris. "Why is she here?"

A squeak of protest escaped their grandmother's lips. *She doesn't need a cookie,* Vale mused. *Xanax, maybe.*

"Why don't you ask me directly?" Vale managed to keep her voice level. She invented a story on the fly. "Don't blame Nana—she didn't know I was coming. I drove in for a visit, totally unplanned."

The fiction didn't soften her sister. If anything, she appeared more enraged. Mount Vesuvius threatening to erupt.

The smile Vale attempted froze in place. "How are you? It's been a long time since we've seen each other."

The friendly rejoinder hardened Blythe's features. "What is this—cordial Vale? Talk about a first. Like you care how I'm doing."

"Cut me some slack, okay?"

"I don't think I will. Why should I?" Stepping into the room, Blythe shoved the sunglasses back into her purse. A shiver of rage swept down her spine. "You're not staying here, Vale. Book a hotel room. Or sleep on the street for all I care. Just leave before I'm back."

The command stung like a slap on the face. "This isn't your house. You don't make the rules."

"I was here first," Blythe snapped, as if settling the matter. She wheeled toward Iris. "I have a thing this afternoon and don't have time to stand here debating. I'm running late."

Iris frowned. "What sort of 'thing'?"

Blythe didn't elaborate. A frigid silence fell upon the room. It was enough to send fiery tendrils of humiliation climbing Vale's neck. Whatever Blythe's plans, she wouldn't reveal them before the half sister she despised.

To their grandmother Blythe said, "I'm going out tonight afterward. It'll give you time to sort this out. Please dump her somewhere. If she's broke, I'll pay. I really can't handle her right now."

Iris paled.

The remark threatened Vale's hold on her anger. Where did her sister get off, assuming she needed a handout? And she wasn't being dumped somewhere like yesterday's garbage. Iris loved them equally. They were both welcome in their grandmother's house.

Blythe strode out. The front door shut with a crack of sound.

Vale grasped for the tattered threads of her patience. Letting Blythe storm off was the smarter choice. Better to hash this out tonight. Reason with her once she returned, and hopefully cooled down. Yet even as Vale chewed over the common-sense approach, fury leaped inside her. Strong, sudden, impossible to ignore. Demanding release.

Setting her feet in motion.

Iris rushed forward, too late. "Vale, stop! Let her go."

Deaf to the plea, Vale bounded outside.

Racing down the steps, she caught up with her sister on the lawn. "What do you want from me?" Trapped inside the dark emotion, she latched on to Blythe's wrist. "If I'd known you were here, I wouldn't have come. Do you think I'm looking for a fight? It's not like I'm trying to infuriate you."

Blythe pulled free. "Well, congratulations." She pushed her away. "You're doing a good job anyway."

"I'm not leaving! Nana is my grandmother too."

"Stop shouting at me."

"I'm not shouting!" Vale realized she was. She tried to get her bearings, a difficult proposition with her sister glaring at her.

"Go home to Pittsburgh. Reschedule your visit."

"I can't."

An impasse, and tension crackled between them. Hatred simmered in Blythe's gaze. It was enough to douse the anger leaping through

Vale. From the corner of her eye, she caught movement behind the living room curtains—Iris peering out, plainly upset. Too upset to risk intervening in an argument between the granddaughters she adored.

"What will it take for you to calm down?" Frustration lifted Vale's palms. "An apology? If that's what you're waiting for, I'm game."

"Don't waste your time. I wouldn't believe you."

"That's not fair. I regret how our relationship worked out."

"No, you don't."

"I do, Blythe. If I could change the way I treated you in the past, I would." The words tumbled out of their own accord. Heartfelt, sincere, they carried Vale a step closer. "I'm not proud of myself."

"Save the speech. Don't you get it? There's nothing you can say to change how I feel."

Gray patches formed half moons under Blythe's eyes. Pain compressed her lips. A young wife concerned about the problems in her marriage, she didn't need more stress.

"I am sorry," Vale insisted, and her voice nearly broke. "For a lot of things."

"I don't care!" Like thunder Blythe's voice rolled across the yard. "Stay away from me."

Turning on her heel, she climbed into the Audi. The screech of tires, and the car sped down the street.

The silence left in its wake threatened Vale's composure.

Why did I follow her out of the house? A reckless move in keeping with the impulsive behavior that had marred their relationship in the past. *Crazy-cakes.* At twenty-nine, Vale possessed the ability to control her emotions. But with her half sister, it seemed she never would.

The living room curtains fluttered back into place. Witnessing the argument would have upset their grandmother. Why had she broken the promise not to cross swords with Blythe? Humiliated, she trudged back toward the house.

A child's voice rang out. "That was worse than a fight at school. I didn't know ladies were meaner than kids."

Vale whirled around.

A picket fence ran between her grandmother's property and the small house next door. On the opposite side of the fence, a girl studied her quizzically.

A fluff of brown hair crowned the child's head. Ketchup spattered the collar of her lime-green top. The round purple glasses perched on her nose were too large for her face. She resembled the cartoon version of a bookworm caterpillar.

"Why were you fighting with Blythe?" the girl asked. "She's really nice. She's married to Booker Banks, you know. He's the best pitcher in the universe. Blythe got his autograph for me."

Naturally the kid knew her younger sister. Blythe lived in Philadelphia. She visited Iris frequently.

"It was nothing," Vale lied. "Just a quarrel between sisters. I'm sorry you heard us."

"You're Blythe's sister? I didn't know she had one." The girl cocked her head like a bird. "You don't look like sisters."

Vale's shoulders sagged. "We're not," she admitted. "Not in the ways that count."

Chapter 7

Near the podium, Blythe waited for her turn to speak.

Beneath a look of calm, her emotions roiled. The shock of finding Vale in their grandmother's living room. The sharp words they'd exchanged. Of all the times to pick for a surprise visit, why was Vale here now?

During the most difficult phase of Blythe's life.

Her energies were consumed by the heartbreaking decision hanging over her like a curse. By the sheer force of will it took not to fall apart completely. Would her sister remain in Philadelphia long enough to watch her world crumble? Having Vale bear witness seemed the cruelest twist of all.

A tremor shuddered across Blythe's shoulders. Subduing it, she glanced furtively at the women surrounding the linen-clad tables in the Ritz-Carlton's banquet room. They wore a variety of stylish outfits for the afternoon charity event. Many favored spring dresses and sleek pantsuits. Others chose pencil-thin cropped pants with silk blouses, their necklaces swinging lightly as they sipped chilled goblets of chardonnay. Several acquaintances waved, and Blythe forced a smile.

At the podium, Stu Gaines spoke passionately about his dedication to research for childhood leukemia. Barrel chested, with a thatch of iron-colored hair and an easygoing personality, the retired Phillies infield coach held the women in his thrall.

He mentioned Booker and the Phillies' current winning streak. Applause rippled across the room. The attention of a hundred women swung briefly to Blythe, as if her marriage to the team's starting pitcher had any bearing on his success.

Eyes downcast, she resisted the urge to bolt from the room. *Just get through this.* Lifting her head, she mentally rehearsed the short speech she'd prepared. *Don't let Booker down.*

The irony of the situation wasn't lost on her. Not very long ago, she'd loved crowds. Adored them, really. The opportunity they gave her to shine, and to bring people together. How she'd sweep into a function with confidence, acting like a shield for her more introspective husband. Now the women casting glances her way only filled Blythe with shame.

During the first year of their marriage, Blythe had thrived in the reflected glow of her husband's celebrity. Booker's fame lent prestige to any charity, and he never declined to help organizations that benefited children. She admired his desire to champion worthy causes. By their second year of marriage, she began appearing in his place during the season, when baseball commanded all his energies. Now she despised the questions posed by curious fans, and the assumptions that marriage to the star pitcher brought only happiness.

Did she enjoy the travel? Were they planning on a family? Did Booker have any hobbies during the off-season?

Blythe answered each question with aplomb. Even though she felt like an impostor. *Was* an impostor, in all the ways that counted.

Wrapping up his speech, Stu winked at her. *Ready?* For a brief, terrible moment, a sensation like falling rushed through her. As if the floor had opened beneath her feet to plummet her into an unescapable well of sorrow. Blythe's vision narrowed to a pinpoint. Summoning the last of her emotional reserves, she strode to the microphone.

Blythe thanked the women for attending. Sticking to the prepared script, she spoke quickly. A jittery despair tightened her chest. She feared stumbling over her words. With thinning determination, she muddled through.

Another round of applause, and Stu escorted her to a table in front. They made small talk with the charity's organizers, the wife of a local oncologist and a rheumy-eyed matron whose old-money wealth funded a variety of cancer research.

Plates of Caesar salad appeared before them.

"Has the flight landed?" Stu asked her.

Regret slowed Blythe's movements as she pressed the napkin to her lap. "They'll be on the ground in just a few minutes." Tonight, Booker would play against the Rockies at Coors Field. For now, he was buying the ruse that she wanted a long visit with Iris.

Stu dug into his salad. "I'm sorry the fundraiser kept you in town."

It hadn't—she'd been avoiding Booker for weeks. Using every excuse at her disposal to put distance between them while she tried to make a decision.

"It's fine. I didn't mind."

The waiter appeared with wine. Ignoring the drink, Blythe sipped her ice water, her stomach queasy. Several women stopped by the table to chat. Thankfully Stu carried the bulk of the conversation.

When the women left, Stu took a sip of his wine. "I appreciate your help." He gave Blythe a warm glance. "If you hadn't been able to come, I would've been doing this solo."

Her phone buzzed, sparing her from responding. Throat tight, she read the text from Booker.

Just landed. Wish U were here.

The room swayed. It seemed to tilt off-center as she reread the message. The threat of tears stung her eyes. Sliding the napkin from her lap, she placed it beside her plate. She needed to escape the banquet room's bright laughter and curious glances.

"Stu, if you'll excuse me for a moment." Blythe pushed back her chair.

He studied her with concern. "Should I walk you out?"

"No. I'm fine. I'll be right back."

With a stiff gait, Blythe strode past the sea of tables. The corridor was thankfully empty. She paced across the thick carpeting until her pulse steadied.

In her palm, the phone vibrated. Another text from Booker.

Babe?

For long seconds, she stared at the text. Felt her heart throb as she finally responded.

I'm here.

Having fun with Iris?

Grief threatened to pull her under. *I'm not having fun, baby. I'm in hell.* She reminded herself that Booker didn't need the piling on. Not from his private life—not until she came to a decision.

Rallying, she typed quickly. She was having a wonderful time with her grandmother. She wished him well at tonight's game and promised to watch.

A last text from her husband—the flight's passengers were beginning to deplane.

The phone went silent.

Returning to the banquet hall, Blythe managed to get through the event. The moment the luncheon ended, she bade Stu farewell and hurried to her car.

Pulling into the late-afternoon traffic, she recalled the lie she'd told Iris about meeting friends for dinner. For days, Blythe had been avoiding everyone in her social circle. Only a great actress could fake happiness—she was anything but. If one of her girlfriends picked up on her mood, they'd pose questions she wasn't prepared to answer.

Driving past her grandmother's house, she spotted Vale's car in the drive. Blythe's heart sank. Did it matter if she issued a dozen ultimatums? None would carry weight. She couldn't force Vale to leave.

Knowing Iris, she viewed the double visit as an opportunity. Would she attempt to mend the relationship between her granddaughters? *Good luck with that.*

Even though she'd fail, Iris would never ask one of them to stay at a hotel. Vale wasn't going anywhere. Blythe considered booking a room for herself. Holing up somewhere quiet while she weighed the pros and cons of staying in her marriage. Or *made* the effort to stay—whenever she mustered the courage to lay everything at Booker's feet, wouldn't the final decision be his?

Quickly she dismissed the idea of staying somewhere. Booker was an A-list celebrity in Philadelphia. What if a reporter spotted her at a local hotel and began asking questions?

Which left too many hours to fill before returning to her grandmother's house tonight. She'd promised Booker she'd watch the game, something she refused to do with Vale present. Where to catch the game instead?

On the next block, she pulled into the lot behind Knock's Pub. Dinner hour, and couples filled the tables for Friday date night. Blythe slid onto a stool at the bar, near one of the big-screen TVs. When the waitress appeared, she ordered a burger she couldn't eat.

Picking at the bun, she realized the deception wouldn't last much longer. She owed Booker the truth.

She'd broken a cardinal rule of marriage. The honorable choice was to seek a divorce, a prospect she didn't wish to contemplate. How could she hurt Booker, the only man she'd ever loved? Yet it wasn't fair to continue this . . . charade. Pretending she could give him the happiness he deserved.

Caught on a knife's edge of indecision, Blythe flagged down the waitress.

Setting her plate aside, she ordered a Jack Daniel's neat.

Chapter 8

At the kitchen sink, Vale glanced out the window. Lights from nearby houses winked in the inky night. Despite Iris's calls and texts, there was still no word from Blythe. The situation left Vale teetering between concern and relief. Concern because her sister's absence weighed heavily on their grandmother. And relief because the animosity between sisters might spark another argument.

After dinner, she'd unpacked in the smaller of the two guest bedrooms. The *pink room*, in her grandmother's parlance. The cozy space featured whimsical, pink-striped wallpaper. A border of roses in deeper hues ran above it, rimming a ceiling painted blush pink. On the bed, the quilt embroidered with ivy and roses was soft from wear. It smelled pleasingly of lavender from a recent washing.

Across the hall, she found the door to the larger guest bedroom— the *yellow room*—firmly shut. Walking past, she went downstairs to join her grandmother. Together they'd watched Booker and the Phillies play in Denver against the Rockies.

On the stove, the teapot whistled. Vale filled two cups with chamomile tea and carried them into the living room. At the bank of windows, Iris stood frowning at the night.

"You might as well stop worrying." Vale handed over a cup. "Blythe will return when she's good and ready."

"I should've mentioned your visit this morning." Worry lines creased Iris's brow. "I didn't give her time to prepare. It *has* been a long time since you've seen each other."

"It wouldn't have mattered. Blythe wants nothing to do with me. If you'd told her at breakfast, she still would've been furious."

"You don't know how she might have reacted. This is all my fault."

"Stop beating yourself up." Vale led her away from the windows. When they were both seated on the couch, she added, "If it weren't for your tests next week, I'd drive back to Pittsburgh immediately. Believe me, I'm not looking forward to dodging my sister for the duration of my stay."

"You won't have to avoid Blythe. I'll reason with her."

An undertaking sure to fail. The last time the sisters enjoyed a semicivil relationship, they'd been children. Iris could lay on a ton of sugar—it wouldn't sweeten Blythe's opinion of Vale.

"Nana, I *do* wish you'd explain about the tests." Vale expelled a frustrated breath. "Why can't you fill me in? I'll feel less nervous if you shed some light on your health issues."

"Stop fretting. At my age, doctors never stop poking and prodding. It doesn't mean I'm dying."

A comment made in jest, but the humor escaped Vale. "I'd still like the details. Think of it as fair trade. It'll keep me from returning Blythe's next insults. Got any Band-Aids for my ego? I'll need them."

"You always were my glass-half-empty grandchild. Why not give optimism a whirl? You might like it." Eyes dancing, Iris took a dainty sip of her tea. "Here's a suggestion—stop viewing your sister as the enemy."

"If I'm a pessimist, then you're too optimistic. Given a chance, Blythe will pitch me off a bridge."

"Nonsense. Your sister doesn't have a mean bone in her body."

The ready defense angled Vale's neck back. "Are you sure about that?" she sputtered. "Blythe was rude to you, Nana. She ordered you to park me in a hotel somewhere. Does she usually issue commands from on high?"

"She didn't mean to be rude. Seeing you after all this time gave her a shock, that's all."

"You may need to rethink your assessment. She's furious I'm staying. Imagine how she'll react when she discovers you *didn't* put me up in a hotel—or dump me on the street. She's spoiled and used to getting her own way."

Iris grunted. "That's your jealousy talking. Good heavens, will you let it rule you forever?"

Heat blistered Vale's cheeks. "I'm not jealous of Blythe."

"I understand the reasons," Iris continued with irritating confidence, "but it's time to let it go. You've spent most of your life clipping the wings of your higher angels. Aren't you tired of fighting with your sister? Not to mention your mother and Grant. None of us chooses the circumstance of our birth. We make do with what we're given."

"I'm not jealous!"

"Oh, Vale. The turmoil and secret heartache we're each born into is long in the making before we draw our first breath. Stop aiming your worst emotions at Blythe. You're both victims in our sad family drama."

The observation loosened the hard stone of anger lodged inside Vale. Flustered, she lowered her elbows to her knees. The truth rolled over her like a wave.

She *was* jealous of Blythe. Of the affection she received from their mother and Grant in ever-flowing abundance. The ease with which she traveled through life.

Until now. Was Blythe seriously thinking about ending her marriage? A divorce would serve as her first mistake. The first loss in a lifetime of wins. The prospect stirred sympathy Vale didn't wish to feel.

The emotion drumming through her put a mix of affection and pity on her grandmother's face. "Your feelings *are* valid," Iris said, "even if they don't serve you well. Nothing about your childhood was normal.

50

Bo moved out before you celebrated your first birthday. Oh, he tried to stick to a visitation schedule. Once he left Philadelphia, those visits became infrequent."

The sadness overtaking Vale shut her eyes. She'd never mustered the courage to ask her mother *why* she divorced so quickly. Bo's constant hopping from one job to the next surely took a toll. His inability to slip into the role of husband and provider. Still, Audrey should've given him a chance to grow into fatherhood—should've given Vale, in her most formative years, the opportunity to thrive in a loving home with both parents.

It wasn't until she began college that Vale gleaned the basics of her parents' ill-fated romance from Iris. The pregnancy was unplanned. Audrey, fresh out of college, had landed a position as an intern at Stern-Belkins, one of the most prestigious accounting firms in the city. When it became clear a baby was on the way, Bo suggested they marry. Despite his aversion to duty, he tried to do the right thing.

While he bounced from one job to the next, Audrey kept them afloat, working through the third trimester of pregnancy. Her water broke during a meeting; Vale nearly made her entrance in a Stern-Belkins conference room. Luckily the ambulance arrived in time.

At sea, Vale opened her eyes. "In my earliest memories, I'm crying. Big, ugly tears as my dad leaves after one of his visits. He never stayed long. Afterward, I felt . . . broken. Like I'd never glue myself back together." The cracks in the foundation of her psyche still frightened her. As if they might cause her to shatter without warning.

"It didn't help when Grant came on the scene. The ink was barely dry on your mother's divorce when he began courting her."

Anger flickered inside Vale. Contrary to her grandmother's assumptions, she suspected Grant had broken up her parents' marriage. Five years older than Audrey, well established—did Grant encourage her to leave Bo?

A theory she didn't share as Iris gave her a consoling hug. "I'll admit, I was stunned when your mother agreed to remarry," Iris said. "I thought she was behaving rashly. Moving from divorce to a new commitment within months."

"It *was* rash."

"And then Blythe came along. You were just a toddler when she was born."

"We were never treated the same."

"No, you weren't," her grandmother agreed, the lines on her brow deepening. There was no mistaking her aversion to discussing truths sure to wound her granddaughter. "That doesn't mean you weren't equally loved."

Disbelief lifted Vale's head. "How can you say that?" She darted an accusing glance. "Mom favored Blythe. Praised her and bragged about her achievements to anyone who'd listen. Grant did too, but that's understandable. She *is* his child."

"Nonsense. Your mother loves you both. It's not in her emotional makeup to love one child more than the other." Distress crossed Iris's features, silencing her for a long moment. Then she added, "Some children are easier to raise. They go along instead of fighting. They follow the rules. Blythe was one of those children."

And I wasn't. Childhood had been a rigged competition, with Blythe winning every round. Unable to catch up, Vale had found creative ways to lash out.

Iris released a tremulous breath. "You turned every one of your mother's requests into a battle. Now that you're all grown up, you might consider how the family dynamic affected your sister."

Vale drew her lips together, considering. It seemed less than charitable that she'd never viewed the situation from Blythe's vantage point. Nearly three years younger than Vale, a silent witness during many of the arguments between Vale and their mother. The escalating series of battles didn't end until Vale reached adulthood and moved out. Did Blythe carry scars from those years?

All families endure private hardships. What the world sees in public rarely mirrors the reality behind closed doors. Vale understood this. Yet she'd never grasped how their tumultuous homelife affected her younger sister.

In the corner of the living room, the grandfather clock chimed the midnight hour.

"It's late, Nana." On the coffee table, her tea had grown cold. Vale picked up the cup. "It's been a long day. We both need to get some rest."

Retrieving her phone from her pocket, Iris studied the blank screen. "I wish Blythe would answer my calls. Why doesn't she pick up?"

"She's fine, Nana. She'll come back when she's ready."

With a sigh, Iris nodded. "Please leave a lamp on. I don't want her coming into a dark house." She started for the stairs.

"Will do."

Vale went into the kitchen to clean up. Her limbs felt leaden as she ascended the staircase. Climbing into bed, she quickly fell into a dreamless sleep.

For an hour, no longer.

Moonlight streamed across the floor. Throwing off the blanket, Vale tried to get a fix on what had awoken her. Then she heard it again—a thumping noise. Louder, now.

Staggering across the darkened bedroom, she tripped on the rug and nearly face-planted. Muttering a curse, she grabbed her bathrobe. At the second-floor landing, she caught a boozy wave of laughter. Blythe's.

A low, masculine voice followed. Not Booker's: the Phillies had played the Rockies tonight in Denver. With her protective instincts on full alert, Vale clambered down the stairs.

In the foyer, she ground to a halt. Confusion stopped her from opening the front door.

Why would Blythe—a married woman—bring a man home?

Chapter 9

Peering through the peephole, Vale gasped. The scene playing out on the shadowy porch strained belief.

Blythe—who'd finished high school without running afoul of their mother's curfew, and sailed through college without one embarrassing shipwreck involving Jell-O shots—was too drunk to walk unassisted. A man half carried, half dragged her forward.

Tall, with reddish-brown hair and the first hint of thickening around the waist, he appeared on the brink of middle age. Good looking, with a wide brow and a strong chin. Fifteen years older than Blythe, easy.

With boozy interest, Blythe leered at him. "My hero." A jumble of curls spilled across her forehead. She'd lost one of her shoes. "Thanks for giving me a ride."

"It's the least I could do."

"Want to come inside?"

"That's the plan. I'll take you to your room."

Vale bristled. Let the sexual antics go on much longer, and they'd wake Iris.

She flicked on the lights. Throwing open the door, she launched onto the porch.

Squinting in the glare, the man looked up. Blythe, reeking of whiskey, seemed unable to focus her eyes.

"Stay where you are," Vale told him. "This is my grandmother's house, not the local brothel. You're not bringing my sister inside and making . . . whoopee."

"Making whoopee?" His gaze sparkled with mirth. "Wasn't the phrase retired in the roaring twenties?"

"You know what I mean."

"I do, and I take offense. If you'll get out of the way—"

"Let her go. I mean it." Vale got in his face. A difficult feat, given his height. "I'll take it from here."

An impasse, and the man smiled with frank amusement. "Don't take this the wrong way," he said, "but the way you tore out of the house with your blonde hair flying . . . I got an image of Tinker Bell ramming against the inside of a mason jar. Do you always come on this strong? It takes some getting used to."

An attempt at a joke, or a clumsy stab at an icebreaker. Vale couldn't decide. She gave up deciphering the mystery when Blythe's knees began to wobble. She lunged forward to catch her.

The man was faster, scooping Blythe up into his arms. "Do me a favor, Vale. Step aside. She's deadweight, more than you can handle. Lead the way—I'll get her to her room."

"How do you know my name?"

On his chest, Blythe's head lolled. "Because I told him you are the *worst* sister in the world. The absolute dregs of humanity."

"She did," the man cheerfully agreed. The late-night confrontation plainly delighted him. "She forgot to mention your territorial nature."

Another joke, and Vale stiffened. "Why don't you stay out of this?"

"Stop telling him what to do." Blythe stuck out her tongue. "Go away."

"Shut up, Blythe," she replied, blocking entry to the house. "I'm doing this for your own good."

To demonstrate, Vale clamped her hands on the doorjambs. She looked foolish, like a physical manifestation of a **DO NOT ENTER** sign.

Some indignities one endured to protect a drunken sibling. After running a bar in Pittsburgh, she'd witnessed too many women make bad choices with men after throwing down enough liquor. *Something I did myself recently. I still blame the tequila.*

At least she hadn't boarded the Stupid Train with a two-carat diamond flashing on her ring finger. If Blythe planned to break her marriage vows, she could schedule her downfall another time.

The man struggled to suppress a smile. "Your reputation precedes you, Vale. Not that I blame you for getting a little amped up."

"Why are you hitting on a woman half your age? Can you see she's drunk?"

"*Half* my age?" He regarded her with mock horror. "You really know how to land the punches."

"Well, you should be ashamed of yourself."

"Why? I'm not here to make whoopee." He took a gander at her scruffy robe and bare feet. His close inspection put heat on her face, which seemed to delight him more. "I'm Emmett McFall," he announced, planting his feet as he strained to hold Blythe. She *was* deadweight. "I'm not the enemy. I live down the street."

"I don't care who you are. Put my sister down."

The command lifted Emmett's brows. Then he surprised her by flinging Blythe over his shoulder.

Nudging Vale out of the way, he strode across the foyer. "Which bedroom?" He began climbing the staircase to the second floor.

"Don't you take 'no' for an answer?" She raced up the stairs behind him. "I didn't invite you inside!"

"Forget the Tinker Bell comparison. You're more like a dog guarding a bone."

The retort Vale readied died in her throat. On the landing Emmett halted abruptly. She nearly careened into him—and her dozing sister, hanging limply across his back.

The commotion had woken Iris. In the hallway above them, she pressed fluttery hands to her cheeks. Her stylish silver-and-violet hairdo stuck out every which way. A neon-pink sleeping mask slanted across her forehead.

"Oh! Emmett!" The strong odor of whiskey wafted up. Repulsed, Iris covered her mouth.

"I was at Knock's Pub with friends and saw Blythe leaving," Emmett told her. "I followed her outside and persuaded her to let me drive her home."

"That was kind of you. She's in no state to get behind the wheel." Iris noticed the sole of Blythe's right foot, blackened with grit. "Emmett, she's missing a shoe! Where is it?"

"I'm not sure. She was hobbling around on one heel when I spotted her leaving the pub."

"I suppose it doesn't matter now." She gestured down the hallway. "Carry her to the yellow room, please."

The friendly exchange deepened the blush on Vale's cheeks. With confusion, she followed them into the bedroom. It *was* plausible that Emmett had come to Blythe's assistance outside the bar. On the other hand, he might've approached her in Knock's Pub and helped her get blitzed.

Trailing close behind, she waited as Emmett deposited Blythe on the bed. The mattress swayed beneath the added weight. Ridiculously, Blythe threw out her arms like a child making snow angels. Then she belched.

Rolling sideways, she giggled. "It's not bedtime. Let's party!"

Vale regarded her grandmother. "I hope you have aspirin. She's going to pay for a night of carousing big-time."

"Yes, she will. The poor baby."

Emmett said, "Can you ladies take it from here?"

"Obviously." Vale narrowed her eyes. "You can leave."

The dismissal put a sparkle in his gaze. "It was nice meeting you too, Vale."

"Go!"

Once his footfalls receded down the stairs, Iris shot her a look. "What's the matter with you? There's no reason to treat Emmett rudely. He's a good friend."

"How was I supposed to know? It was dark when I spotted him on the porch with Blythe. I couldn't tell if he was getting handsy with her."

"Emmett wouldn't take advantage of your sister. He's a good man."

"Don't take this the wrong way, Nana—you're no expert on the modern dating scene. Mix booze with a willing woman, and most guys think 'game on.'" With disgust, Vale recalled her night of stranger-sex in Pittsburgh. "Trust me on this. I know what I'm talking about."

"Then I suggest you find a better caliber of man to date. Responsible men don't take advantage of women."

Tiring of the discussion, Vale surveyed the bedroom. "Let's get Blythe ready for bed. Does she have pj's or something?"

"Check the closet."

A row of neatly hung clothing accosted Vale. Even the accessories—belts, scarves, a gold handbag—were carefully placed on hangers. She grabbed a lace-encrusted nightgown.

"Nana, can you sit her up? Let's get her undressed."

Nodding, Iris approached the bed.

Blythe slapped her away. "Make Vale take out the garbage." Apparently too much booze was leading her on a stroll down memory lane. "I get stuck doing *all* her chores."

"What is she talking about?" Iris sent nervous fingers to her brow. She discovered the sleeping mask tangling with her hair and stuffed it into a pocket of her robe.

"You don't want to know." During their teenage years, Vale had often saddled her younger sister with her chores. "She's really drunk, Nana."

Blythe was also veering toward belligerence—a downside of too much liquor in the occasional patron at the Crafty Cocktail. Vale had seen more than her share of those customers at the bar's closing time.

Getting her ready for bed might take some effort.

"On second thought, let me handle this." Plucking off Blythe's lone shoe, Vale tossed it aside. "Why don't you go back to sleep?"

"Are you sure you don't need my help?"

Blythe took a poorly aimed swipe at the curls tumbling across her face. "It's Vale's turn to vacuum the living room. Make her get her lazy butt moving."

Grinning, Vale shooed her grandmother from the bed. "I've got this, Nana. Go on."

With visible relief, Iris padded from the room.

Taking her time, Vale managed to inch her sister up onto the pillows. The effort drew Blythe's attention from the ceiling. Her eyes slowly blinking, she canvassed Vale's face with irritation. Then with interest. When a tiny flicker of warmth crossed her features, it stirred the memories in Vale's heart.

During childhood she'd often helped her sister dress. Holding pants as Blythe stepped in. Steering tops over her head and lacing up her shoes. Sweet moments of intimacy before Vale—burdened by their mother's criticism and chafing beneath the questions other children asked—learned to shield her emotions.

Why is your last name different from Blythe's and your mom's? By Vale's first years in elementary school, Bo's visits were unpredictable. But he never would've allowed Grant Wittman to adopt his child. Vale wore the name Lightner with defensive pride—and unspoken shame.

Running from the memory, she gently leaned Blythe forward. "Lift your arms."

"I can't. I'm too tired."

"No, you're stubborn. You're enjoying this at my expense."

"I'm sleepy." Blythe rolled sideways. Vale drew the shirt over her head and unclasped her bra.

The nightgown rippled past Blythe's neck. Her eyes drifted shut as Vale eased her arms through. Removing the skintight jeans took longer. Blythe, succumbing to a bout of giggles, refused to cooperate.

"You really are a pain." Vale wedged the jeans down past her sister's thighs. "FYI, you owe *me* an apology for putting me through this."

"I don't owe you anything."

She flung the jeans to the floor. "Yeah? Well, tell me this. Why were you flirting with Emmett on the porch? You were coming on to him." With irritation, she pulled down the bedspread and the sheet. "I thought you had more sense."

"It's none of your business."

"You're married. You're not supposed to go to bars solo and pick up men."

"Oh, shut up already."

"No, you listen to me. I mean it, Blythe." After she tucked her sister in, she sat on the side of the bed. "I don't care what's gone wrong in your marriage. You took a vow, and it ought to mean something. At least it should mean something while you're wearing Booker's ring. You want to make dumb choices? Go right ahead. But you owe it to Booker to at least wait until—"

She cut off as Blythe slipped her hand out from beneath the sheet.

Blythe's features were suddenly relaxed, her eyes open with childlike wonder. She curled a finger through a lock of Vale's golden hair. The gesture was intensely familiar. She'd often played with Vale's hair when they were children, flung out together on the grass. Or on nights when lightning streaked the sky and, frightened, she climbed into Vale's bed.

Their gazes merged. When Blythe spoke, her voice was more fragile than dreams.

"Remember when you taught me to fly?" she asked.

"Of course I remember." Affection mixed with the sorrow growing heavy in Vale's chest. "You were three years old. You were scared about learning, but I promised to keep you safe. It was the only way to get you to take a leap of faith. You weren't exactly a brave kid. Not when it came to trying something new."

"You *did* keep me safe. We had fun."

"Yeah. We did."

Blythe's eyelids began to close. Sleep wanted to take her. Fighting the urge, she drew them open. "Where were we?"

"At the playground across from the library." It had been a beautiful spring afternoon. A day full of promise, like the lives they had yet to lead. "We were with the babysitter."

"Which one? There were so many."

Vale searched her memories. "Her name was Glendy. She smelled of licorice and gave us candy on the sly. You liked her. I did too. She worked at Stern-Belkins with Mom and your dad before she retired—a receptionist."

"She didn't mind you teaching me to fly?"

The weight of remembering bowed Vale's head. "She thought I was trustworthy. You did too."

Vale had been, on that day. Taking Blythe by the hand to lead her to the swing set. Helping her climb into the wide vinyl seat and guiding her hands onto the swing's heavy chains. *Hold tight.* When Vale pushed her forward, Blythe chortled with delight. They played until the sun dipped low in the sky, and the other children scampered off as the dinner hour neared. It was just the two of them as Blythe discovered the thrill of breaking past gravity's hold.

"I want to feel that way again." Blythe let her eyes drift shut. "Free. Happy."

"You will. Just put in the effort. You'll get your life back on track."

"I doubt it. I've messed everything up. I can't fix it."

An opportunity, and Vale seized it. "Did you do something to hurt Booker? It's okay if you did. Nobody's perfect, right?" The impulse to help was unexpected. Vale welcomed it gladly. "If you need a sympathetic ear, I'm happy to listen."

"You can't help. Nobody can."

The remark fell into an uneasy silence. Disappointed, Vale turned off the lamp. Moonlight spilled across the bed in icy waves.

Blythe groaned. "Make the room stop spinning."

"Sorry, I can't. It'll stop in a little while."

"What if it doesn't?"

"Go to sleep, Blythe." Before second thoughts intruded, Vale kissed her lightly on the cheek. The affection put the smallest hint of pleasure on Blythe's face.

She was nearing the door when her sister spoke again.

"Vale?"

"Yes?"

"Thanks for tucking me in."

Chapter 10

In the lot behind Green Iris, the delivery van rolled to a stop. Two men got out. They began ferrying plants to the shop's back door.

Vale parked nearby and hurried over. "Sorry I'm late."

The younger of the two sported the beginnings of a mustache. "Where's Iris?" He frowned. "She handles the Saturday morning deliveries."

"She's not here." Last night's theatrics with Blythe had taken a toll. It took some convincing before Iris finally agreed to sleep in and let Vale open the shop.

The younger man ambled closer. "Who are you?"

"Her granddaughter." Vale held up the key. "I'll let you in."

In the stockroom, pots and gardening supplies took up much of the space on the twelve worktables. An unusual sight—plainly the dual visits by her granddaughters had taken precedence over Iris's normally keen organizational skills. Vale directed the men to put the day's shipment on an empty table.

Potting soil trailed across the floor. It led to a large ceramic pot, where someone—probably her grandmother's business partner, Detta Green—had recently transplanted a lushly green parlor palm. Near the front of the stockroom, other houseplants waited in a pretty row for placement on the sales floor.

Long established in Philadelphia's Queen Village, the two-story shop also carried vegetable plants suitable for container gardening, cacti and succulents, miniature roses, and a wide variety of terra cotta and ceramic pots. Wandering out front, Vale breathed in the moist air. She surveyed the rustic shelves brimming with greenery and the wide display window with its vibrant arrangement of standing and hanging plants. During her difficult childhood, she'd loved working in the shop beside her grandmother.

"Vale, hello!"

Keys jingling, Detta Green strode through the front door. Stout, sixtyish, with deep smile lines framing her mouth, Detta continued to work at the shop full-time. Her close friendship with Iris went back decades; they'd first met in a grief support group after losing their husbands. To Vale, Detta was like a generous auntie, quick to dole out advice and affection in equal measure.

She caught Vale in a tight hug. "I'm thrilled you're back in town!" Releasing her, she flashed a winning smile. "Do you need help finding an apartment? Say the word, and I'll begin the search."

"Slow down. I've missed you too, but I'm only visiting."

"Do you want to break my heart?" With mock fury, Detta stomped her foot. "You've been living in Pittsburgh long enough. Sell your portion of the Crafty Cocktail to your father. Move back to Philadelphia."

Inwardly Vale winced. There was nothing left of the bar to sell. Even the furnishings were toast.

"I'll never understand how Bo convinced you to go into business with him," Detta added. "Running a bar, staying up half the night—I don't know how you stand the hours."

"Detta, pressuring me won't do any good. I can't just pick up and move back."

"You're only twenty-nine. You can do whatever you please. The best years of your life are still ahead of you. Come work for us—we'll promote you to manager. Even with a part-time staff, running the shop is tiring for two women nearing retirement."

"My grandmother has ten years on you. *She's* nearing retirement. I can't imagine you slowing down."

"How do you know what I'd like to do? Maybe I'm dreaming of traveling nonstop. I've always wanted to see Thailand. I hear the street food is fabulous."

To Vale's knowledge, Detta rarely left Philadelphia—or the shop. "Are you serious?" She was more of a homebody than Iris.

Detta's eyes twinkled. "It depends. Will you come work for us?"

A teenage girl entered the shop, sparing Vale from answering. A boy about the same age came in next. The weekend staff.

After Detta put them to work, Vale followed her to the stockroom. Together, they ferried the newly delivered plants onto the sales floor. Outside several customers milled about, waiting for the shop to open.

"Where's your grandmother?" Detta added a golden pothos to the plants in the display window. "We open in ten minutes. It's not like her to arrive late on a Saturday."

Lowering her voice, Vale explained about the night before. Summing up, she added, "I doubt Nana got much sleep after we put Blythe to bed."

"What a terrible experience for you both."

"I'm worried about my sister. Blythe was totally blitzed. She's always been levelheaded. I never would've guessed she'd drink to excess."

The observation furrowed Detta's brow. "This isn't the first time."

"What do you mean?"

Gesturing her forward, Detta marched to a corner of the store. Her posture indicated this wouldn't be a pleasant conversation.

Once they were out of earshot of the employees, she said, "Please don't share this with your grandmother. She's worried enough about your sister as it is."

"Share *what*, Detta? FYI, you're scaring me."

"Earlier this month, I ran into Blythe in a restaurant here in Queen Village. I'd gone in to pick up dinner. I spotted her alone at the bar, finishing her third martini."

"How do you know how much she had to drink?"

"The bartender hadn't removed the other glasses. It was after seven o'clock—the place was busy. Your sister looked ready to slide off the barstool. Seeing her like that kicked the wind out of me."

Pity for her sister wove through Vale. "What did you do?"

"Paid for my takeout and her bar tab. Then I insisted on driving her home. She was too drunk to make a fuss. Thankfully she'd taken Lyft to the restaurant. She wasn't in any shape to get behind the wheel."

The story washed Vale's stomach with acid. Last night, Blythe *had* nearly driven home while under the influence. What if her grandmother's neighbor hadn't stopped her? In retrospect, Vale shouldn't have given Emmett McFall a hard time. He deserved her gratitude for bringing her sister home safely.

She thought of something else. "When you got to her apartment, how did Booker react?"

"He wasn't home—game in Atlanta. During the season, Blythe used to accompany him to nearly all the away games. Not this year, according to your grandmother. If she's out drinking whenever he's out of town, how would he know?"

"He wouldn't."

"Which is why someone close to Blythe must talk to her. I would, but it's not my place to intervene." Worry inked Detta's toffee-colored eyes. "Perhaps you should. I'm not saying Blythe has a drinking problem. Not yet, but this can't go on. Whatever's bothering her, she's more apt to talk with someone close in age. You *are* her sister."

Overwhelmed, Vale studied her feet. What was the likelihood her half sister would listen to her counsel? For a few brief moments last night, she'd nearly felt close to Blythe. As if the interlude they'd shared could melt away the years of animosity.

Nothing has changed. Once Blythe dragged herself out of bed today, she'd feel hungover and testy. It was unlikely she'd remember the sweet conversation about Vale teaching her to fly on the swing set—a day from the dawning years of their childhood when the bond of love held them close.

"Detta, my sister won't confide in me. You know we don't get along."

"Can't you put aside the bad feelings and make a fresh start?"

"I'd like to," Vale said, astonished by the sincerity rimming the admission. She *did* want a do-over. One long overdue but impossible to achieve. "It's not that simple. Blythe has no reason to trust me. We're practically strangers. Besides, I'm not staying long enough to fix everything that's gone wrong between us."

"You won't know unless you try. You *are* here, Vale. When was the last time you and Blythe stayed under your grandmother's roof together?"

"I honestly can't recall."

"Then consider this an opportunity." Detta started toward the door, to flip the OPEN sign. From over her shoulder, she added, "Make the attempt to mend the relationship."

The bell chimed as several customers walked in.

Glad to get to work, Vale approached a middle-aged couple shopping for a patio garden at their condo. As she helped them select plants, she privately sifted through Detta's words, sensing the truth in her advice. Iris planned to speak with Blythe about her troubles. But wouldn't it be easier for Blythe to unburden herself to someone closer in age? If the opportunity arose, Vale resolved to make the effort to reach out to her sister.

Soon the shop bustled with people. A third part-time employee, a bespectacled gentleman with a cloud of white hair, arrived at ten o'clock. He wore a smart tweed blazer and a bow tie. With a nod to Detta, he positioned himself on the shop's second floor, where shelves of miniature roses and vegetable plants suitable for container gardening were located.

At half past eleven, Vale spotted Iris near the sales counter. Wending her way up the crowded aisle, she waved. "How long have you been here?" She gave her grandmother a peck on the cheek. "I didn't see you come in."

Iris stashed her purse beneath the counter. "I've just arrived. I hope Detta isn't upset by the delay. I hate letting her down."

"She's fine. I handled the morning delivery and explained about Blythe. How is she this morning?"

"Still asleep, poor baby. I left a bottle of aspirin on her nightstand." Iris stifled a yawn. "I can't shake the fog in my head."

"Detta just brewed a new pot of coffee. Would you like a cup?"

"I'll get it." Iris glanced at her watch. "You can't stay."

"Sure I can. I'll help out until closing."

"I appreciate the gesture, but Ana was called in to work. Her normal babysitter isn't available. Will you watch Natty for a few hours? She's no trouble at all. I told Ana you would."

Vale studied her with puzzlement. "Sure . . . if you'll tell me who's Ana. I'm guessing Natty is her daughter."

"Ah. Right. You haven't met them yet." A sheepish grin crept across her grandmother's lips. "They moved in next door about a year ago. Ana lost her husband in Afghanistan. Natty is her only child. A delightful girl—Natty wears purple eyeglasses that are too big for her face. They make her resemble a curious baby owl."

"Or a cartoon version of a bookworm caterpillar," Vale murmured. "I met Natty yesterday."

"You did?"

"She witnessed my shouting match with Blythe on the front lawn. Actually, I did most of the shouting. Blythe made her feelings known without raising her voice, at least not until the end." Dismay lifted Vale's shoulders to her ears. "After Blythe drove off, I *did* apologize to Natty."

"Oh, Vale. When will you learn to control your temper?"

"Hey, I wasn't the only one fired up yesterday. Blythe was too."

"Because you followed her out of the house! If you'd stayed put, there wouldn't have been an argument in my front yard."

"All right—you win. I should've stayed inside."

"I'm not keeping a scorecard, pumpkin. I just wish you'd think before you leap." Iris fiddled with the buttons of her pink spring sweater. "Speaking of apologies, please extend one to Emmett if you see him in the neighborhood. I sent him a text this morning, but you should follow up. You were beastly to him last night."

"Which is why I'm planning to dodge him." *Mostly,* Vale mused, *because I wouldn't know how to frame the apology.*

"Gutless." Iris gave her a small push toward the stockroom. "Make sure your sister is fine before going over to babysit Natty. If Blythe's awake, encourage her to eat something. It'll help her feel better. You have some time—Ana isn't expecting you for another hour."

Chapter 11

A deep quiet enveloped the house. Hovering by the stairs, Vale considered checking on her sister. She decided against it. Better to let Blythe sleep.

The rumble of her stomach urged Vale into the kitchen. This morning, she'd skipped breakfast. An afternoon of babysitting lay ahead. She made a turkey and swiss sandwich, then went out back.

The gardens behind her grandmother's house balanced lush green hideaways with riots of color. Curving beds of azalea and rhododendron hugged the slate patio. On the arbor leading away from the cozy space, thickly vined roses hung heavy with buds. A stone walkway cut through the rectangular strips of lawn. On either side of the property, a privacy fence ran between the adjoining houses.

Beneath the Japanese maple, the beginnings of a new flower bed were taking shape. Carved in a half-moon shape, the patch of ground waited for the arrival of shade-loving plants. Nibbling on her sandwich, Vale wondered if Iris had left the bed unfinished once she learned of Blythe's marital troubles.

Pacing in a slow circle around the tree, Vale recalled this morning's conversation with Detta. Perhaps Blythe didn't have a drinking problem yet, but addiction often began in fits and starts. Drinking alone was a warning sign. On at least two occasions she'd done so—last night and when Detta found her downing martinis in Queen Village. Were there other occasions when Blythe used liquor to numb her emotions? With the baseball season in full swing, Booker seemed oblivious to the change in his wife's behavior. Nothing stood in the way of Blythe cultivating a destructive habit.

If not for last night's events and Detta's troubling story, Vale wouldn't know either.

Despite the emotional divide separating them, she didn't wish to stand by idly while Blythe succumbed to addiction. Sisters were supposed to protect each other.

Strolling toward the house, she pondered last night's tender exchange. Could she steer their relationship onto a better path? Finding a way past the rancor and the years of mistrust was a daunting task.

She stepped into the kitchen to find Blythe digging ice out of the freezer. A combative air surrounded her. On a positive note, she'd donned jeans and a tank top. She'd also run a brush through her thick curls.

"I'm glad to see you're awake." Vale spiked her voice with good cheer. "Would you like an omelet? I'll whip one up for you."

"Don't bother."

Setting her plate in the sink, Vale hazarded a more thorough glance. "How do you feel?" Her sister's normally olive-toned skin looked patchy with fatigue.

"Like I've been put through a meat grinder—twice."

"It'll pass."

"Not fast enough."

Turning away, Blythe dumped ice cubes into the center of a dish towel. Rolling the towel shut, she pressed it to her forehead. No doubt she preferred her solitude, and the desire to escape the kitchen grew strong. Holding her ground, Vale began unstacking the dishwasher.

"Should I brew coffee?" She clattered plates into the cupboard. "The caffeine might help."

"Please don't." Cradling the ice pack, Blythe sank onto a chair. "I won't be able to keep it down."

"How about ginger ale? It'll settle your stomach."

"Sure."

While she filled a glass, Blythe scrolled through her phone. The headline for last night's game in Denver popped onto the screen.

Vale placed the ginger ale before her. "Did you catch the game? The Phillies were incredible—especially Booker. The Rockies didn't stand a chance against his pitching. He must be on top of the world this morning."

"I wouldn't know. We haven't spoken."

"You haven't called to congratulate him?" The remark was close to prying, and Vale sent an apologetic glance. "I guess I assumed you would."

Blythe regarded her with impatience. "It's three hours earlier in Denver. Booker's probably in the shower. Not that I plan to call him later."

"Why not?" *Also not my business.*

"Booker won't pitch again until next week, but the team has another game tonight against the Rockies. He's superstitious on game days. Eating the same high-protein breakfast, putting in twenty minutes of meditation before he goes to the ballpark—during the season, pro athletes deal with a lot of pressure. I stay out of his way."

"It sounds like a lot of pressure for both of you."

The remark, meant to soften, brought an unintended consequence. Blythe's expression grew stony.

"Vale, I'm not comfortable discussing my marriage with you. I can see you'd like to help, or you're striving to get on my good side."

"Both, actually." Vale took a tentative step closer. "Last night when I tucked you into bed, there was a moment when I thought we connected. The way we did when we were kids. Before everything went wrong between us. Can we build on that? I'd like to."

Lowering the ice pack, Blythe gasped. "You put me to bed?" Her mouth thinned. "You must be kidding."

The reaction made Vale feel exposed, foolish. She managed to blot the disappointment from her face.

"I don't remember much about last night," Blythe was saying. "Not beyond getting into Emmett's car. I assumed he dropped me off."

"You're missing a few key moments after he brought you home. Big ones." When Blythe flashed her a look, Vale held up her palms. "Hey, I *am* trying to help."

Blythe's gaze hardened. "That's great. You want to help? Start by telling me when you're going back to Pittsburgh. Today would be good."

"I haven't decided."

"Well, you should leave immediately. I'm going through a hard time and don't need the added stress."

Vale struggled to suppress her anger. "I don't have a firm date set." She flirted with the idea of explaining about their grandmother's upcoming tests. If Blythe understood the situation, she'd back off. Wouldn't Iris need moral support from them both if the tests revealed a problem? Yet breaking her grandmother's confidence didn't appeal. Given Blythe's marital troubles, they'd agreed not to tell her.

Choosing a different tack, Vale said, "You need your privacy—I get it. I'll stay out of your way. I'm planning to put in hours at Green Iris while I'm here. At dinnertime, I'll take off if you need time alone with Nana. You'll hardly see me."

"You aren't needed at the plant shop. Nana has a part-time staff, and you have a job in Pittsburgh. Reschedule your visit."

"I can't."

The ice pack landed on the table with a *thunk.* "You're unbelievable." Rage broke on Blythe so strong, she appeared ready to launch to her feet. "Don't you see you're in the way? I'm dealing with issues you can't understand because you're flighty. You never stuck with a job when you lived in Philadelphia. Now you and Bo are running a bar that

I'll bet is always on the verge of bankruptcy. You don't know the first thing about making good choices, or commitment, or what it's like to have your marriage on the rocks. All you think about is yourself. You're shallow and self-centered—just like your father."

Blythe's voice broke. On a sob, she scooped up the ice pack.

She hurled it with surprising force. Vale leaped sideways, bumping into the counter as the pack grazed her shoulder. Smacking into a cupboard, it burst open. Ice skittered across the floor.

"Leave Bo out of this!" Vale's anger flared. "What about *your* father? Grant is an opportunist. He has absolutely no morals."

"What are you talking about? My father is a good man. Don't you dare try to tear him down."

A challenge, which Vale took up readily. "Get real, Blythe. Grant caused my parents' divorce. He was seeing Mom while she was still married to my dad."

"That's not true!"

"Oh please. It was awfully convenient, how he popped the question right after they'd divorced. Too convenient, if you ask me. He knew Mom wanted a do-over, and he was happy to supply one." For years, the unsubstantiated theory had gnawed at Vale. Now she took a sickly pleasure in the shock it stamped on her sister's face. "I'm sure that's how it went down. Grant started an affair with Mom, then encouraged her to divorce Bo. I hated him for destroying my parents' marriage. I still do."

Venom bled through the declaration. It stole the oxygen from the room.

Blythe studied her with glittering ire and a strange satisfaction. Beneath the force of her regard, Vale was struck with the sudden awareness that she'd lost the upper hand. How, exactly, wasn't clear.

But the emotion flashing through her sister's eyes warned she'd miscalculated. Badly.

Pushing away from the table, Blythe rose on unsteady feet. "Get your facts straight." She gave a look like thunder. "Bo divorced Mom. My father didn't have anything to do with it."

"You're wrong."

"Don't take my word for it—call Bo. Maybe he'll tell you the truth. You could ask Mom, but you've treated her like a pariah for years, and she may not want to talk about it. Bo divorced her because she wouldn't take seriously his dream of owning a bar. She begged him to find a more stable occupation. He refused. Then he filed for divorce."

Confidence rimmed the explanation. It cut through Vale's assumptions.

Floundering, she managed to meet Blythe's gaze. "How do you know what happened between my parents?"

"I can't believe you have to ask."

"Tell me."

"Mom gave me the details when I was in high school. I was curious, and she didn't hesitate to share the story. I'm sure she would've told you too if you hadn't spent every minute fighting with her."

The weight of the heated exchange congealed the air between them. Vale searched for a retort. She was unable to rally one.

Blythe wasn't finished. "Here's some advice. Stop going through life with blinders on." She gave a short, mirthless laugh. "Or can't you stop rewriting history? Bo chose to leave Mom—and you."

Uncertainty washed through Vale. Abrupt, painful, it stole the breath from her lungs. Was Blythe's version of the past accurate?

The triumph curling her lips held the answer.

It was enough to send Vale fleeing from the room.

~

Vale's purse lay on the foyer's console table. Snatching it up, she ran outside. Scrambled down the porch steps, her throat tight.

On the sidewalk, a woman in a floppy sunhat steered her toy poodle to the base of a tree. Brushing past, Vale took long strides away from the house. Clammy perspiration sprouted on her brow. Pulling out her phone, she checked the time. In five minutes, she was due to babysit Natty.

Wavering, she stared unseeing at the street. It made sense to check Blythe's version of events. Let it go, and she'd never stop wondering.

With thin resolve, she dialed her father. On the second ring, Bo picked up.

"Hey, blue eyes. How's your grandmother? I miss you. It's been—"

"Dad," she said, breaking in. "There's something I need to know."

"Sure. What's up?"

The sun beat down, a merciless glare. Escaping the light, she darted into the shade of an oak tree.

"Vale? Are you there?"

She leaned heavily against the trunk. There was no simple way to ask. *Why even go there?* The truth could sting, like a self-inflicted wound.

"Did you divorce Mom?" she blurted. "I've always assumed it was the other way around."

"Why does it matter now?"

"Because my family has been broken my entire life. I can't repair the damage if I don't understand the reasons."

The waver in her voice put Bo on guard. "It was a long time ago," he said carefully. "I really don't want to go into it."

A dodge, and her heart thumped out of rhythm. "Then it's true. You walked out on us."

"I couldn't be the husband your mother wanted. Or live up to her demands."

"So you left."

An uncomfortable pause. In the background, Vale caught a woman's voice. Bo muffled the phone as he spoke to her.

When he came back on, he said, "Can we talk when you get back? This isn't a good time. I, uh, have company."

"Don't worry about it, Dad," Vale said, her voice barely a whisper. Why prolong the conversation? She'd already learned the ugly truth. "I'll talk to you later."

"The offer stands. Once you're back in Pittsburgh, if you want—"

"Forget it. There's no need. I'll talk to you soon."

Hanging up, she swiped at her eyes.

Chapter 12

A bitter taste bloomed in Vale's mouth. Staring at the silent phone, she struggled to get her bearings. Why had she assumed she understood the particulars of her parents' divorce? Why hadn't she asked? During the last four years while she worked beside her father, there had been many opportunities to discover the truth. Were there other secrets Bo had kept from her? Details from his past he kept hidden out of shame or guilt?

There wasn't time to think about it now. She'd promised to babysit the girl next door. Picking up her feet, she hurried down the sidewalk.

Natty's mother stood on the front stoop of the nondescript brick ranch. Shielding her eyes, she scanned the street with ill-concealed worry.

Spotting Vale, she waved. "I can't thank you enough for babysitting in a pinch." Ana smiled with relief. "If you hadn't agreed, I would've been in a bind. It's hard to find a babysitter on short notice."

"It's no problem." After the argument with Blythe and the upsetting phone call with her father, Vale welcomed the diversion. Watching a child on a Saturday afternoon beat having another spat with her sister or brooding over secrets Bo should have revealed long ago.

"You live in Pittsburgh?"

"That's right."

"From what Iris tells me, she's been looking forward to your visit." Ana held open the door. "Can you stay until five thirty? I'll finish work by then."

Vale followed her inside. "Of course. I don't have plans this afternoon."

The living room was a small, cramped space. A faded bedsheet hung across the window like a drooping sail. Across from the threadbare couch, a small flat-screen TV balanced precariously on a corrugated box. A Nintendo Switch and a PlayStation shared space on the coffee table with a book bag, a bowl of potato chips, and an American Girl doll.

The doll was a wretched sight. Ink circled one of its eyes. Someone had shaved off a chunk of its hair, and dark stains peppered the gingham pajamas.

Catching her appraisal, Ana sighed. Thin, with deep frown lines, she wore the furtive expression of a woman accustomed to hard times. From the looks of the house, she was barely scraping by. Vale made a mental note to refuse payment for watching Natty. It seemed the least she could do.

"We found the doll at a garage sale." Picking it up, Ana smoothed a palm across the bald spot on the doll's head. "It's not in great shape, but Natty didn't mind. I can't even guess why someone would shave off part of a doll's hair."

"Boredom, I suppose."

"Such a shame. It's an expensive toy." She returned the doll to the coffee table. "My daughter is in the kitchen. Please don't worry about the mess. I'll clean up when I get home."

A mad science experiment seemed underway in the kitchen. The pan sizzling on the stove threw specks of grease into the air. Cereal trailed across the counter like a colorful river. Beside a sink heaped with dishes, a can of ready-made spaghetti spilled its contents.

At the counter, the adventurous Natty balanced on a step stool. "Are you leaving, Mom?" Focused on her task, she slathered peanut butter on a chunk of french bread.

"In a moment." Ana turned to Vale. "This is my daughter, Natty."

"We've met—briefly."

"You have?"

"Yesterday, in the front yard. I was . . . talking with my sister. Your daughter heard us, by the fence."

Natty snorted. "You weren't talking to Blythe. You were yelling at her." She pointed the knife accusingly, and a glob of peanut butter plopped to the floor. "I guess it's okay. She was yelling too."

Ana folded her arms. "Natty, you know better than to eavesdrop on an adult conversation. Sisters don't always get along, even when they're all grown up."

"Like I'd know. I don't have a sister. I'd settle for a brother if he let me pick what to watch on TV. It's no fun being an only kid."

While she complained, smoke began to rise from the pan. Approaching, Vale peered inside. Two link sausages were burning.

"Natty, can I help you make lunch?" She slid the pan off the heat.

"I'm okay."

"What are you making?"

Ana chuckled. "You don't want to know. My daughter gets awfully creative with the cuisine."

Natty scooped up a handful of cereal. With a grunt, she pressed the cereal into the peanut butter. "Vale, are you hungry?" Wielding a pair of tongs, she dropped the charred sausage links on top. "I don't mind sharing."

Not on your life. "I've had lunch, but thanks."

Ana said, "Don't worry about the dishes. Natty will help me take care of them tonight."

"Mom, don't forget to ask her!"

"I appreciate the reminder, sweetie." Ana pulled her wallet from her purse. "Vale, I hate to be a bother. Mullaney's sent the text right before you arrived. Do you mind driving up for Natty's scrip?"

"My inhaler." Natty thumped her narrow chest. "I have asthma."

Mullaney's was a neighborhood institution. The compounding pharmacy drew children year-round to its old-fashioned soda fountain.

During her own childhood, Vale had spent many leisurely hours sipping milkshakes in one of the cherry-red booths.

She accepted the cash. "We'll drive up after Natty finishes eating," she promised.

Ana left, and Natty carried her plate to the table. With relish, she bit into the sandwich. Hiding her distaste, Vale surveyed the dishes piled in the sink. A quick inspection revealed a dishwasher on the blink: splotches of mold dotted the inside of the appliance. Grimacing, she slammed it shut. She began removing the dishes in the sink.

With interest Natty watched her. "What are you doing?"

"Cleaning up." Vale filled the sink with soapy water. "It won't take long."

"The guy is supposed to fix the dishwasher. He never does."

"What guy? A repairman?"

"No. The man we rent from. Our . . ."

"Landlord?"

"Right!" Natty swiped at her eyeglasses, frowned. "Something's wrong with my specs."

Chuckling, Vale removed them from her nose. Spots of grease dotted the lenses. "Word to the wise. Don't stand over the pan when you're cooking something greasy. It'll do a number on your eyeglasses."

"Thanks. I'll remember."

Vale dunked the eyeglasses into the soapy water, then rinsed them clean. Drying them slowly, she took care not to scratch the depressingly thick lenses. With myopia of this degree, Natty couldn't see past her nose.

When she steered them back onto Natty's face, wonderment rounded the child's mouth.

"Wow." She blinked theatrically. "That's better. Everything's crystal clear."

"You're welcome." Vale got to work on the dishes. "How old are you anyway?"

"I turned nine last week. Mom bought me a jumbo cupcake and a new swimsuit for summer." Natty pulled a sausage link from the sandwich's gloppy mess and bit off the end. "How old are you?"

"I'm twenty-nine."

"That's pretty old."

"You think?" Grinning, Vale shook her head. "Some days I *do* feel road weary."

Finishing the sausage link, Natty licked her fingertips. "Are you married?"

"Not yet."

"Do you have a boyfriend?"

"Nope. Do you?"

"Mom says I'm too young, but I like boys sometimes. Except Jared. He makes fart noises with his armpits and sticks chewing gum under his desk. He's disgusting." Natty took another bite of her sandwich. "How much money did Mom give you? Can I get a chocolate sundae at Mullaney's?"

"You can, but not with your mother's cash. I'll treat."

"Great!"

After Natty finished her meal, they walked next door to Vale's car. Blythe's red Audi was gone. Would she spend Saturday night drinking in the bars? A sinking feeling accosted Vale as she helped Natty fasten her seat belt. If Blythe was determined to continue the destructive behavior, there was no way to stop her.

The soda fountain in Mullaney's Pharmacy buzzed with activity. Twin boys with matching buzz cuts were flicking jelly beans down the counter, harassing the other children seated on barstools. A harried-looking woman with a baby on her hip swept past; she paused long enough to drill the twin demons with a hard stare before striding toward the toiletry aisles.

All the booths were occupied. In the one nearest the front, three teenage girls snapped photos of their beaming faces.

"Why don't we pick up your scrip first?" Vale suggested. "There might be an empty booth when we get back."

"Sure," Natty agreed.

Several paces from the pharmacy, a niggling sensation lifted Vale's eyes. Dismay brought her to a standstill.

The pharmacist—his reddish-brown hair distressingly familiar—finished administering a shot to a man seated in a chair near the counter. She groaned.

Natty's brows puckered. "What's wrong?"

"Nothing. Everything." Was it too late to beat a fast exit? Emmett McFall hadn't seen her. "Never mind."

"You look kind of sick."

"I'm having a weird day." She reached for Natty's hand. "Change of plans. Why don't we get ice cream first, and pick up your inhaler later?"

Or never.

The opportunity to avoid detection vanished. Emmett looked up. Their gazes locked, setting butterflies loose in Vale's stomach.

Natty ran toward him. "Hi, Emmett!"

"Are you here to pick up your inhaler?"

"Yep."

His attention veered back to Vale. Shrinking beneath his regard, she recalled the insults she'd volleyed at him last night. She'd capped off the impolite behavior by ordering him from the house. *Beg his forgiveness, then get out of here.* She wasn't quite sure how to phrase it.

"Vale, you won't believe this," he said, clearly enjoying her discomfort. "I was just thinking about you. Or, more precisely, about how you owe me an apology."

"Thanks for the reminder."

His eyes danced when she blushed. "What are you doing running around with my favorite pipsqueak?"

"I'm watching her this afternoon."

"You're Natty's babysitter? Interesting."

"Why interesting?" she tossed back, irritated by his chatty ease with a truly awkward situation. Not to mention the butterflies he'd unleashed inside her. In fairness that was her problem, not his.

"I had you pegged for a career in law enforcement or Homeland Security."

"Is that a joke?" When he nodded, Vale pointed at herself. "This is me *not* laughing."

"You *do* have a territorial nature, as evidenced by your behavior last night." Emmett folded his arms. "I'm not telling you anything you don't already know."

Natty followed the interplay like a fast-moving tennis match. "Do you know each other?"

Ignoring the query, Emmett leaned close. "Have you composed that apology yet?" His cologne was spicy and warm, and Vale breathed it in willingly. "I'm waiting."

The man smelled great, but his gall was unbelievable. Even if she *did* owe him an apology.

"Get comfortable." She couldn't tame her naturally defensive streak. "You'll have to keep waiting."

"Fine. I will."

The grin he flashed nearly took her hostage. But flirting in his professional capacity as Mullaney's pharmacist seemed a talent not yet mastered. With a start, Emmett noticed the customers queuing up in line. Many of them watched the exchange with interest.

The glee vanished from his features. In a professional voice, he said, "I'll get that scrip."

Vale paid the cashier for the inhaler. With her dignity in tatters, she led Natty to the soda fountain. It would've been the better part of valor to apologize. A simple feat to accomplish if Emmett hadn't been intent on teasing her. And flirting—the natural fallout of a mutual attraction. Like it or not, she found him attractive. Older than the men she usually dated, but she couldn't lump his age into the minus category. It didn't help that he smelled great too.

Natty ordered a double-scoop sundae with extra sprinkles. They found a booth near the corner.

"How do you know Emmett?" she asked between mouthfuls.

"Let's talk about something else. *Anything* else."

"Can't you tell me?"

Vale stole a glance toward the pharmacy. "It's too complicated."

"I've known Emmett forever." Natty lifted her chin with haughty authority. "My mom worked here when she took classes to become a legal secretary. She worked at Mullaney's for a long time. When we needed to move, Emmett helped us get a new house."

The disclosure piqued Vale's interest. "The house you're living in now?"

"Emmett knows the owner. If Mom saves up enough money, the guy will let her buy the house. We won't have to move around anymore. Emmett also helped Mom study for her citizenship exam when she worked here."

"Are they dating?" Vale couldn't resist asking.

Natty scooped up ice cream, then left the spoon hovering near her lips. "They're just friends." A surprising glint of maturity sparked in her gaze. "Do you like Emmett? He's a free bird. You should put the moves on him."

A grin tugged at Vale's lips. All things considered, it seemed he'd already put the moves on *her*. Why else tease her about her territorial nature? *Verbal sparring: stage one of attraction.* A convenient means to keep the feisty hormones at bay. On further reflection, Vale realized he'd been flirting last night too. In her agitated state, she'd missed the signals. *My bad.*

Natty brightened. "Will you ask him out? If you're too shy, I'll help. Write him a note and I'll take it to him. Just don't write anything sexy, like those YouTube videos—*Make Him Your Boy Toy.* I googled some of the words. They were totally disgusting."

Vale opened her mouth, then closed it again. It was best not to inquire about the words Natty had looked up. Whatever happened to childhood innocence?

The internet, that's what. And easy-to-bypass parental controls.

Natty's budding matchmaking skills were a problem. To deflect them, Vale nodded at the empty bowl. "Would you like another?"

"You've already treated once. Shouldn't I pay if I'm having seconds?"

"With what? Your good looks and charm?" Vale winked at her. "Wait here. I'll be right back."

A group of chattering teens crowded before the soda fountain. At the other end of the store, Emmett stood behind the pharmacy bay explaining something to a silver-haired matron. It warmed Vale, the way he took his time answering the woman's questions. He also possessed a nice build. For a man on the cusp of middle age, he clearly worked out regularly.

Reaching the head of the line, Vale ordered the ice cream. When she returned to the booth, Natty was pecking away on her phone.

Vale placed the ice cream before her. "Who are you texting?"

"Emmett."

"You have his personal number? That's convenient." *Or problematic.* "What are you talking about?"

"You, what else? Emmett says you're nice. I asked if he likes blondes. The older girls at school say lots of guys do."

Vale tried to rein in her curiosity. "What's the verdict?" she asked, letting the emotion run wild.

Scanning his reply, Natty grinned. "He says blondes are nice, especially when they're spicy." Puzzled, she wrinkled her nose. "What's that supposed to mean? Pizzas are spicy. Hair isn't."

"Never mind."

"Hold on. There's more." A long text, apparently. Natty read slowly.

"Don't keep me in suspense." A ridiculous burst of excitement dived through Vale. "What else is he saying?"

"He'll accept your apology if you buy him coffee tomorrow morning. He's off on Sundays, so you can pick the time. Starbucks is on the corner, right by the shoe store." Natty waved her spoon due west. "When should I tell him you'll be there?"

"Stop texting—and stay put. I'll be right back."

"Where are you going now?" The words were barely out when the proverbial light bulb flashed above Natty's head. She gave the thumbs-up. "Good luck!"

A fizzy determination propelled Vale toward the pharmacy. *There's no harm in seizing an opportunity.* During the four years she had spent managing the Crafty Cocktail, she'd had precious few chances for a social life. Why not remedy the situation?

She liked Emmett. The feeling was clearly mutual.

A matron paid the cashier for her scrip. Emmett pivoted, to return to the dispensing area.

Vale waved, stopping him in his tracks. His face lit up.

With her confidence threatening to flee, she motioned him into the shampoo aisle.

"Dating isn't a good idea," she blurted, "but I'm game if you are."

"I'm game." Lowering his voice, Emmett leaned closer. "Why isn't it a good idea?"

"I don't live in town."

"Yeah, I've heard. Iris mentioned she'd like to convince you to move back to Philadelphia. If she's planning to strong-arm you, should I offer an assist?"

"Totally up to you, but it won't matter. You see, my life is up in the air. I'm not sure what I'm doing, other than apologizing to you for acting like a horse's ass last night. You did my sister a favor, driving her home from the bar. I shouldn't have assumed you were putting the moves on her."

"Especially since I'd rather put the moves on you."

The husky admission startled her. From the looks of it, Emmett was startled too.

In her chest, the fizzy determination morphed into exhilaration. "Are you always this direct?" she asked.

"No. Never. I've got to admit—it feels good." Emmett rocked back on his heels. "Forget about meeting for coffee tomorrow. Do you have plans tonight? I'd love to take you out to dinner."

Chapter 13

With a frown, Vale studied the two dresses laid out on the bed. Neither appealed. Why hadn't she packed something nicer?

In February she'd purchased the balloon-sleeve maxi dress online. The bargain-basement price should've offered the first clue that she was throwing away good money. The polyester blend felt scratchy against her skin, and the roomy waist swam on her. Even with a belt, the dress looked three sizes too large.

The second choice was no better. The block-print, A-line dress—a wardrobe staple from her midtwenties—barely covered her thighs. Flashing acres of skin on a first date would send the wrong message.

Nervous tension dived into her belly. It was nearly six thirty. Emmett would arrive in half an hour.

Downstairs, footfalls sounded. They made their way up to the second floor. Her grandmother appeared in the doorway.

Vale nodded in greeting. "You're late. I thought you'd return from Green Iris an hour ago."

"We had a few stragglers at closing. I offered to throw them out of the store. Detta wouldn't hear of it. She never turns away a potential sale." Iris leaned against the doorjamb. "Where's Blythe?"

"I haven't a clue. She left in the early afternoon and never came back."

"Some of her girlfriends have been trying to get together with her. I hope she's meeting them for dinner, not out drinking alone. I can't bear a replay of last night."

"Giving yourself an ulcer won't help. Blythe isn't a child. She'll do what she wants."

"She doesn't know what she wants. Hence the erratic behavior." Iris managed a weak smile. "Speaking of children, how did it go with Natty?"

"Great. She's sweet. I told her mother to give me a call if she needs help next week. I refused payment—I got the impression Ana is hardly making ends meet."

"That was kind of you." Kicking off her shoes, Iris plucked wearily at her pink compression stockings. She looked ready for a hot bath. "Do you mind if we settle for leftovers tonight? I'm not in the mood to cook."

Picking up the A-line dress, Vale held it to her waist. Should she risk flashing too much thigh? It seemed a better option than showing up in a dress three sizes too big.

"I'm sorry, Nana. You'll have to dine alone. I have a date."

"You're going out?"

"With Emmett."

"Emmett McFall?"

"The one and only." Vale sent Iris a mildly disapproving look. "Why didn't you mention he's a pharmacist at Mullaney's? I ran into him when I took Natty to pick up her inhaler."

"And he asked you out?"

"Not immediately. First, we embarked on the standard mating rituals. He teased me, and I was sassy. We both needed a refresher course on flirting, but it didn't matter. At least not to Natty—she caught something in the air other than pollen."

"The whiff of romance?" Delight brought her grandmother into the bedroom.

"She wanted to fix us up. We took matters into our own hands." Vale flung the dress back onto the bed. "There's only one problem. Emmett is taking me somewhere near Washington Square. Most of the restaurants there are fancy. I have absolutely nothing suitable to wear."

With distaste, her grandmother appraised the choices. "You can't wear either of these. You didn't pack anything nicer?"

"I don't *own* anything nicer. The only time I get marginally dressed up is when you fly into Pittsburgh. We never go out for a bite anywhere fancy."

"Wait here." Iris swept out of the room.

She returned with a pool of crimson-red fabric fluttering in her arms. Knee-length, with delicate cap sleeves, the dress shimmered as she held it up for Vale's inspection. She'd also brought along a pair of strappy black heels.

Vale shooed her back. "Nana, I can't borrow Blythe's clothes! She'll read me the riot act in ten different languages."

"You're borrowing the outfit, not stealing it. I'm sure she won't mind."

"She *will* mind. Where I'm concerned, she isn't feeling charitable." Unable to resist, Vale approached. She trailed her fingers across the silken fabric. On a sigh, she let her hand fall back to her side. "We had another argument today. Worse than the one yesterday."

The revelation slumped Iris's shoulders. She wanted her granddaughters to mend their rift. Nothing mattered to her more, and Vale knew she'd failed her. Retreating to the dresser, she chastised herself for allowing the heated exchange to escalate. Why hadn't she walked away instead?

"What were you arguing about?"

"How long I'll stay in Philadelphia. Blythe made it clear she wants me gone. It didn't end there." Scooping up a hairbrush, Vale coasted it through her long hair, thankful for the repetitive motion's calming effect. "The spat devolved into a comparison of our fathers. Mostly of their faults, real and imagined. Blythe was happy to set me straight."

"About what?"

"A misconception I've carried around for years. I didn't know my dad ended the marriage. I've always believed the divorce was Mom's idea. How could I have been so stupid? I knew Blythe was telling the truth once I called my dad for confirmation."

A muddy silence overtook the room. The dress rippled in crimson waves as Iris placed it on the bed.

"Oh, Vale. Your sister shouldn't have brought up the divorce. I'm sure she assumed you knew the specifics."

"I didn't. I never once broached the subject with Mom. I assumed she chose Grant over my dad. And I was furious about her choice. It never occurred to me that my dad wanted the divorce." The news still grated against Vale's heart. "Nana, why didn't you ever set me straight? You knew I blamed Mom. I've done nothing but complain about her since childhood."

Regret sifted across Iris's features. "Perhaps I should have. I assumed Bo would tell you at some point, after you moved to Pittsburgh. I'll wager he made the attempt but never followed through."

"I'm angry he didn't."

"You're not angry, pumpkin. You're hurt."

Vale tossed the brush aside. It clattered across the dresser. She *was* hurt. And confused. What other assumptions regarding her family were in error? Her understanding seemed more fragile than a sandcastle built near the rumbling surf.

The prospect unsettled her. "I had a right to know," she said. "Why didn't Bo tell me? We worked together daily. I deserved to know how the divorce really went down."

"You may be upset that Bo never explained, but your hurt lies deeper. Vale, the divorce is at the root of your unhappiness. Like many children, the break between your parents made you feel abandoned. You're all grown up now, but the feeling is still there. It's never left you."

"Bo *did* abandon me."

"Then ask yourself this: Does it serve your interests to pass judgment on decisions he made decades ago? Should you overlook the relationship you enjoy with him now, out of bitterness? Your parents were young when they split up. Younger than you are now."

"They were," she stubbornly agreed.

The compassion in Iris's gaze deepened. "Don't hold this against your father. It's not easy, disappointing a child you've grown to love. And Bo *does* love you. He may not have discovered how much until you went into business together. He's certainly aware now."

The explanation began to soothe Vale. Unlike the rest of her family, Iris never criticized Bo. She accepted his failings. She accepted them with the knowledge that he possessed good qualities too. She never gave Vale the impression her devotion to her father was misplaced.

"Secrets are corrosive," her grandmother added. "They wear away the love we share. I'm sorry Bo didn't set you straight. I'm sorry I didn't either."

The affection softening her grandmother's features stung Vale with guilt. *What right do I have to criticize Bo? I keep secrets too.* Mostly out of fear of revealing her failures. Her inability to find her own dreams and build a good life.

Determined to start fresh, Vale said, "I haven't been totally honest with you. I should've said something the minute I arrived. The thing is . . . my life in Pittsburgh isn't going well. In fact, it's a mess. The Crafty Cocktail—"

"Burned down," Iris cut in. "The bar is gone."

Vale inhaled a startled breath. "You *know*?"

"And there's no insurance money to rebuild. Your father didn't renew the policy." With faint pity, Iris shook her head. "Bo is the finest bartender in Pittsburgh, but he lacks common sense."

Vale exhaled swiftly as the pieces clicked into place. "He told you?"

"Who else would I call when you refused to answer your phone? You were incommunicado for days. It didn't take long to pull a confession from Bo. He told me everything." Iris puffed up her chest like a frigate bird assured of its dominance. She looked inordinately pleased with herself. "I assumed you'd broach the subject eventually."

"I've been afraid to." Laughter escaped Vale's throat. "Don't get the wrong idea, okay? The loss of the Crafty Cocktail doesn't give you license to badger me about moving back to Philadelphia. I hate living five hours away from you, but I don't get along with Mom and Grant—or Blythe. It's easier, living in Pittsburgh."

"It's gutless," Iris muttered. Shrugging off her sudden irritation, she looked up brightly. "You *should* come home, but let's not discuss it now. What time is Emmett picking you up?"

"Soon."

With an encouraging smile, Iris retrieved the crimson dress from the bed. "Now stop fussing and lift your arms. I promise, Blythe won't mind if you borrow the dress. I'll see to it."

Relenting, Vale stepped forward. Iris steered the dress over her head. The cool fabric rippled down to her knees. Murmuring with satisfaction, Iris zipped up the back.

With a gasp, Vale looked in the mirror. The dress subtly hugged her breasts and hips. Against the rich color, her hair glistened like threads of gold.

"This isn't too sexy?"

"You look drop-dead gorgeous." Iris fetched the two-inch pumps. "Try them on."

They fit perfectly. As Vale clasped a thin gold necklace on her neck, the doorbell rang.

"I'll get it, Nana."

If she needed further confirmation of her appeal, Emmett's gaze supplied it. His eyes swept down her body in a thorough and hungry pursuit. An uncommon feeling of triumph spun through her.

A lopsided grin rose on his lips. "Thank you."

"For what?"

"Agreeing to dinner. A better alternative than meeting for coffee."

She hesitated. "Thank *you* for accepting my apology."

"My pleasure." Above his expertly knotted tie, his Adam's apple bobbed. He looked younger then, unable to hide his excitement. "Do you like French cuisine? I've booked us a table at Rue de Jean."

"I'm not familiar with the restaurant. I'm sure I'll love it."

Vale wasn't disappointed. Tucked on a side street in the Society Hill neighborhood, Rue de Jean brimmed with tantalizing scents and the murmur of conversation. Chubby wall sconces washed the room in amber light. A zinc-topped bar occupied the center of the restaurant. Round tables sheathed in linen, with vases of colorful gerbera daisies on top, clustered around the bar.

After they were seated, Emmett scanned the wine list. "Should I order a bottle?"

"Please don't on my account. I love wine, but it gives me an awful headache."

"You may have an intolerance to the sulfites. Would you like a cocktail?"

"No, thank you. I guess I'm allergic to most liquors," she admitted. "Headaches, stuffy nose—it takes the fun out of drinking."

"Do you like Pellegrino?"

"Perfect."

Two glasses of the sparkling water appeared before them. When Vale couldn't decide on an appetizer, Emmett selected three dishes— steak tartare, foie gras, and a sublime truffle potato soup.

"Tell me about yourself," he said as they sampled the treats. "What do you do?"

"Until recently, I owned a bar in Pittsburgh with my father."

Amused, he leaned back in his chair. "A bar owner with an aversion to drink. That's not something you hear every day."

"Well, opening the Crafty Cocktail wasn't my grand vision. My dad owned a bar in Cincinnati that didn't do well. When he moved to Pittsburgh, he asked if I'd go into business with him. I jumped at the chance." Vale took a hasty sip of Pellegrino, her throat suddenly dry. "We did a good trade until the fire."

Emmett's brows lifted. "Arson?"

"Stupidity, most likely. The night of the fire, my dad stayed after closing with some of his friends. A regular thing, most Saturday nights."

"When will you reopen?"

"Never. Dad let our insurance policy lapse."

Surprise leaped across Emmett's face. "You must be furious with him."

It occurred to Vale that the particulars of her parents' long-ago divorce bothered her more. A business loss versus the scars from childhood. There really was no comparison.

"I was upset," she admitted. "I'm getting over it. Growing up I didn't see much of my father. Starting a business together gave us the chance to connect in a meaningful way."

"What will you do now?"

"Scour the Pittsburgh want ads for a new job. I hate the thought of losing my independence, but I don't have the funds to launch another business."

"Why not look for work in Philly? You have management experience. Landing a job here will be easy." Emmett flashed a persuasive smile. "There's a man in town who'd like to continue seeing you."

"You're not up to long-distance dating?" she teased.

"If that's my only option, I'll take it." His eyes caught hers, spreading heat across her skin. "Last night, when you stormed out of your grandmother's house, I knew this could lead to something. *Would* lead to something if I didn't let the chance slip away. If you hadn't come into Mullaney's today, I would've taken the initiative. Shown up at Iris's door and asked you out. The big opportunities . . . you don't pass them up."

A potential suitor unafraid to state his intentions boldly. An intimidating discovery, and Vale wasn't sure how to react. Emmett, it seemed, was supremely confident.

"I can't promise how long I'll stay." Considering, she smoothed her palms across the linen napkin on her lap. "My grandmother has sidelined my plans for now."

"What do you mean?"

Iris's health issues were private, but Emmett *was* a pharmacist. He followed a medical code of ethics.

"She's going in for some tests." Vale knew she could rely on his confidence. "She'll begin them at the hospital this week."

"Is it serious?"

"I hope not—she won't share the details. I'm planning to stay until we get the results. Longer, if the tests reveal anything to worry about." Vale took a last spoonful of soup, then set the spoon aside. "What I hadn't bargained on was running into my sister. Before I drove in, my grandmother conveniently forgot to mention Blythe is also visiting."

Emmett nodded to the waitstaff; they began clearing away the appetizers. A fragrant plate of coq au vin appeared before Vale. Across the table, Emmett's gaze remained trained on her as the waiter set down the plate of blanquette de veau.

Once they were alone, his lips quirked into a grin. "Vale, you're an interesting mix. To all outward appearances, you're prettier than a fairy princess and just as ephemeral. Underneath? You have real grit."

"I'll take that as a compliment."

"My intention, of course." Compassion flickered across his face as he lifted his fork. He left it hovering above his meal. "Why is Blythe convinced you're the worst sister in the world?"

Under normal circumstances, the question would sting. Yet the openness of Emmett's gaze, his warmth, lowered her defenses. Despite his attraction to her, Vale sensed his desire to offer something equally valuable: his friendship. Whatever she chose to confide, he'd treat the revelations with sensitivity and care.

"Blythe has good reason for her low opinion of me," she admitted, glad suddenly to unburden herself. "I was the older sister she wanted to look up to. I never passed up an opportunity to bully her or make her life miserable. I was cruel, in a zillion ways."

"Why were you so hard on her?"

"If you ask my grandmother, she'll say I was jealous. The full story is more complicated."

Picking up her fork, Vale absently poked at the coq au vin. An expensive meal paid for by an engaging man she *would* like to see again. Dutifully, she took a bite. The pungent chicken melted in her mouth.

After finishing another bite, she returned her hands to her lap. Emmett, plainly eager to hear the rest, seemed oblivious to his meal.

"My sister and I have different fathers," she explained. "Blythe's father, Grant, raised us both, and Blythe has always excelled. It's intimidating, having a sister who makes all the right moves while mostly I . . . react. I've never planned my life well."

"Your mother favors Blythe?" Emmett guessed.

"I don't blame her." The memory of Audrey's favoritism sent a sharp pang through Vale. She hid the injury behind a smile. "My mother and Grant are both accountants—precise, balanced, pragmatic. Blythe takes after them. I'm less focused. The woman with the scattershot approach to life."

"Is that a fair characterization? Listen, we've all gone through periods where we spend too much time reliving the past. Letting old hurts stand in the way. Been there, done that. I've found that when I put my energy into mapping out my future, everything else falls into place."

The observation struck her as accurate. "Do you have siblings?" she asked.

"Two sisters. Both younger, married, and with kids. Delany, the youngest, is an orthodontist in West Kensington. She shares a practice with her husband. My other sister, Libby, is a pediatrician in North Philly. She's currently on maternity leave—she's just had her second child, a boy." At last, Emmett noticed his meal. Between mouthfuls, he added, "My sisters are great, but I *do* wish they'd stop nagging me about following them into wedded bliss. They're relentless."

"You've never come close?" Not a first-date query, but he'd grown animated. She knew he wouldn't think she was prying.

"I was engaged in my early thirties. I broke it off."

"Cold feet?"

Her interest softened his gaze. "Not even a little," Emmett said. "My fiancée was still in love with her ex-husband. A typical case of unfinished business. They'd married quickly and divorced just as fast."

"I'm sorry."

"Don't be. A broken engagement is better than dealing with a mistake after the fact." With an air of celebration, Emmett lifted his glass of Pellegrino. "I wish them the best."

They clinked glasses, their eyes catching over the rims. Vale admired the way he trod into his past with ease. Like a child discovering new adventures in a familiar wood.

Without becoming mired in the brambles.

"Teach me that trick," she blurted, suddenly keen to learn. "How do you deal with the past and move on?"

"Simple. Choose to live in the present." Pausing, Emmett held her gaze like an embrace. A smile rose on his lips. "Everything worked out for the best. My lost fiancée remarried her ex. They have three children—triplets."

Vale laughed. "They'd better start saving. They'll need *three* college funds."

Chapter 14

Outside the breeze had kicked up, fluttering the daffodils arranged in stone planters before Rue de Jean. The moon, fat and golden, hovered in a cloudless sky.

The night was too lovely to waste. They drove down to Race Street Pier to join the passersby strolling beside the Delaware River. The pier's terraced promenade featured amphitheater-style seating and lush plantings, including three dozen trees that rustled in the night air. Above them, the lights trimming the Benjamin Franklin Bridge scattered glimmers of color across the inky waters—blue, green, purple—in a rainbow display that captivated Vale.

"I'd forgotten how much I love it here." She brought them to a standstill.

"The bridge or Philadelphia?"

"Both. On weekends, I used to visit craft fairs with my grandmother, and I've always loved walking near the river." She gestured to encompass the pier. "Sometimes Nana and I would drive in from Media just to take a stroll."

"You're close to Iris."

"She's always played the role of mediator. Or rescuer, whenever I needed to escape the house." A powerboat glided across the river, too far away to make out the people inside. Vale let it hold her attention for a moment before she cast Emmett a curious glance. "You mentioned your sisters. Are your parents in Philadelphia?"

"They live in Chestnut Hill. Dad was a pharmacist, now retired. Mom's an ultrasound radiographer at Chestnut Hill Hospital. She bakes the best pecan pie you'll ever taste. She's originally from Louisiana."

"Choosing a career in medicine must've been a no-brainer for you."

Emmett chuckled. "Medicine is in our DNA. I chose to follow in my dad's footsteps because I like the day-to-day interaction, building relationships with my patients. They know the local pharmacist is available to answer questions in a hurry."

The wind gusted, lifting Vale's hair, spinning it away from her shoulders. Nearing, Emmett captured a heavy lock and hooked it behind her ear. His fingers lingered on her neck, igniting tiny fires. Too quickly, he lowered his hand.

"What was it like, managing a bar?"

"Hard," she admitted, wishing he'd touch her again. "Sometimes I wouldn't get to bed until four in the morning. I've never been able to train myself to sleep during the day. I got a real education in sleep deprivation."

"You're not a night owl? I assumed you were."

"In my perfect world, I climb into bed every night at ten o'clock with a book."

"I *do* read in bed. Books, the newspaper, the *Economist*—and my Kindle is fully loaded." Emmett let his hand steal back into her hair. When she shivered, the corner of his mouth curved with ill-concealed pleasure. Yet he kept up the banter, asking, "Do you like burgers and hot dogs?"

An odd question to pair with his gentle foreplay.

I like kisses. Never had Vale waited this anxiously for a first kiss. As if this moment with Emmett were a gift she'd never expected to receive. Most of her previous dates had squandered the first kiss, launching directly into making out—and suggesting they spend the night with her.

Crude, clumsy attempts. No wonder those first dates never led to a second.

With daring, Vale coasted her palm across his chin. "Everyone likes burgers and hot dogs." She delighted in the way her touch hitched his breathing. "Why? Are you inviting me over to grill out?"

"Tomorrow afternoon. If you'll come, I'll add some great side dishes to the menu. Do you mind a threesome?"

"Who else is coming?"

Emmett's hands were back in play, sliding down her back, making her dizzy. "I'm Natty's babysitter tomorrow afternoon," he explained, steering her into his arms. He seemed perfectly comfortable blending light conversation with heated caresses. "Ana's working her second job for one of the food-delivery services. I can never recall which one. She's determined to build up her savings account."

"Natty mentioned Ana's side jobs. She's hoping to buy the house they're renting."

"She's determined to give Natty a permanent home."

Spinning, Vale lifted her face. "I'm happy for them both." She let her attention hang on his lips. "From what Natty told me, they've moved around a lot."

"Yeah, too much. Natty likes her new school. She wants to stay."

"I hope it works out."

Dropping the subject, Emmett canvassed her features. "So you'll come?"

"On one condition." Pleasure tumbled through Vale. "Stop talking and kiss me."

Complying, he bent his head.

Chapter 15

From the hallway's second-story window, Iris watched Blythe sprint down the stone path away from the house.

On the sidewalk Blythe paused to warm up in the blush-colored dawn. She lunged forward with her right leg, then with her left, arms raised above her head. Next came stretches—a standing quad and a lateral squat. She performed each movement with the fluid grace of an athlete.

In high school and college, Blythe had played a variety of sports, trying her hand at tennis, soccer, and basketball in her determination to keep off the extra pounds that had plagued her through adolescence. The jogging habit came later, not long before she met Booker. Their romance blossomed during early-morning runs near the Delaware River and along the leafy trails of Forbidden Drive.

Blythe still worried about her weight.

Iris recalled the blustery March when the first pimples sprouted between Blythe's eyebrows like tiny, angry volcanoes. At eleven, Blythe had thrown herself into copying Vale's use of cosmetics. She dabbled unsuccessfully with eyeliner and layered her lashes with enough mascara to resemble a spotted owl.

The blight of acne scuttled this predictable form of hero worship. To cheer up her younger granddaughter, Iris took her shopping. Jeans, blouses, and skirts were carried into the department store dressing room. Ignoring the clothes, Blythe stared forlornly at the mirror.

Why is Vale pretty and I'm not?

Grandmothers excel at providing caring and comfort, and Iris stuck to the classic script. She recited her granddaughter's attributes: the beauty of her wide-set eyes and full mouth; the glossy tumble of her curls; her popularity at school and ability to earn perfect marks in every subject.

None of the assurances pacified the child. Trapped in Vale's shadow, Blythe saw only how she lacked her sister's physical gifts. Vale's sun-kissed hair and flawless skin. Her lithe, feminine build that drew the feverish attention of youths, and the interest of men, wherever she went. Blythe never glimpsed the scars Vale hid behind terse comments and black, flashing looks—a teenager wounded by Audrey's rash choices and Bo's unreliable behavior.

Remorse throbbed beneath Iris's rib cage. During those tumultuous years, her intervention might have made a difference. Yet she'd never confronted Audrey.

Time and again, Audrey had silenced her conscience to tangle with carnal desire. Her secret life—a wedge thrust between her daughters—drove the girls apart. The trysts, of which they were unaware, made them competitors, not allies. The injury didn't end there. Audrey weakened Vale's self-confidence and belief in herself. In contrast she coddled Blythe. She encouraged her perfectionist streak while making her unable to rally when life meted out its predictable defeats.

As if grooming Blythe for excellence might erase the passion that lured Audrey for years.

Drawing from the reverie, Iris returned her attention to the window. On the sidewalk, Blythe finished the warmup. Sprinting down the street, she disappeared beneath a curtain of leaves. The morning jog usually lasted about twenty minutes.

Long enough.

Vale was still asleep. After last night's dinner with Emmett, she'd returned in an uncommonly good mood, handing Iris the dress to return to Blythe and then going promptly to bed.

Blythe had stomped up the staircase past midnight after spending another night at the bars. At least she'd gone out jogging this morning.

The decision gave Iris hope as she padded into Blythe's room. The door shut with a soft click. Appraising the space, she swallowed down the sharp tang of shame. Creeping around an adult grandchild's room wasn't admirable. Given the circumstances, it *was* necessary.

By the window, Blythe had positioned the card table she'd lugged up from the basement. On top lay the Sony turntable she'd bought for Iris last year after discovering her collection of Motown LPs growing dust in the attic. Gladys Knight, Marvin Gaye, Diana Ross—the bluesy arrangements and soulful vocals captivated Blythe, especially the songs heavy on sorrow.

Turning away, Iris strode to the dresser. One by one, she sifted through the drawers. Panties, bras, stacks of neatly folded tops—with a tug, she pulled open the bottom drawer. Beneath three pairs of jeans, her fingers brushed against cool metal.

Wedging out the framed wedding portrait, she sighed. In the photo, Blythe wore miles of white chiffon. Her joyous face tilted up to Booker's. He looked dashing in a black tux, his attention riveted on his new bride.

Iris checked the impulse to place the portrait on the dresser. Remembering herself, she tucked it away. How to explain the intrusion if Blythe discovered she'd been snooping around?

It's nothing, peaches. I rummaged through your bedroom to check if you're hiding booze. Your late uncle Darren had a problem with liquor. He didn't get sober until his fifties. Have I mentioned it? These issues can run in families.

On the nightstand, Blythe's laptop hugged the base of the lamp. Her smartphone sat on top, blinking out a message. Taking care not to read it, Iris reached for the nightstand's skinny drawer.

A scrip for sleeping medication rolled forward and another of melatonin, three-milligram tablets. A sleeping mask, three tubes of lip gloss, and a pack of chewing gum—Iris pushed her fingers toward the back of the drawer. Her heart fell as she retrieved a box of blue velvet and snapped open the lid. The two-carat engagement ring and platinum wedding band caught glints of the morning light. Blythe had stopped wearing the rings whenever she was in the house, as if practicing for the day when she'd put them away forever. She only slipped them on before going out at night.

A quick check of the closet revealed nothing worrisome. No bottles of whiskey tucked behind the dresses or flasks of vodka hidden on the top shelf. Only the sleeping pills gave Iris pause, but the bottle appeared full. Hopefully Blythe would get her marriage on better footing and throw the meds out.

Checking the time, Iris swept back through the room. Confident everything was in its place, she hurried downstairs. She made a cup of tea and poured a glass of water. The sun was rising above the treetops as she walked out to the porch.

Blythe appeared soon after, panting from the run. Beads of sweat glossed her brow. Ascending the steps, she regarded Iris warily.

"Can we talk?" Iris held out the glass.

"Where's Vale?"

"Still asleep." She smiled brightly. "By the way, I let her borrow one of your dresses. I'm sure you don't mind. The red silk."

"Why did she need it?"

"For a date last night."

Blythe accepted the glass. "When she wakes up, tell her to keep the dress. It's too tight on me." She settled into a wicker chair. "I'm not even sure why I packed it."

"Why not tell her yourself? A peace offering of sorts." When her granddaughter's face fell, she added, "Your sister mentioned the argument. Blythe, there are lines you should never cross. Frankly, I'm surprised at you."

"Please don't launch into one of your heart-to-hearts. I feel awful about ten different ways—" Cutting off, Blythe took a long sip of water. Her eyes were distant when she set the glass down. "I shouldn't have told Vale that Bo divorced Mom. I assumed she knew. It really threw me . . . She didn't have a clue. She took the news hard."

"You hurt Vale."

"It wasn't intentional. We've been at odds for years, but that doesn't excuse my behavior. For reasons I'll never understand, she idolizes Bo. I shouldn't have torn him down." Blythe rubbed her arms, as if scouring away the shame. "I just wish she'd leave. Go back to serving drinks at the Crafty Cocktail and pick another date to visit you."

"You aren't being charitable. Besides, I'm not sure there's much for her to go back to." Blythe didn't know about the fire at the bar. There was no reason to fill her in. Why put more arrows in the quiver when she might take aim at Vale again? Treading carefully, Iris said, "You're not the only one going through a difficult phase. Vale is too. She has a lot to sort out."

"What, exactly?"

"If you're curious, talk to her. I can't break a confidence."

"Can't or won't?"

"Does it make a difference? The point is, I'm trustworthy. With Vale's secrets, and yours." For emphasis Iris leaned closer. When her granddaughter's eyes lifted, she said, "Peaches, why don't you confide in me? You've never hesitated to seek my advice in the past. Why is now different? Begin with the reason you're considering divorce. I thought you and Booker were happy."

"We were." Blythe's attention shifted away. She tucked a stray curl behind her ear. "Booker still is, at least for now. I haven't found a chance to talk with him. With the baseball season in full swing, he needs to focus on the game. I don't want to put his career at risk, but the pretending is hard. I owe him the truth."

"What about counseling during the off-season? You've only been married for three years. All couples face difficulties. Talking it out with a professional can help."

"Oh, Nana. This isn't something counseling will fix." Pain suddenly crossed her face—and fear. She resembled a woman caught in rip currents far from shore. At risk of going under. "I can't give Booker what he needs. Believe me, I've tried. I'm not . . ." An agonized silence took her voice.

Bewildered, Iris reached for her hand. "You're not . . . what?"

"Worthy of him."

Refusing the affection, Blythe wound her fingers into a tight knot. Her knuckles whitened beneath the effort to contain her emotions.

"Blythe, you *are* worthy. Why would you think otherwise?"

"Because all marriages come with conditions. Agreements you make, both directly and implicitly. It doesn't matter if you don't spell out all your expectations before you tie the knot. They still matter. Like they would in any contract between adults."

"How does love fit into your grand equation? You make it all sound . . . cold-blooded."

"In some ways it is. When people marry, they enter the union with expectations. I can't live up to my side of the bargain."

"Why not?"

Frustration burst across Blythe's features. "Would you stop grilling me already? I love Booker—I hate the thought of leaving him. But if I stay, am I only delaying the inevitable? Eventually he'll realize I've failed, and he'll leave *me*. He'll go, and I won't be able to blame him. Because I'm not the wife he deserves."

The admission pulled Blythe to her feet and carried her to the porch railing. She leaned heavily as her composure broke. Her back heaved with sobs. The impulse to comfort her nearly brought Iris forward.

A dark thought seized her, rooting her in place.

What have you done?

Blythe was the child molded by Audrey. The one she spoiled and smothered with the affection she couldn't share equally between her two daughters. They were alike in many ways.

In too many ways, perhaps.

The memories wheeled before Iris, unbidden and despised. Audrey wiping the distress from her expression when Grant entered a room. Summoning a smile. The bonds holding her family together growing weaker each time Audrey succumbed to her worst impulses.

Was Blythe making the same mistake?

Chapter 16

Deliciously hot water pummeled Vale's back.

It was a rare treat. In her apartment in Pittsburgh, the water never heated past lukewarm. Showering consisted of a mad dash to finish before chilly droplets prickled her skin. Bathing until the steam turned the bathroom into a sauna was a luxury. As was sleeping until noon. Vale couldn't recall the last time she'd done so.

Taking her time, she washed her hair with Blythe's rosemary-mint shampoo. She lathered her body with the milk-and-honey bath gel her grandmother kept on hand. After last night's date with Emmett, she felt good. Stepping from the shower, Vale reminded herself that long-distance dating rarely worked out. Still, there was no harm in savoring Emmett's company until she returned to Pittsburgh. She looked forward to seeing him again this afternoon.

Toweling off, she perked her ears for the Motown songs that had woken her. They were no longer playing. Was Blythe downstairs? Vale padded into her bedroom after grabbing a robe. If they bumped into each other, she resolved to avoid another spat.

On the nightstand, her phone jingled with a new text. There was no message—just a series of weary-face emojis and a screenshot of paperwork from Pittsburgh's fire department. Guilt nicked her. The forms were scattered across the glass coffee table in Bo's apartment.

She dialed her father.

"Should I drive back tomorrow?" she asked when Bo picked up. They hadn't spoken since her abrupt call yesterday about the divorce. "I didn't know there'd be a lot of paperwork. I can come in for the afternoon and help plow through it. I shouldn't have dumped everything on you."

"You're not dumping anything on me. I just thought you'd get a kick out of seeing bureaucracy in action." Relief colored her father's voice. He was clearly glad to hear from her. "I'll finish digging through the forms today. I'll drop the stack off to the fire department tomorrow."

"Any news on the cause of the fire?"

"Nothing definitive yet. The fire department *is* sure the blaze started in the back of the building. In a wall, behind the bar's kitchen. Something about the burn pattern made them rule out arson. Not that I understand half of what they tell me."

"I'm glad it wasn't arson." A possibility Vale hadn't seriously considered.

"Me too. I'd hate to think some underage kid torched the place because we wouldn't serve him." Bo chuckled. "We've seen our share of fake IDs, right?"

"Too many."

An uncomfortable pause, and she feared he'd circle back to their conversation about the divorce. She was still stinging from the discovery that he'd left her mother—not the other way around.

As if sensing her unease, Bo cleared his throat. "I'd better get back to the paperwork."

"Let me know if there's anything I can do."

"Just have fun with Iris. I'm sure she's missed you. How's she doing?"

"She seems fine. I'm trying not to worry."

"Give her my best."

"I will."

After she hung up, Vale put on jeans and a floral blouse with pretty shell buttons. Emmett was expecting her soon for the cookout.

In the living room, there was no sign of Blythe. The pillows on the couch appeared recently plumped, and the lemony scent of furniture polish carried in the air. Wandering into the kitchen, Vale spied a gardening trowel on the counter beside a freshly brewed pot of coffee.

She grabbed a cup and went outside. Beneath the Japanese maple, she spotted the wheelbarrow loaded with bags of gardening soil. Quickening her pace, she discovered her grandmother on hands and knees jabbing at the hard earth with a gardening claw.

"Nana, why don't you work on the bed tomorrow? I'll help you finish when you return from the hospital." A stone popped from the ground, whipping past Vale's ankles. "Detta won't care if I leave Green Iris before closing. Mondays are never busy."

"I appreciate the offer, but I'd rather tackle this today."

"When do your tests begin tomorrow?"

"Early." Setting the gardening claw aside, Iris heaved a clump of dirt from the ground. She flung it out of the way. Glancing up, she surveyed Vale's outfit. "You look nice. Are you going somewhere?"

"To Emmett's. He's grilling burgers and hot dogs."

"Two dates in less than twenty-four hours. Sounds auspicious."

"It's not a date. Natty will be there too. Ana has to work."

"Call it what you'd like. If a man invites you over to his house, it's a positive development."

Snatching up the gardening claw, Iris attacked the ground with sharp jabs. Another stone popped loose, pinging her in the shoulder. She fell back on her bottom, muttering beneath her breath.

"Nana, what's bothering you?" Vale wrenched the tool from her fist. "You're not gardening. You're on a rampage."

"I'm upset."

Unease trilled through Vale. "About the tests? Please let me go with you tomorrow. I'll skip work at the shop. You shouldn't be alone."

"I'm not worried about the tests."

"Then what is it?"

The query met with silence. Head bowed, her grandmother scanned the ground as if searching for something valuable. Like her normally sunny disposition.

"Nana?"

With a grunt, Iris struggled to her feet. "I'm worried about your sister. Or I'm furious with her." Rubbing her back, she cast an irritated glance at the house. "I can't decide."

"Where *is* Blythe? I didn't see her inside."

"She's on the front porch stewing in her own juices. With good reason, in my opinion."

Vale folded her arms. "I'm getting the feeling you and Blythe had a heart-to-heart this morning." One that didn't go well, obviously. It would explain Iris's testy mood. "What else did I miss by sleeping in?"

"A lot," Iris said dryly. "I'm worried your sister has done something disgraceful to put her marriage in jeopardy."

"Something more serious than maxing out her credit cards?"

"Obviously." Iris picked up a stone and tossed it into the wheelbarrow. "Blythe has always been sensible. Ethical. There are lines I assumed she'd never cross. Now it appears she has, and I'm heartbroken."

The hairs on Vale's neck lifted to attention. *She's implying Blythe has been unfaithful.*

The notion didn't fit, not for someone like Blythe. She negotiated life with a strict moral compass. Growing up, she'd followed their mother's every rule. Even in high school, she'd been incapable of telling Audrey the most insignificant white lies—about whether a friend's parents would supervise a party, or where a boy planned to take her on a date. She'd missed out on parties *and* dates when her truthful accounts didn't meet with their mother's approval.

Even as the objections raced through Vale, doubt pierced her ready assumptions. Could she accurately gauge her sister's behavior? They lost touch before her move to Pittsburgh. Blythe was practically a stranger.

Iris said, "I thought it would be easy to get your sister to confide in me. Of course, I presumed her marital problems weren't complicated. Young couples argue over the silliest things. Often a cooler head can intervene to set them on a better course. Blythe's situation, it seems, is anything but simple. She's caught up in an untenable situation."

"Wait. Did she confide in you or not?"

"Indirectly."

"That's not good enough. You're jumping to conclusions."

"Vale, I wasn't born yesterday. I can read between the lines." Iris picked up another stone. With impressive force she flung it toward the fence. "Now I don't know what to do. Booker is such a devoted husband. There's no doubting his love for Blythe. If she's been dishonorable, how can I lend advice? I'm so angry!"

This change of opinion was striking. To Vale's knowledge, Blythe never earned their grandmother's censure. Whatever she'd indirectly revealed—out of guilt or by accident—she'd given Iris the impression that she'd lost her moral compass.

Because she's running around on Booker. What other conclusion made sense?

Vale gave her grandmother a quick hug. "Whatever Blythe did, you won't help matters by making her feel worse," she pointed out. "What if you read her the riot act, and she packs up to stay with a friend? If she leaves, we can't help her at all."

"We?" Iris shuffled back a step. "Since when are you interested in helping Blythe?"

"She is my sister. I don't like seeing her this . . . unglued. If I can help untangle the mess she's making of her life—well, I'm in. Totally."

"Then we'll help her together." Surprise blended with relief in Iris's gaze. "You're unpredictable, Vale—in a good way."

The conversation came to an abrupt close. Behind them, the fluff of Natty's hair appeared on the opposite side of the fence. The child managed to bring her face into view, undoubtedly by standing on tiptoes.

"Vale, are you ready? Emmett says he's firing up the grill."

Vale gave a thumbs-up. Then she told her grandmother, "They text. Emmett also watches her periodically."

Iris lowered her voice to a whisper. "I do too when Ana's regular babysitter isn't available. Blythe has too, now and again. Last year she helped Natty decorate her Christmas tree. Ana worked double shifts through the holiday season, poor thing."

Dropping the subject, Iris approached the fence. "Hello, Natty."

"Hi, Mrs. McClintock! Are you coming too? Emmett made lots of food."

"Oh, I'd rather not." She gestured toward the Japanese maple. "I'm in the middle of a project."

"That's too bad. You're missing out on some great eats."

"I'm sure I am. But you enjoy."

"I will."

Inspiration struck and Vale said, "Natty, why don't you ask Blythe to join us? She could use the diversion."

"Sure! Where is she?"

"On the front porch moping."

Natty cocked her head to the side. "What's 'moping'?"

"Never mind. Just convince her to come. Don't take no for an answer."

"I won't!"

After the child dashed off, Vale regarded her grandmother with triumph. "You see? I'm a natural peacemaker. With a little practice, it'll become second nature."

Iris grunted. "Don't stand in line for a gold star just yet. If I award one, it will go to Natty. You've never seen her in action. She'll lay on enough sugar to persuade Blythe." Iris snatched the coffee from Vale's fist and took a long sip. Handing back the mug, she added, "I nearly forgot—Blythe is giving you the red dress."

"No way."

115

"She says it's too tight on her."

"You covered a lot of ground this morning. What else did you discuss?"

"You want the details? Ask your sister."

Pivoting away, Iris returned to her gardening. Vale started for the house.

When she reached the foyer, Natty announced, "She's coming!"

Unable to contain her excitement, the child swayed back and forth. Blythe—seated on the stairs—appeared more subdued. She wore no makeup. Vale noticed the telltale puffiness beneath her eyes.

She'd been doing more than moping on the front porch. She'd been crying.

Natty scooped up Blythe's tennis shoes. "What do you like better, hamburgers or hot dogs?" She placed them before her.

"Oh, I don't have a favorite." Blythe spiked her voice with false cheer. She failed to wash the sadness from her features, and her lower lip wobbled. "What about you, Natty? What's your favorite?"

"Burgers, definitely. With ketchup. I hate mustard. It smells funny and tastes worse."

"I don't think so."

"You like mustard?"

"Sometimes." Slowly Blythe reached for her shoes. "It's great on corned beef."

Natty's foot tapped an impatient rhythm. "Do you need help? I'm good at lacing up shoes."

Aware her sister needed space, Vale steered Natty toward the door. "Let's give Blythe a minute." She ushered the child onto the front porch. "Tell Emmett he has another guest for the cookout. We'll meet you there soon."

"Why can't we walk down together?"

"Natty, go on. We'll be right behind you."

Chapter 17

Once Natty clambered down the porch steps, anxiety carried Vale back inside.

Blythe stood before the foyer mirror. With sulky movements, she pulled her curly hair into a ponytail. The silence grew oppressive; she seemed no more certain on how to interact than Vale. During their long-ago childhood, they'd enjoyed companionship at random intervals, the moments of closeness dictated by Vale's mood. Those interludes hadn't left a deep enough imprint to guide them now.

Vale offered a smile. "There's no hurry. Take all the time you need."

"It was sweet of Natty to invite me." Blythe smoothed nervous palms down her jeans. "Thanks for sending her ahead."

Whatever Blythe had discussed with their grandmother this morning, it had left her shaken. She looked wan, nearly disoriented. A tear spilled down her cheek.

Rummaging around in her purse, Vale found a packet of tissues. "Why don't you dry your eyes?" She held one out.

Blythe hesitated. She seemed unwilling to accept the smallest token from the older sister who'd often treated her like the enemy. Or perhaps the offer of assistance—a glaring spotlight on her struggle to master her emotions—injured her pride. Either way, her indecision created a rare opportunity.

Boldly Vale approached. With careful movements, she dried her sister's cheeks. Incredibly, Blythe didn't flinch at her touch.

With childlike obedience, she allowed Vale to fuss over her. The tacit consent flooded Vale with unfamiliar memories. Cradling a sobbing Blythe after her first try on roller skates ended in disaster. Bandaging her knee after she took a spill off a bicycle. Memories hidden so deeply, Vale wasn't aware she'd kept them until now.

Blythe said, "I'm not sure how to deal with the new and improved Vale. What happened to your famous temper and your snark?"

"I grew out of the snark." Vale swept the tissue beneath her sister's damp eyes. "My temper is a work in progress. Sometimes it gets the better of me."

Blythe remained perfectly still as she took this in. "Did you tell Natty to invite me to Emmett's, or was it her idea?"

"Why does it matter?"

"Stop dancing, Vale. Answer the question."

"Inviting you was my idea. For the record, Natty was all in. I'm sure Emmett is too. If you need proof, I'll send him a text for confirmation."

"You're still dancing." Snatching the tissue from Vale's grasp, Blythe stuffed it into her pocket. "Why do *you* want me to come?"

The question nearly put Vale on the defensive. Would her sister forever view her every move with suspicion?

She chose the direct approach. "You need cheering up, and the cookout will be fun. I have a feeling you and Nana were arguing this morning. Which is strange enough. I didn't know you ever disagreed."

"We don't, usually."

"I'm not prying. I just thought you needed a diversion."

Blythe offered a rueful glance. "Vale, about our argument yesterday . . ."

"Let's not go into it now."

"No. I need to say this." Blythe took a steadying breath. On the exhale, she said, "I was out of bounds, mentioning your parents' divorce.

I thought you knew, but that doesn't excuse my behavior. We've had lots of disagreements in the past, but we've managed to keep our fathers out of it. What happened between your parents is none of my business. I hope you can forgive me for bringing it up."

The sincere apology took Vale aback. She felt her throat pinch with emotion.

"Forgiven and forgotten," she managed.

"Thanks."

With satisfaction she noted the trace of relief on her sister's features. "Thank *you* for the stunning silk number. It's officially the nicest dress in my wardrobe." If they were steering their relationship onto a better path, it helped to lighten the mood. "The dress is practically new. Are you sure you want to part with it?"

"I can barely pour my curves into it," Blythe admitted. "I'm sure it looks better on you."

"Then let me pay you."

"It's a gift, Vale. I don't want your money." Blythe slid her phone into her pocket. "Are we going or not? We shouldn't keep Emmett and Natty waiting."

An unexpected camaraderie led them outside. The street sang with activity. The buzz of lawnmowers whirred across patches of lawn. A group of children were decorating the sidewalk with chalk.

Before Emmett's brick Tudor, Natty paced in a glum circle.

"Finally!" With impatience she flapped her arms. "Emmett promised to start grilling once you got here."

Vale ruffled her hair. "You must be hungry."

"I'm starving." Skipping up the front steps, Natty pulled open the door. "Well, come on." She darted off, and Vale heard a sliding glass door swish open in the back of the house.

Emmett came into the foyer, a dish towel slung over his shoulder. "Hey, there." He brushed his fingers across Vale's wrist. "I hope you brought an appetite."

The remark barely registered as she took in her surroundings. "Your house is beautiful."

The foyer was painted in a light shade of lime as welcoming as a new day. The walls of the living room shimmered in a deeper grass-green hue. Behind the leather furniture arranged in the living room, a bookcase climbed to the vaulted ceiling. Vale wasn't sure what she'd expected, but Emmett's home was no thrown-together bachelor pad.

The compliment pleased him. "Thanks." Looking past her, he appraised Blythe standing just inside the door. "It's good to see you, Blythe. I'm glad you can join us."

"Thanks for letting me tag along." Unease crowded Blythe's face. "Is there anything we can do to help in the kitchen?"

She seemed about to add something else. A mention of his assistance Friday night, no doubt, when he'd driven her home from Knock's Pub. Finding the right words seemed an obstacle. Vale searched for a way to rescue her.

Emmett beat her to it. "Vale can help me finish up dinner." Once they entered the kitchen, he provided Blythe a means of escape, adding, "Would you mind giving Natty an assist? She's setting up the croquet field in the backyard. She's not sure where to place the wickets."

The suggestion eased the tension flitting around Blythe like bothersome flies. With a nod, she went out back.

The moment they were alone, Emmett drew Vale into his arms. "I enjoyed last night," he said. "The most fun I've had in a long time."

"Me too," she agreed, her attention centering on his palms coasting across her back. "It was a wonderful evening."

"If you have an adventurous palate, there's an Israeli restaurant I hear is great. Why don't we go sometime this week?"

"I'd like that. I've never tried Israeli cuisine."

"Both of my sisters are fans of the place. I'll check when we can get a reservation." Letting the topic go, he dipped his nose into her hair. "You smell great." Brushing his lips across her ear, he sent warmth tumbling through her. "You taste even better."

He kissed her slowly and thoroughly, making her breathless. When he drew back and Vale opened her eyes, she found him canvassing her features with an intensity that made her dizzy. She was inexperienced with attraction this immediate and consuming. The lightest touch—the mere tangling of their gazes—created something thrilling and combustible.

Instinctively, she leaned against him. She wanted nothing more than another kiss, another delicious moment to drink him in.

But Emmett wasn't a young man falling headfirst into love. Erasing the passion on his features, he pivoted away. He tossed the dish towel on a nearby counter.

From over his shoulder, he asked, "How did you manage it?" From a drawer, he retrieved two serving spoons. "With your sister, I mean. I'm surprised she's joining us for the cookout."

"Call it a moment of inspiration—one that would've failed without Natty's help. She's a master at little-girl lobbying. Blythe couldn't refuse."

"Blythe seems awfully low. I suppose she misses Booker. Marriage to a pro athlete can't be easy. All those away games."

"I'm sure it's not," Vale replied carefully. Her sister's marital problems were private. Her attraction to Emmett didn't warrant revealing the secret.

Letting the subject go, she surveyed the kitchen. A bank of windows looked out on gardens lovingly tended like her grandmother's. Tall, whitewashed cupboards, stone flooring, a rustic table of golden oak—she could pitch a tent and stay in this sunny room forever.

"How long have you lived here?" She noticed a head of lettuce by the sink and began washing the leaves.

"Nearly ten years. The place was a fixer-upper when I bought it." Emmett handed her a tomato, a cucumber, and a knife. After she got to work, he pulled a bubbling casserole from the oven. The rich scents of potatoes au gratin spiked the air. "I tackled most of the renovations myself. YouTube is a great resource if you're a novice at setting in tile or hanging drywall. Not that I can take all the credit. My brothers-in-law pitched in whenever their schedules permitted."

"It must be wonderful, living somewhere long enough to make it your home."

"You've moved around a lot?"

Nodding, Vale began slicing the cucumber. "I've never stayed anywhere more than two years. My first apartment was the absolute pits. I moved in with two other girls I met online. We were crammed into a one-bedroom in South Philly with heating that barely worked and a fridge that went on the blink monthly."

"Sounds dismal."

"Blame the inexperience of youth—we were all just out of high school. There was only one full-size bed. We took turns sleeping on a moldy couch we picked up cheap. The following year, my roommates signed another lease. I found somewhere better to live."

Emmett, retrieving a platter from the fridge, came to a standstill. "You were living independently at eighteen?"

"By choice." Having him view the decision as tragic would diminish Vale in ways she refused to analyze. "I didn't get along with my mother or my stepfather. Moving out solved the problem."

"They didn't ask you to stay?"

The question was a blade, scraping against the hateful memories. Vale recalled the sense of helplessness swamping her when she threatened to move out. Neither her mother nor Grant protested. They stood frozen, glaring at her. As the silence lengthened, shock leaped through her. Then Audrey, pulling out of her stupor, threw her hands in the air.

Fine, Vale. You don't want to live here? Get out of my house.

"It wouldn't have made a difference." The memory ate at her composure, but Vale kept her tone light. "We fought constantly. I was tired of their nonstop criticism. I knew it was time to go."

His expression fluid, Emmett set the platter on the counter. "Did your mother and stepfather help you out financially?"

"Sure. Whenever I asked," she said, hating the lie. On the few occasions when she couldn't stretch a paycheck to make the rent or buy food, she'd asked her grandmother for help. She never would've approached her mother and Grant, and risked their refusal. "I wasn't destitute, Emmett. I worked two jobs and learned how to get by without much sleep. I learned to live frugally. My mother and Grant *did* pay for college, although they weren't pleased when I kept dropping out. It took forever to earn my bachelor's."

Leaning against the counter, Emmett crossed his arms. His fluid expression settled into something unreadable. A stronger, harsher emotion he seemed unable to suppress. For an easygoing man, the change was remarkable.

"Who wouldn't keep dropping out of college?" he snapped. Sparks glittered in his eyes, and she realized he was struggling to subdue his anger. "Most kids aren't ready to live independently right out of high school. My parents were still helping me *after* I'd completed my doctoral degree in pharmacy. If parents have the means, they should put their children first."

"They *did* help—by paying my tuition." Vale wasn't sure why she was defending them. It seemed laughable, pathetic. "The first years were hard, but I adapted."

"You never should've been in the situation where you *needed* to adapt. Learning how to manage cash, paying for rent—I never could've pulled off that feat at eighteen. When I wasn't living on campus, I lived at home. Thanks to my parents, I was able to focus on my studies. Even with their help, it was a tough slog."

Outrage had lowered Emmett's voice. She knew he wasn't angry with her. His fury was directed at her mother and stepfather. He viewed them as uncaring if not outright negligent.

"Not every family operates like yours, Emmett. You were fortunate." As Vale uttered the words, the unspoken questions tightened her throat. *Were Audrey and Grant negligent? If they were, then Bo was too.* She felt her eyes burn. "That doesn't mean I made a mistake. Lots of kids move out right after high school. It's not uncommon."

"You didn't make a mistake, Vale. Your parents did."

Parents. The awful hurt centered in her chest, and she nearly laughed. A better choice than succumbing to tears. The year she turned eighteen, Audrey and Grant celebrated dual promotions at Stern-Belkins. Bo wasn't even around. He'd remarried and moved with his third wife to North Carolina. He'd divorced soon after, returning to Pennsylvania near Vale's twentieth birthday.

"Hey, don't cry." Steering her from her thoughts, Emmett cradled her face. Then he brushed his nose across hers. "I didn't mean to upset you. I have no right to judge your family."

Vale released a gurgling laugh. "You don't," she agreed.

"I should keep my opinions to myself. Hard to do in my line of work. Some days, I dispense more advice than medicine." He trailed gentle fingers across her neck. "Can you forgive me?"

When his arms tightened around her, Vale rested her cheek against his chest. "There's nothing to forgive. We come from different backgrounds, that's all." Without thinking, she brushed her damp nose across his shirt. She gasped, embarrassed.

Grinning, Emmett reached for the dish towel. He finished drying her face with the same tenderness she'd displayed with Blythe earlier.

Swiftly, he kissed her. "All better?" He seemed unwilling to let her go.

She draped her arms around his neck. "I'm great." She longed for another kiss.

"Let's never argue. I hate seeing you unhappy."

"All couples argue. We can't agree on everything."

Emmett pulled her in closer. "Are we a couple?" He chuckled against her neck. "That was fast. Not that I'm complaining."

Were they? Pleasure and worry mixed inside Vale. It was risky, falling in love too fast. Diving in before they knew each other well.

Natty burst into the kitchen.

"I'm *starving*. Are we *ever* going to eat?"

They pulled apart like teens caught making out.

Natty's jaw loosened. "Are you getting mushy in here?" She looked genuinely offended. Nose wrinkling, she thumped her chest. "There are kids present. Keep it PG-13, okay?"

Blythe came in behind her. "You're not thirteen," she informed Natty. "You're nine. If you're watching PG-13 movies, I'm telling your mother."

"I don't watch that stuff!"

"Good to hear. Now, do me a favor. Set the picnic table. The plates and silverware are already outside."

"Okay—I'm going." Natty slammed the door on her way out.

With an assessing eye, Blythe watched Emmett fumble with oven mitts. He finally shoved his hands inside. On the way to the oven, he bumped into the counter. A serving spoon clattered to the floor.

Vale's face prickled with heat: Emmett's hair was tousled. Like he'd just rolled out of bed.

When did I run my fingers through his hair? Probably while yearning for another kiss.

Oddly, the pheromones leaping through the kitchen didn't persuade Blythe to retreat. They energized her. Or amused her. It was hard to tell.

Taking charge, she said, "Emmett, why don't you start the grill?" When he nodded, she handed him the platter of beef patties and then opened the fridge. She found the package of hot dogs and placed them on top. "Vale and I will finish up in here."

Emmett strode out.

Cheeks burning, Vale returned to work on the salad. Donning the oven mitts, Blythe withdrew a casserole of baked beans from the oven.

She gave Vale an appraising glance. "He's quite taken with you."

The feeling is mutual. Vale tossed a handful of cucumber slices toward the bowl, missed.

"He's nothing like the men I usually date. Not that I date very much." The slices dived to the floor.

Blythe picked them up. "Is that a good thing, or bad?" She tossed them into the sink.

"Good. Definitely. He's authentic. He can also be intense. Sometimes Emmett gets a look in his eyes that makes me feel like . . ."

"What?"

The tomato Vale attempted to slice sprang loose. It rolled off the cutting board. "Like he's the hunter and I'm the unsuspecting rabbit."

Blythe caught the tomato a thin second before it hit the floor. "It looks to me like 'intense' is just what you need. Not all men play games. Especially if they're thinking about taking a romance to the next level." Nudging Vale aside, she finished the salad. "You're not bothered by the age difference? Emmett must have ten years on you."

"I haven't really thought about it. We've only had one date."

"Two dates. This afternoon counts. I'll bet Emmett's planning to corral you into a third date this week."

"He *did* mention taking me to an Israeli restaurant."

With interest, Blythe looked up. "I've never had Israeli food. Is it good?"

"According to Emmett, it's great. I guess I'll find out later this week."

"Oh. Wait. I have tried Israeli cuisine. It's similar to other Middle Eastern fare with lots of feta cheese, dates, and lamb dishes. And lots of tomatoes and parsley. Tahini is one of my favorites—have you tried it?"

"I'm not sure."

"It's made with sesame seeds. There's an Israeli restaurant in Atlanta that makes tahini to die for. I order it every time we eat there. I love Atlanta. It's such a fun city . . ."

Vale stared in wonder as Blythe prattled on. The conversation was utterly normal, the sort shared by sisters everywhere. She'd never discussed men with Blythe, or Israeli cuisine, or anything of importance. Not since they were children, and how many issues of consequence do children share? They'd waded through puberty without each other's love or reassurance; they'd become women alone, never sharing their exploits or whispering about secret loves. It seemed unimaginable that Blythe was now flinging open the doors to conversation.

As if there'd never been a break in their affection. As if this simple, startling moment were normal, like a thousand days before it.

It was a start.

Chapter 18

A welcome calm entered their grandmother's home.

Sunday's barbecue couldn't heal all the wounds between sisters. Even so, Vale and Blythe settled into a peaceful rhythm. No arguments broke out. There was no more discussion of when Vale would return to Pittsburgh. On Monday, their grandmother left early for the hospital. Iris was still upset regarding her suspicions that Blythe had run around on Booker. Still, she managed to keep a polite tone as she strode past her younger granddaughter.

While Vale readied for work at the plant shop, Blythe offered to make breakfast. She whipped up a batch of blueberry pancakes. While they ate, they were unable to get the wind under the sails of their conversation. Still, the experience was pleasant. The next morning Vale reciprocated, making omelets they shared over slightly easier conversation. When Blythe met with an old friend from college on Wednesday night, Vale dusted and vacuumed both of their rooms.

On Thursday afternoon, Vale returned from Green Iris to find her laundry hamper empty. Her freshly washed jeans and blouses were arranged in neat stacks on the bed. That night, she went out with Emmett to the Israeli restaurant. She brought home a slice of cheesecake for her grandmother—Iris's favorite—and a box of chocolate-and-currant rugelach for Blythe. It seemed a victory when the lure of sweets prodded Blythe from her bedroom, where she'd been camped out listening to the more tragic songs from Motown's classic playlist.

To Vale, the improvement in their relationship was a gift. As she sampled the rugelach with Blythe, she began toying with an idea. What if they went out together soon? Since they were getting along on the domestic front, why not expand their horizons with a social activity? A sisters' night out might cement their new friendship.

Iris—still simmering like a pot nearing a boil—thanked Vale for the cheesecake and left the kitchen without even a glance at Blythe.

Her behavior didn't improve over the weekend. If anything, it worsened as they began the new week. Iris went to the hospital for her mysterious tests or worked short shifts at the shop with a dark cloud brewing around her. She didn't seem eager to confront Blythe over her suspicions. Yet she'd given her younger granddaughter the cold shoulder enough times that Blythe—still going out most nights and preoccupied with her own troubles—was beginning to notice.

Near dawn that Wednesday, a storm raced across the sleeping neighborhood, and a persistent tapping invaded Vale's dreams.

Dragging herself from bed, she padded to the window. Outside the trees swayed in the lashing rain. She wasn't due at the shop until nine o'clock. There was still time to sleep, but she needed to speak to Iris. Mostly to ensure she didn't make the détente between sisters impossible to achieve.

Vale knew her grandmother was convinced Blythe had been unfaithful. Her marriage was teetering by no fault of Booker's. The blame for its dissolution, if it came to that, rested solely with Blythe. Vale suspected this was true. Yet she didn't see the sense in punishing Blythe for wrongs she may have committed—which Iris did each time she responded with a snappish comment or left the room when Blythe entered.

Coming to a decision, Vale tiptoed down the hallway.

The main bedroom swam in a sea of shadows. Behind the partially shut curtains, rain thumped against the windowpanes. Once her vision adjusted to the dim light, Vale approached the four-poster bed. Pillows tumbled every which way against the headboard. Beneath the chenille bedspread, Iris lay curled on her side.

Vale climbed beneath the covers. "Nana." She bent toward her grandmother's ear. "We need to talk."

A gargled snort. Iris burrowed deeper in her contented sleep.

"Nana, wake up."

The command unleashed an impressive bout of snoring. It cut off as Iris rolled onto her back, her sleeping mask askew.

Giving up on the delicate approach, Vale flicked on the lamp. Her timing was impeccable: at the same instant, thunder bellowed across the roof. The windows shuddered.

Iris shot up in bed. She ripped the mask from her face, her startled gaze finding Vale.

"Are you *mad?*" She lasered Vale with a look of pure fury. "I was asleep! What are you doing here?"

Mischief tugged at Vale's lips. It was cruel to rattle Iris. *It's also fun.*

"Jeez, Nana. You used to invite me into your bed all the time. If I couldn't sleep, you'd read stories."

"You were young. We read stories in the evening. The one time I let you crawl into my bed during the middle of the night, you gave me the thrill of a lifetime. And *not* in a good way. I should've checked your pocket before you crossed the threshold to my room."

"What did I have in my pocket?"

"A frog you found in the backyard. You'd kept it hidden all day."

A strange accusation, and Vale laughed. "Are you making this up? I never brought a frog to your bedroom."

"You most certainly did. You named him Jeremy. You assumed if you gave the creature a name, I'd allow you to keep it. Such nonsense. I spent a good ten minutes chasing that energetic little beast around my room before I caught it."

"I don't remember Jeremy the frog."

"You were five, in one of your more disobedient phases. Your father had blown into town unannounced and spent less than an hour visiting with you. Bo shouldn't have bothered at all. After he left, you insisted on spending the night at my house."

That much of the story made sense. Often Vale had demanded to stay with her grandmother after Bo's infrequent visits. Even as a small child, she'd been aware that something about his visits injured her relationship with her mother and Grant.

"So I viewed Jeremy as my consolation prize? I'm impressed I was able to sneak him into the house without you catching on."

"You were a stealthy child. I'm lucky you didn't find a snake slithering around my petunias instead of Jeremy. It would've scarred me for life." Plumping up the pillows, Iris arranged herself in a more comfortable position. "Enough about your fascinating childhood. Why are we having this clandestine meeting at"—she peered at the nightstand clock—"six in the morning?"

"I want you to release Blythe from your arctic chill. I get that you're upset with her, but you haven't said two positive words to her in days."

"Or negative ones either." Iris tilted her chin defiantly. "I've been resisting the urge to read her the riot act. That counts for something."

"It counts for nada."

"I disagree."

"Nana, do you remember what you told me when I first came to Philly? Don't fight with Blythe. Outside of the first few days, I've held up my side of the bargain. I really have."

"I know. You've done great, pumpkin."

"You wanted me to stay out of the way so you could get to the bottom of her marital troubles. From what I can tell, you *did* broach the subject in a tentative way. The weekend after I drove in, remember? Only now you're treating Blythe like a pariah."

Iris plucked her sleeping mask from the bedspread. "You're right," she agreed, winding and unwinding it around her wrist. She couldn't seem to keep her fingers still. "I'm disappointed in her, but my behavior isn't helping matters."

"No, it's not. Especially since your reaction is based on supposition. It's not like Blythe made a confession. Or am I missing something?"

"I know what I know." With unexpected pique, Iris pitched the sleeping mask off the bed.

"Which is what? You're positive Blythe is running around on Booker?" Tired of sidestepping the issue, Vale attacked head-on. "Nana, it happens. Not everyone who recites marriage vows follows through on the promise. Blythe is married to one of the best pitchers in Major League Baseball. What if she didn't understand the sacrifices that entails? During most of the year, Booker is playing or practicing with the team. If Blythe cheated—and we have no proof—maybe she did because she's lonely. You're treating her like she's done murder and dumped the body in your basement."

Iris bristled. "You condone her behavior?"

"People cheat, Nana. I'm not saying it's okay. I *am* saying that sexual desire can short-circuit a person's common sense. It can be overwhelming. We like to believe we're reliably in charge and our sex drive is easy to suppress. Maybe it is, for some people. Not for everyone."

A hush fell between them. The rain tapping against the windows slowed in tempo.

Her grandmother patted her hand. "When did you become so wise?"

Vale couldn't believe she needed to ask. "I owned a bar. Some of the regulars switched partners on a weekly basis. We had to install extra lighting in our parking lot just to stop customers from getting laid in their cars. And I've watched my father skate through too many relationships."

"Beauty is your father's curse. When Bo flashes those pearly whites, it spells doom for any woman in the vicinity."

Vale couldn't disagree. "He's addicted to the conquest—and the payoff. I've also waited on people at the Crafty Cocktail who make the stupidest decisions *before* they order their first drink. More often they make incredibly dumb choices after they start drinking." Vale studied the shadows filtering across the ceiling. Then she added, "I've made the same mistake."

"That's hard to believe. You don't even like to drink."

"It only happened once. I'm still angry with myself."

Iris blinked. "When?"

"A few days after the Crafty Cocktail burned down." Vale wished she could erase that day. Blot it from the calendar of her life. "Too much tequila, and an attractive man buying all the rounds. If I hadn't been upset about the bar, I never would've gone home with him." Letting it go, she looked swiftly at her grandmother. "Whatever Blythe has done, I'm sure she regrets it. She can't begin to forgive herself—and hopefully save her marriage—if you're casting judgment. Will you let it go?"

With a sigh, Iris climbed out of bed. "I'm turning over a new leaf, starting this morning." Clearly chastised, she made an X over her heart.

"Good. We don't have much time."

"Don't worry, pumpkin. There's time to reason with Blythe."

"I'm talking about Mom and Grant. Once they return from Aruba, will Blythe feel cornered and make a rash decision? It's not like they won't notice she's camped out in one of your guest bedrooms." Apprehension jolted Vale as she steered her feet to the floor. "When *are* they coming back?"

"Not for another ten days. They got a deal on a time-share, compliments of Ira Stern and Libby Belkins. Your stepfather was recently promoted—again."

Like I care about Grant's career. "Perfect. You'll channel your normally sunny disposition, and I'll give my plan a go." A feeling of self-congratulation sent Vale's apprehension fleeing.

With interest, her grandmother studied her. "What plan?"

"Well, Blythe wants to surprise you by tackling your attic. It hasn't been sorted and deep-cleaned in ages."

"Good heavens. Is she serious? The attic is a dead zone. I've stopped visiting."

"Good to know because she won't get too far. I'm taking her out tonight. Don't tell her—I'll persuade her after I come home from Green Iris. Do you think Detta will mind if I clock out early? I have a big night planned."

Iris shrugged into her robe. "Detta won't care if you leave in the middle of the afternoon. I'm going in. We'll have more than enough staff."

"Don't you have more tests at the hospital?" Last weekend, Vale was sure she'd mentioned another round.

"They've been rescheduled," Iris said breezily. "I'll finish the entire lot on Friday."

Chapter 19

Blythe stepped inside the apartment on Rittenhouse Square.

Their sumptuous home in one of Philadelphia's swankiest neighborhoods still felt like a spread in *Architectural Digest,* in which it had appeared. No dirt marred the gleaming travertine floor. The sofa, swathed in ivory velvet, appeared untouched. On the slipper chairs covered in raw silk, there wasn't the smallest crease. With misgivings, Blythe recalled her excitement when she'd first married Booker and thrown herself into decorating their new home.

She hadn't understood that Booker's fame would afford them every luxury except time.

For spring training, they rented an apartment near BayCare Ballpark in Clearwater. During the baseball season, their lives revolved around Booker's game schedule. With 162 games played in 180 days, they rarely invited guests over for dinner. During the off-season, they visited his family in Des Moines before flying on to Hawaii for intensive rest and relaxation. Then they returned to Clearwater for the onset of the next season.

The pace took a grueling toll. Dropping her keys into her purse, Blythe walked slowly toward the main bedroom. Living with a pro athlete was difficult and hectic and often lonely. Yet if she decided to end her marriage, she'd miss every precious minute of her life with Booker.

Talk to him. In the hallway, she squeezed her eyes shut. *Tell him how you've let him down.* The charade had gone on long enough. Pretending their marriage wasn't crumbling diminished them both. If the situation were reversed, would Booker delay talking to her? *No. He's too honest and straightforward to rely on deceit and lies.* In all the ways that counted, he was as open and simple as the land of Iowa cornfields where he was born.

Blythe wavered with indecision. Tonight, Booker would pitch against the Milwaukee Brewers. A home game with the stadium packed with adoring fans. How to reveal the tragic facts now? Her timing was lousy. She'd crush every assumption they'd made about their marriage when he needed to stay focused on the upcoming game. *If the Phillies lose tonight, it's on me.*

Talk later this week? With growing frustration, she recalled the series of away games filling the roster. Nearly a full week with the team out of town. It was today, or nothing. *Nothing, then. I'm not going to break the team's winning streak by dumping the truth on Booker this morning.*

What choice was there but to continue stalling? To continue the farce until it became impossible to do so.

A feeling of hopelessness led her into the main suite. Eyes downcast, Booker strode out of the bathroom, his thoughts undoubtedly centered on tonight's game. The sight of him gripped Blythe with love so fierce, she felt momentarily dizzy.

Droplets of water clung to Booker's thick, sandy-blond locks. His torso wore a sheen of dampness. Buttoning his jeans, he started toward the dresser. Halting, he noticed her.

A slow smile quirked the corner of his mouth. "Babe."

The endearment filled her with longing. Blythe couldn't stop her feet from carrying her forward.

Booker nuzzled her close. "I hoped you'd drop by before I left for the ballpark."

"I would've called but I knew you were in the shower." On game days, he followed a schedule with exacting precision. He ate the same breakfast, and he always showered twenty minutes before leaving for the field at noon.

"I missed you in St. Louis." The Phillies had just finished a four-game series against the Cardinals. "Some of the other wives asked about you."

Smiling, Blythe hid her unease. She'd been avoiding the other wives, for fear one of them would clue in to her marital woes.

"What did you tell them?"

"That you're tired of chasing me across the country for every game. You've done more than your share."

"It wasn't too bad in the beginning. Now the jet lag gets to me."

"Once we start a family, you'll have a built-in excuse to avoid the road. I know you're tired of jumping across time zones." Booker paused, a muscle in his jaw tensing. He cupped the side of her face. "No pressure, Blythe. I just didn't want to give you the impression I'm so wrapped up in the game, I've forgotten about our plans."

Pain splintered through her. "I know you haven't."

They'd made so many plans during their first year of marriage. When to build their dream home, how many children they'd have—Booker had laughed when she'd announced the desire to have four children. Two boys and two girls, all endowed with their father's athletic prowess and her emotional intelligence. Booker, the son of Iowa farmers, was an introvert. He'd never expected a childhood love of baseball to carry him to the pinnacle of fame. Beneath the warmth of Blythe's more sociable nature, his natural reserve was beginning to thaw.

If they divorced, would Booker retreat into his shell? Would it shatter his confidence, and his ability to play? *If I leave, it will destroy me too.* Blythe's love for him tightened her arms around his waist. He deserved more than she could give, and she didn't want to hurt him.

"No pressure," he repeated, misreading her reaction. "I know this is hard for you. We never talk about it . . . Maybe it wouldn't do any good if we did. I know you've been upset."

"I'm fine," she replied automatically.

He studied her closely. "How was the visit with your grandmother? Are you coming home tonight?"

"That's why I stopped by," she replied, improvising on the fly. "Booker, I'd like to stay at Nana's awhile longer. Vale is in town." She declined to add that they'd been staying together at their grandmother's for nearly two weeks now.

His brows lifted. "You want to stay *because* Vale has turned up?"

Dry-mouthed, she nodded.

"You can't stand her. I've never even met your half sister." In the placid Banks family, everyone got along. "I'm lost here. What's changed?"

"Everything. I know it sounds strange, but I'm starting to get along with Vale. Believe me, I'm surprised too." Blythe gave him a warning look. "And please don't refer to her as my half sister. She's my *only* sister."

"Got it." Booker planted a kiss on her forehead. "Babe, if you're reconnecting with Vale, it's a good thing. Don't let me stand in the way. When *are* you coming home?"

"In about a week, I guess. I'll keep you posted."

"What about tonight? Are you coming to the game? I'm sure the other wives would like to see you."

She hated disappointing him. "Do you care if I watch at my grandmother's house? I thought I'd start deep cleaning her attic this afternoon. Tonight I'll relax with Nana and Vale." When he shrugged in tacit agreement, she quickly added, "It's almost noon. You have to get to the ballpark."

"Right." With regret, he let her go.

Chapter 20

Peeling off the dirt-flecked T-shirt, Vale stretched her sore muscles. At Green Iris, she'd waited on customers nonstop, ringing up flats of spring vegetables, flowers, and herbs. When she wasn't manning the cash register, she'd carried houseplants to patrons' cars. A busier Wednesday than normal, even for late April. Iris was still at the shop. After they closed, she planned to have dinner with Detta in Queen Village.

Rummaging through the dresser, Vale searched for a suitable top. The temps were forecast to become chilly tonight. She selected a long-sleeve sweater and slipped it on.

She'd already bought the tickets and filled up her gas tank. Emmett was disappointed he wouldn't see her tonight, but he'd sent a flurry of encouraging texts. Assuming she convinced Blythe to go out, they'd enjoy their first sisters' night out together.

The soulful music of the Temptations' pop hit "Just My Imagination" drifted down from the attic. Evidently Blythe had carried their grandmother's record player and LPs upstairs for her cleaning spree.

The attic blazed with light. Three floor lamps were arranged around the room. A stepladder leaned against a wall. Apparently, Blythe had used the ladder to reach the fixtures running the length of the pitched roof to put in new bulbs. The windows beneath the low-slung rafters were free of grime, adding to the illumination. In the center of the room, Blythe sat amid a circle of boxes and bags.

"Is it bright enough in here?" Vale joked.

"Light is the best line of defense." With a lopsided grin, her sister held up a can of bug spray. "I don't mind tackling Nana's attic, but I hate spiders. They give me the willies."

"Seen any?"

"Not since I lit up the attic like Christmas."

Vale joined her on the floor. "No worries. If any spiders crawl out of hiding, I'll deal with them."

"You're a lifesaver." Blythe pushed a box forward, urging her to look inside. "I found some of the board games Nana bought for us. They're dusty from storage, but they're practically brand new."

Shame pricked Vale as she withdrew a bright-pink box. Pretty Pretty Princess, one of Blythe's childhood favorites. Throughout their childhood and adolescence, Iris had searched for ways to encourage her granddaughters to play together. Board games. Arts and crafts. Puzzles. The efforts failed miserably. Vale rarely agreed to play with her younger sister. If left alone together, she was more inclined to whisper hurtful comments or scald Blythe with dark looks.

There *were* occasions when Vale was nearly civil. But her moods had fluctuated constantly. They ebbed and flowed around the frequency of her battles with their mother, and the degree to which she missed Bo. She'd taken out her rage and grief on her younger sister.

Banishing the memory, Vale asked, "Should we give the board games to Natty? She doesn't have many toys."

"That's a great idea. Maybe we can peel her off her Nintendo Switch and PlayStation."

Vale returned the game to the box. "When I babysat last weekend, she played Gelly Break nonstop. I was convinced I was hearing the game's slurpy sounds for hours afterward."

"She spends too much time alone. Not that I blame Ana—she's holding down two jobs."

"What's Natty's regular babysitter like?"

Blythe closed the box, pushed it aside. "A nice woman, but older. She's probably happy to leave Natty parked in front of video games."

"You know, there are lots of our toys stored up here. The trick is finding them." Vale surveyed the bags and dusty cartons scattered beneath the eaves. "Roller skates, kid-size gardening tools, jump ropes—we should let Natty pick through the stuff."

"I haven't run across any of our other toys. At least not yet."

Vale studied the boxes surrounding her sister. "What have you found?"

"Tons of Nana's old clothes and enough knickknacks to stock a rummage sale. Glassware, old bedding, a toaster manufactured before we were born—I had no idea Nana was a serious pack rat."

"I could've let you in on the secret. She's been meaning to clean out the attic forever."

"Well, I can't sort through it all today. When I *do* finish, I'll take everything Nana doesn't want to Goodwill. Tomorrow or Friday." Blythe frowned at a chipped casserole dish before placing it in the donation pile. "Probably not on Friday, come to think of it. I'm meeting a friend from college for dinner. If all else fails, I'll get to it next weekend."

Curiosity got the better of Vale. "Blythe, you've been staying at Nana's for nearly two weeks. Doesn't Booker wonder when you're coming home?"

It came as a relief when her sister gave no reaction. The query wasn't out of bounds.

"We've already discussed it," Blythe admitted.

"When?"

"This morning." Briefly her eyes searched Vale's, as if gauging how much to share. Looking away, Blythe opened a bag, withdrew a musty stack of tablecloths. "I drove over to our apartment, a few hours after you and Nana left for the shop."

"I thought you were . . . you know. Steering clear of your husband for now."

Impatience flickered across Blythe's features. "I haven't decided what to do, but I can't avoid Booker indefinitely. I didn't meet him at the airport earlier this week when he flew in from St. Louis. We've hardly spoken on the phone, and I don't want him to worry. He's pitching tonight." She let the silence grow full before adding, "I told Booker you were in town."

"Why would that matter?"

"He knows we have a history of *not* getting along."

"We're starting to," Vale countered.

The urgency in her voice—the hope—stilled Blythe's hands. A dash of muted pleasure crossed her face.

"Which is exactly what I told him." She returned the tablecloths to the bag. "Booker doesn't mind if I stay longer."

Vale blinked. "You told him you wanted to spend time with me." A statement not a question, and she savored a moment's triumph.

Patching up their relationship mattered to Blythe too.

Still, the disclosure made her sister uneasy. Throwing her attention on a box, she began tossing out sheets of Bubble Wrap.

"Extending my stay is no great hardship on Booker. Our time together is limited during the season." Blythe frowned suddenly. "I hope you don't mind I used you as an excuse. Having you come into town . . . it gave me the perfect alibi."

The attempt to backpedal nearly dashed Vale's hopes. *Given our history, why would Blythe make it easy on me?* She needed to earn her sister's trust.

"I don't mind at all. Whatever works." Seizing the opportunity, she offered a winning smile. "Tell you what. Tomorrow I'll skip work at Green Iris. They have a bigger staff on Thursdays—I won't be missed. We'll tackle the attic together."

"It's a big job. You're sure you don't mind?"

"I'm happy to pitch in, just not now. I'm beat. Why don't we go out for a bite? There's a place on Pattison Avenue I've been meaning to visit."

A fiction, and she quickly added, "The best pizza in Philadelphia—I used to go there all the time before I moved to Pittsburgh."

"I have a weakness for pizza."

I know you do. "Then you're in for a treat." Blythe's love of pizza with a thick, chewy crust went back decades.

"Pattison Avenue . . . the restaurant is near the Sports Complex?"

Vale wiped her features clean of artifice. "I suppose. Does it matter?"

"Not really." Blythe rose and turned off the music. Brows furrowing, she slipped the LP back into its jacket. "I don't know, Vale. Why don't we get a pie delivered? I promised Booker I'd watch the game tonight."

"Let's watch from the restaurant. The walls are plastered with big-screen TVs. Besides, there's nothing better than a pizza right out of the oven."

"Who gets to pick the toppings?"

"You do."

"No anchovies. I know you like them, but the smell makes me sick."

Vale hated anchovies. During childhood she'd ordered them only to make Blythe squirm.

"No anchovies. I promise."

Within minutes, she'd prodded her sister out of the house and into the car. Rush-hour traffic into the city was heavy. Cars moved at glacial speed as they approached the South Philadelphia Sports Complex.

Blythe, however, was a trusting soul. They'd joined the stream of cars entering Citizens Bank Park before she realized she'd been duped.

"This is *not* a pizza shop." She threw an accusing glance. "Why weren't you straight with me?"

"Because you would've refused to come. You would've climbed into pj's and watched the Phillies play from Nana's couch. Or gone out drinking and watched alone. No offense, but you've done enough barhopping lately."

Blythe huffed out a breath. "That isn't the point. You shouldn't have lied."

"Oh come on. Don't you want to see the game live? Thanks to your talented husband, the Fightin' Phils are on a winning streak."

"I know their stats, Vale. They're having a great season." A grudging response, yet Blythe couldn't hide the excitement in her voice. "Where are we sitting?"

"Upper deck, along the first-base side." Sadly, this was nowhere near Section 121. According to Iris, who'd attended past games with Blythe, the team's family section offered prime views overlooking the batter's box. "If you're dodging the other baseball wives, I've got you covered. We'll enjoy the game from the wilderness—I couldn't afford better seats."

Blythe's eyes rounded. "How do you know I'm avoiding the other wives?"

Pulling into a parking spot, Vale chuckled. "Because I'm your sister. Whenever you're troubled, you hide." She pocketed the keys. "You aren't sure what to do about your marriage, and you aren't great at faking happiness."

Chapter 21

The stadium teemed with fans.

From their bird's-eye view in the upper deck, they cheered as the Phillies picked up an early lead on the Milwaukee Brewers. Booker was a marvel to watch, throwing fastballs that made the fans roar. Each time he strode to the pitcher's mound, Blythe's loving gaze clung to him.

The display of emotion was both touching and pitiful. Touching, because the affection Blythe made no effort to hide sent hope surging through Vale. Such deep and tangible affection held the promise of new beginnings. Surely it was easier to convince a woman still in love with her husband to save their marriage.

Yet the display of emotion was also pitiful. Why consider leaving a man you adored? Only a woman burdened with guilt would do so.

Finishing her hot dog, Vale cast her sister a quick glance. "What's he like in real life?"

"Booker? He's quiet, mostly. He loves camping and backpacking, although we don't get much chance. Only during the off-season. Booker is levelheaded. Focused. Like most pro athletes, he keeps a rigorous schedule. When to eat, sleep, exercise."

"Sounds like more self-control than the average mortal can handle."

"He enjoys every minute of it."

"What about the celebrity? Has it gone to his head?"

"Oh, Booker loves the fans. Being the center of attention and doing interviews . . . not so much. He does enjoy the charity work, knowing his fame benefits worthy causes. Especially the charities for childhood literacy and cancer research."

"Do you like his family?" Vale knew little about his private life.

"They're great—down-to-earth. For six generations, his family has farmed a large tract of land outside Des Moines. Booker calls his parents nearly every day. His brother too. Short phone calls, but he likes to stay in touch. They're all very close."

"How did you meet?"

Blythe placed her untouched hot dog on her lap. "Literally by accident, on Forbidden Drive. I'd just taken up jogging. Hauling my butt out of bed at dawn every day. Which is laudable, I suppose."

"*Every* day? Talk about going overboard. Aren't you supposed to ease into a new workout routine?"

Blythe shrugged. "When you need to peel off ten pounds, you want quick results. Except that by the end of the third week, I was hitting the trail on fumes. Half-asleep, totally in the zone. Totally *not* paying attention. I came around a bend too fast and ran smack into Booker."

Charmed by the tale, Vale laughed. "Talk about a memorable first meeting." With effort, she pulled her attention off her sister's forgotten hot dog. Her stomach rumbled in protest. "Then what happened?"

"After he scraped me up off the pavement?" Catching Vale's hungry appraisal, Blythe handed over the hot dog. "I was stumbling through an apology when Booker asked me out."

On the pitcher's mound, Booker went into his windup. He launched a curveball. The batter swung hard, missed. Striking out, he flung the bat aside. Vale and Blythe surged to their feet. They joined the crowd in raucous cheering.

They sat back down, and Blythe resumed the story. "When I ran headlong into Booker, I had no idea he was a Major League pitcher. He'd recently signed with the Phillies. He hadn't met anyone in Philadelphia who wasn't associated with the team. He'd been with the Cubs since the beginning of his career."

Vale bit into the hot dog. "How long did you date before he popped the question?"

"Five months. We married six months later."

"Talk about a whirlwind romance."

Nodding, Blythe clasped her hands. She looked away. "I'm sorry we didn't invite you to the wedding."

The apology was sudden and sincere. It warmed Vale more than she expected.

"Why would you?" She refused to let the past stand in the way, not when they were getting along so well. "Back then, we weren't even speaking. It's not like I expected an invitation." She neglected to add how much the snub *had* injured her.

"Booker was against the decision." Blythe shifted uneasily in her seat. "He believes nothing should come before family."

"He sounds like a great guy." Vale finished the hot dog.

"He is."

"You still love him. It's a fair guess he loves you too. Isn't that reason enough to stay together?"

The remark hovered between them for an uncomfortable moment. Then irritation crowded Blythe's features. A warning that the observation—no matter how well intended—crossed the line.

Foolishly, Vale plowed ahead. "All marriages go through hard times," she said, considering the reasons Blythe may have cheated on her husband. "Whatever has gone wrong, why not fix it? You still care about each other. Swallow your pride and work it out."

"Since when are you a marriage expert?" Blythe snapped the words out.

"Don't get testy. I don't mean to criticize you."

"Have you ever been in a serious relationship? I'm not talking about short-term dating—I'm sure you're a pro at shallow relationships, Vale.

You're gorgeous. Men will line up whenever you want them. I'm talking about serious commitment. Have you *ever* stuck with a man for any length of time?"

The accusations struck like well-aimed darts. Wounded, Vale struggled to reply. Working a barkeep's hours prohibited dating. The few men she did meet were disappointments. *Not Emmett, though.* But his affection would fade once she returned to Pittsburgh.

The deeper reason didn't bear contemplating. Yet it seized Vale's thoughts.

I'm not worthy.

Throughout childhood, the confirmation had arrived in soul-crushing ways. From her mother and Grant when they treated her like an inconvenience. From Bo, who rarely came around. A child who isn't cherished views all the relationships to follow with doubt. With the expectation of failure.

I'm not worthy of love. Men sense it, and it drives them away.

The belief made her bright with anger. "Stop making this about me," Vale snapped. "How many disappointments have you dealt with, Blythe? None that I can see. There are no roadblocks in your perfect life."

"My life isn't perfect."

"Yeah? Well, from where I'm sitting, it's close. Your father spoils you, and Mom does too. You've landed one of the best pitchers in MLB history and the guy is head over heels for you. And now you've done something you're ashamed of. Here's a tip, little sister—we all screw up sometimes. What matters is how you handle your life after it has gone off the rails."

"You'd know about screwing up. You've had loads of experience." Her sister's face settled into a dark sulk. "All the more reason *not* to dole out advice."

"Oh please. Blythe, you've been numbing yourself with booze. Hitting the bars alone, getting drunk—you're ashamed of something you've done to put your marriage at risk."

"Where do you get off, assuming you know what I've done?"

The false indignation nearly made Vale laugh. Were most unfaithful spouses this obvious? Claiming innocence instead of vowing to change? She wondered if cheating on Booker was the true source of Blythe's fury. Did the blemish on her well-executed life burn deeper?

Grappling for a reasonable tone, Vale said, "Ask Booker's forgiveness. If you can't find the courage to tell him what you've done, then keep your secrets. Work on forgiving yourself and move on. Just don't walk out on a man who's committed to spending his life with you."

Blythe's mouth tightened. She seemed ready to launch another barb. Eyes blurring, she looked away instead.

A frigid quiet surrounded them as they watched the next innings. The iconic fifty-two-foot replica of the Liberty Bell lit up and rang out three times as the Phillies scored one home run after another. When fans leaped up to cheer, the sisters remained in their seats. The seventh inning broke the team's momentum: with Booker out of play and a relief pitcher stepping in, the Brewers scored on back-to-back home runs.

By the top of the eighth inning, Blythe looked despondent. Sullen, unresponsive, she curved into her seat like a butterfly folding in on itself. Her impassive gaze roamed the stadium. Without the expectation of Booker pitching another inning, her interest waned.

Desperate, Vale searched for a way to remedy the situation. *Why didn't I keep my mouth shut?* She'd only managed to push Blythe to the verge of tears.

At the bottom of the eighth, Vale darted an apologetic glance toward her sister. "Should we go?" There seemed no reason to stay. "We'll catch the final score at Nana's."

"Sure."

Several other fans wended through the parking lot. Older couples mostly, getting a jump on the evening traffic. Blythe strode ahead. Giving her space, Vale followed.

They climbed into the car. The engine rumbled to life. Vale reached to shift the car into drive.

Blythe's hand shot out. It landed on the steering wheel. The gesture was quick, sure, colored with anger. Her eyes no longer glistened with tears.

Defiance lit her gaze. "Why do you hate me?"

"I don't hate you." Confused, Vale sensed an undercurrent—a grievance eating at Blythe that was in no way related to her marriage.

Blythe yanked the key from the ignition. "It started when you were fifteen." She pocketed the key. They weren't going anywhere until she decided. "Before then, I couldn't predict your behavior. Sometimes you treated me decently, sometimes you didn't. It was a hell of a way to grow up—never knowing when my big sister would pull out the rapier comments and slice right through my ego. Did you know I wet the bed?"

The question took Vale off guard. "What?"

"You heard me. I wet the bed until fifth grade, thanks to your erratic behavior. Even after I stopped, I worried the bedwetting would start again. I didn't go to my first slumber party until high school. *That's* how long I worried."

Shame and surprise collided inside Vale. She felt sick, unmoored. "Blythe, I didn't know."

"Of course you didn't. I wouldn't have the risked the taunts if you had found out. In retrospect, it's a miracle I didn't wake up in sheets soaked in urine when you were fifteen. When your behavior stopped fluctuating between good and bad. When it became utterly cruel." Blythe polished her tone to a brittle sheen. "So, I'm asking. What happened that year to make you hate me?"

Chapter 22

Self-loathing gripped Vale.

She locked her eyes on the windshield. *What have I done to Blythe?* Sorrow tore loose the unwelcome memory from high school. *Why did I treat her with contempt?* The memory she kept dammed up in the furthest reaches of her heart.

"I'm waiting," Blythe said. "Something happened to change you that year. In March, when you were fifteen. Right around the middle of the month. Afterward, you never said a decent word to me again."

The parking lot seemed to gyrate as a wave of vertigo caught Vale unawares. Dizzy, she lowered her forehead to the steering wheel. She wasn't prepared to remember the angry teenager she'd been. The tyrant who'd taken out her rage on her younger sister.

"You were an easy target," she said, desperate to end the conversation. "Someone I could push around who wouldn't push back. I shouldn't have lashed out at you."

A disturbing energy filled the car. Snapping and sparking. Gaining strength with her sister's determination to understand.

"Tell me the rest," Blythe demanded.

Against the steering wheel, Vale shut her eyes. A nauseating cluster of stars whirled across her vision. In her ears, her pulse beat unevenly.

"I can't, Blythe. It's too hard."

"What is?"

"Talking about it."

A concession, and Blythe's tone lost its edge. "I knew it. Something *did* happen to make you change. We aren't leaving until you explain."

The terrible hush lengthened. From inside the stadium, cheering resounded. It seemed misplaced, out of sync with the sadness pooling between them.

"Please, Vale." Blythe lowered a palm to her back. "I need to know."

Her fingers began moving in gentle circles, the comfort unexpected. Undeserved. Swallowing down her surprise, Vale lifted her head. The stars whirling before her began to recede. It was a relief when the vertigo passed.

The shame, however, didn't abate. Given the injury she'd inflicted on her sister, Vale expected to carry it for the rest of her life.

"Something *did* happen that year. Right before spring break." Her mind jolted back in time. To the thrust and parry of the heated conversation between her mother and stepfather. As if Audrey and Grant were materializing in the car's back seat, their argument still ongoing, as clear and vivid as on the day Vale overheard them. "It was late, after eleven o'clock. You were asleep in your room. Mom and Grant must've assumed I was in bed too. I went downstairs to grab something to eat. I nearly walked in on them, arguing in the kitchen."

"About you?" When she nodded, Blythe shrugged. "What else is new? They argued about you all the time."

"This time was different. I'd been in trouble at school again. Skipping classes, starting fights. You father was tired of it. I'd never heard Grant so angry. He wanted me shipped off to my father."

Audrey, we have our daughter to consider. Once Vale leaves, Blythe will finally have a normal upbringing. Let Bo finish raising Vale. We've done more than our share.

"My dad was blowing off steam," Blythe said, coming to Grant's defense. "He never would've let you go. You were already in high school, and Bo moved around too much to give you a decent homelife. My dad knew that."

Vale lowered her eyes. Blythe didn't cite love in her energetic defense. Because Grant didn't love Vale. Throughout the years he raised her, he treated her with cool civility. Nothing more.

She recalled her mother's response.

Don't you think I'd like to ship Vale off? I would, in a heartbeat. I'd pack her bags myself if I thought Bo could take care of her. He can't handle a teenage girl. What choice do I have but to keep Vale with us?

Something inside Vale threatened to crumble. "Grant's opinion of me didn't matter." Shoring up her resolve to get through this, she added, "What set me off—what changed how I treated you—was Mom's reaction. Oh, she pointed out fast that I couldn't live with Bo. Not because she cared. Not because she loved me and couldn't bear the thought of sending me away. Mom felt *obligated* to keep me."

"You're being unfair. You don't know how Mom felt."

A short, mirthless laugh escaped Vale. "She viewed me as a chore. If she'd thought Bo could deal with me, she would've handed over custody immediately."

"Does she know you overheard the argument?"

"I've never told her what I overheard. Why would I?"

Blythe seemed ready to pose another question. Then recognition broke across her face.

"Wait. I remember that week." She looked up suddenly. "A few days before spring break, your father came into town unexpectedly. Bo was living in Lexington at the time. Per his usual, he didn't call ahead—he just showed up at the door. Mom and my dad had just come home from work. I was in the living room, finishing my homework. You were in your room when the doorbell rang."

Startled, Vale searched her memories. Had Bo visited that week? She couldn't recall. Only the argument between her mother and Grant stood out in her mind.

"I don't remember seeing my dad."

"You did, and you were thrilled. Bo took you out for a burger. It was crazy. He drove all the way from Lexington, but only spent an hour with you. A typical move for your father—blow into town, then leave just as fast."

The scarring conversation she'd overheard must have blotted out the visit. "Are you sure, Blythe?"

"Why would I make it up? I hated your father, Vale. I hated the way he upended our lives. Whenever he came around, it caused so much pain for Mom. For my dad too."

Now it was Vale's turn to protest. "Why would his visits affect them? He never stayed long."

"He didn't have to. Bo was like a tornado—unpredictable, causing havoc. For weeks after one of his random appearances, Mom and my dad weren't themselves. Short-tempered, exhausted—like it took all their stamina just to get our lives back to normal. You never noticed. All you cared about was yourself."

Fleeting images wheeled through Vale. The house thrown into discord after one of Bo's visits. Lots of slamming doors and sour looks. Much of the friction arose from her but not all. Her mother and Grant barely kept a civil tone if she spoke to them. Blythe, often confused by the change in atmosphere, spent hours zoning out in front of the TV.

"You're right," Vale murmured. "I didn't notice."

Grimly, Blythe stared out the passenger-side window. "It doesn't matter now."

It did, and regret burdened Vale. What else had she overlooked from those difficult years? She was too worn down in the moment to puzzle it out.

"Blythe?"

"Hmm?"

"Give me the keys. I'll drive us home."

Without breaking her survey of the night, Blythe tossed them across the seat.

Chapter 23

On Thursday morning, heavy rain swept Philadelphia. The inclement weather kept shoppers away from Green Iris.

Despite the offer to help Blythe clean the attic, Vale chose to go to the shop. After last night's harsh words at the ball game, she knew Blythe didn't want her around. Soon after Iris left for the shop, Vale followed her out.

Without customers milling about, Vale kept busy with odd tasks. She felt dreadful about Blythe.

Her grandmother and Detta spent the morning in the stockroom. Not once did they venture out. Vale was grateful for the chance to nurse her thoughts in private.

To kill time, she washed down the display window and its elevated, tiled floor. She arranged new houseplants to put on show—a tall dracaena with gold-edged leaves; three smaller rubber trees with thick, purplish leaves; and a variety of hanging plants. She added colorful pots of double begonias to the display, as if the cheery flowers might brighten her mood.

Next, she swept both floors of the two-story shop. With the broom's every stroke, her thoughts flicked back to her sister. Would Blythe speak to her today? In a burst of frustrated energy, Vale fetched a ladder from behind the sales counter. Dragging it around the main floor, she watered all the hanging plants, whether they needed a good dousing or not.

The exertion didn't lift her mood. Keeping busy *did* make her feel marginally useful.

At noon, the sales floor was still empty. With no other tasks to occupy her time, Vale returned to the stockroom.

And scudded to a halt.

Twelve shiny metal tables, in three cramped rows, took up much of the storage room. Normally the tables were kept free of plants, their surfaces ready to sort and tag a new shipment of ceramic pots, gardening supplies, or houseplants before they were moved to the sales floor. They were also used to transplant the occasional fig tree or spider plant that had overgrown its pot.

Never had Vale seen all the tables crammed to bursting. Until now.

Rectangular flats of leafy vegetables covered each gleaming surface. Which didn't make sense. No deliveries were scheduled today.

Iris paced before the first row of tables. "Detta, is this your idea of making a killing?" She threw her palms skyward. "Why didn't you tell me about the delivery?"

"I wanted to surprise you. One of our suppliers was overstocked. I got the flats at cost."

"Have you lost your mind? We're supposed to make purchasing decisions together."

"You weren't here. You'd gone to . . . the hospital," Detta said slowly, as if speaking in code. She glanced at Vale hovering in the doorway before giving Iris a significant—and mysterious—look. "If you'd been around, I wouldn't have decided alone."

"Why didn't you call me? I was having tests, not surgery."

"I didn't want to be a bother."

Iris waved an irritated hand to encompass the rows of green. "*This* is a bother. If you can't grow a backbone, let me deal with our suppliers." Striding down the second row, she plucked at her violet-streaked hair. "We don't have space to put everything on the sales floor. Even if we did, when have we *ever* sold eighty flats of vegetables in a week? We can't leave half the merchandise back here."

"We'll make room. Let's rearrange the palms on the first floor. They're too spread out as it is."

"We display houseplants on the first floor. Customers expect to find vegetables upstairs." Iris flicked a dark-green leaf in one of the flats. "This is pumpkin, Detta. No one in Philadelphia grows pumpkin."

Detta straightened her beefy shoulders. "Someone might." Her patience was growing thin.

"On a balcony? Our clientele are city dwellers, not pioneers."

They were perilously close to shouting.

Vale stepped between them. "Stop arguing. I'll have Miranda and Teddy help me reorganize the second floor." The teenagers worked part-time and were due in this afternoon. "We'll fit in whatever we can. If the unsold flats end up in the garbage next week, so be it."

An observation that seemed of no importance as both Detta and Iris trained their eyes on her. Why were they staring? Vale checked if her bra straps were showing. They weren't.

"What's with you two?" She took a self-conscious swipe at her cheek.

Detta's brows climbed her forehead. "The mute speaks."

"I'm not mute. I've been . . . thinking."

"You've been a grumpy-pants since you came in this morning." Detta patted Vale's cheek with the delicacy of a mama bear taking her cub to task. "My first thought was 'menstrual cramps.' Young women are beastly when their monthly arrives. You know what I did after I clawed my way to menopause? Cleared my house of pads and tampons and then splurged on a two-pound chunk of Belgian chocolate. I binged on it for a week." Brightening, Detta rocked back on her heels. "How was last night? Did you and Blythe enjoy lots of sister-bonding at the game?"

Iris rolled her eyes. "Detta, are you stupid? She has 'disaster' written all over her face. It's plain her grand scheme didn't work out."

"Not even a little," Vale agreed.

Her grandmother frowned. "Well, that explains why Blythe is back in her cave. If she starts having pizza delivered to my guest bedroom, I'll have to draw the line. It's not healthy for a grown woman to spend all hours moping." To Detta, she added, "I woke up this morning to Marvin Gaye blasting through the house. I love Motown, but I'm not sure how much more I can take."

"I'm here for you." Detta moved in to hug Iris.

Swatting her away, Iris regarded Vale. "What *did* happen last night between you and Blythe?"

"We got into a sticky conversation about our childhood and my dad. It was upsetting. Strange too how our memories are so different. Like we grew up in different households." Swallowing down her nerves, Vale plowed forward. "When I was growing up, did Bo's visits bother Mom? Blythe insists they did. Which doesn't seem right. I mean, why would Mom care? She had Grant, a great life—she was pulling down six figures at Stern-Belkins. Grant was too, and they'd bought their dream home. She'd achieved everything my dad couldn't give her."

Iris and Detta exchanged a look.

Then, oddly, her grandmother walked to the end of the row of tables. A folding chair screeched in protest as she dragged it from the wall and sat down.

She looked winded. As if Vale's questions had forced her to run from memories she couldn't abide.

Detta took up the gauntlet. "Your sister wasn't exaggerating, Vale. Bo's visits *were* hard on your mother. The way he'd pop in unannounced . . . she didn't take it well. I'm not saying Bo caused her ulcer, but he didn't help. Whenever he showed up, your mother's behavior was nearly manic."

"Hold on. My mother had an ulcer?"

"She didn't get it under control until you and Blythe were grown up."

Vale wasn't used to feeling pity for Audrey. Yet the emotion nudged past her sense of grievance.

"What do you mean, 'her behavior was close to manic'?"

"It *was* manic," Iris put in. "After one of Bo's visits, Audrey pushed herself nonstop. Working late at Stern-Belkins, cleaning the house at odd hours. She got by with so little sleep, I worried she'd have an accident. I love my daughter, but I've never understood her. Not something I'm proud to admit, but there it is." Her face was pinched when her eyes found Vale's. "You're lucky you didn't inherit Audrey's drive. People who push themselves too hard often land in an early grave."

Vale wasn't sure she agreed. *With a little more ambition, I might stop drifting. Find my life's dream, and never let go.*

"What about Grant?" she asked. "Did Bo's visits affect his health too?"

Sadness deepened the lines framing Iris's mouth. "As much as your mother's. His blood pressure is now under control, but his cholesterol is still a problem. He takes statins. Unfortunately, they don't work as well as they should. Grant sees a cardiologist every six months." At the question rising on Vale's features, she added, "No, this isn't all Bo's fault. Grant should improve his diet, and your mother creates many of her own problems. However, they *are* three adults who've made choices that hurt each other."

"It shouldn't be that way."

"The human heart is complicated, Vale. Even when a marriage ends, strong emotions can remain. Your mother didn't stop loving Bo right away. Not enough to want him back—she's nothing if not realistic—but the feelings were still there."

"But she fell hard for Grant. Look how quickly they married."

"Yes, she loves Grant. They have a lot in common. They've built a good life together. Still, it took Audrey a long time to get over Bo. He's charming, witty, and too handsome for his own good."

There was no denying the assessment. Bo was like a sun god, drawing women into his orbit. He captivated them with his easy smile and boyish good looks. Still, it was startling to learn that Audrey wasn't immune to his charms. Even *after* the divorce.

Iris's phone chirped. Picking up, she retreated to the back of the stockroom.

Detta took the opportunity to reassure Vale. "The drama from the past is long over." She took Vale's hand and gently squeezed her fingers. "You're all grown up—those headaches with Bo's visitation don't matter now."

"I suppose lots of blended families deal with similar issues."

"They do, and they get through it. Put it out of mind. There's enough going on in your life, Vale. Don't waste time worrying about the past."

The fresh scent of parsley wafted from one of the flats. Absently Vale plucked off a sprig. Holding it to her nose, she sorted her thoughts. Nearly five years had passed since she'd seen her mother and Grant. The infrequent phone calls they traded never broached the difficult topic of her upbringing. Habit compelled her to defend her father. Now unexpected compassion for her mother and Grant surged inside Vale.

"How *are* Mom and Grant?" she asked. "Health-wise, I mean."

"They're in better shape than many couples in their fifties. Oh, they both put in too many hours at Stern-Belkins. But they *have* begun taking more vacations. The trip to Aruba isn't their only vacay this year. They're talking about a trip to Europe in the fall."

"I'm glad they're doing well."

"You can see for yourself when they get back. You *are* staying for a few more weeks, aren't you?"

Detta began to add something else. Her attention lifted past Vale's shoulder.

"Grant and Audrey are booking a flight home." Iris snapped her phone shut. "They're cutting their vacation short."

~

"Thanks for offering to make dinner at my place." Emmett draped his jacket over a kitchen chair. "Your text was the high point of my day."

Vale retrieved the chicken tenders she'd bought from the fridge. "I have an ulterior motive. There's a comedy on tonight I'd like to catch."

"We'll snuggle on the couch. I'll make popcorn."

"Sounds great. I need serious down time."

An understatement. Since learning that her mother and Grant were on their way back, she'd battled waves of anxiety. About seeing them for the first time in years. But mostly about how their return would affect Blythe. After the failed girls' night out, she seemed more fragile, barely acknowledging Iris when they got home from the shop and ignoring Vale altogether. They'd found her pacing in the living room, her eyes red-rimmed from crying.

A meaningful glance from her grandmother had telegraphed to Vale that her presence wasn't needed. She'd left before Iris disclosed that Grant and Audrey were arriving home soon.

How would her sister react to the news?

She became aware of Emmett hovering beside her. "You're a million miles away," he said. "Is everything all right?"

"Everything's great." Putting her sister out of mind, she reached for the cutting board. "Are you hungry?"

"You bet. I skipped lunch—Mullaney's was crazy busy. I swear, every senior in a ten-mile radius stopped by to pepper me with questions." He snatched a chunk of pineapple from a bowl near the stove. "You didn't have to go to all this trouble, Vale. We've both had a long day. We could've gone out."

"And fought over the check? I have a feeling you wouldn't have let me pay."

"Not on your life. 'Wining and dining' is my department. A man intent on wooing a beautiful woman doesn't let her foot the bill."

Wooing? The term was quaint, like *making whoopee*—the phrase Emmett had teased her about the night they met.

"It's my turn to do the wooing." Vale cut a zucchini into slices. "I can't afford to take you out to dinner. Not while I'm sponging paychecks off Detta and my grandmother. Do you like chicken stir-fry? It's the only dish I know how to make."

"I'm sure I'll love it." Steering the knife from her hold, Emmett set it on the cutting board and took her into his arms. He kissed her slowly and thoroughly, steeping her blood with longing. When he finished, he held her at arm's length. "This is a first."

Vale eased out of his hold. "Our first home-cooked meal?" Continue making out, and she'd never finish the meal's prep.

"Our first time alone. No waiters bustling around in the background, or Natty underfoot. I have you all to myself."

The remark was heartfelt, sincere, and in no way suggestive. Emmett wasn't in a hurry for intimacy. Vale knew instinctively he wouldn't risk his heart—or hers—unless their romance proved enduring.

She gave him a gentle push. "Go upstairs and change into something comfy."

"I'll be right back."

The moment he disappeared, Vale rechecked her supplies. She'd rushed through the grocery store so quickly, she worried she'd forgotten something. *Water chestnuts.* Muttering under her breath, she rummaged through the cupboards. Where was Emmett's pantry? Darting around the table, she checked the built-in cabinetry on the far wall.

Like its owner, the pantry was meticulously organized. Soup, containers of organic stock, a wide assortment of canned fruit—three cans of water chestnuts were stacked beside a glass container of rice. Which she'd also forgotten to purchase.

She was adding water to a pot when Emmett returned in a softly worn jersey and sweatpants. Another first: she'd never seen him in knock-around clothes, with his hair tousled. A new wave of longing swept through her.

He caught her lingering appraisal. "What can I do to help?" He looked pleased.

"Do you have a wok?"

"Ana borrowed it last winter."

Vale laughed. "Ask for it back!"

"I would, if Natty wasn't into Asian cuisine. I've been meaning to pick up a new one."

"Got something else I can use?"

"This should work." He found a large skillet and placed it on the stove. "How's Iris? Any word on her tests?"

"She'll finish the last batch tomorrow."

"Will she get the results next week?"

A tactful query, the subtext easy to detect. *When are you going back to Pittsburgh?*

The answer eluded Vale. She didn't want their relationship to end. She didn't like feeling boxed in either. The fire at the Crafty Cocktail was too fresh. Losing the bar had turned her life upside down. Why consider staying, on the chance their romance would deepen? She'd gambled on a business venture with Bo and lost.

Taking another risk didn't appeal.

"Hey."

Emmett's voice was a low murmur, drawing her from her thoughts. Vale realized she was standing frozen by the sink, the water running.

"Vale, I'm not pressuring you." He took the handful of snow peas from her grasp, tossed them on the counter. "I'm trying to understand your plans."

"They're still up in the air." More so now that Audrey and Grant were flying back from Aruba. "If Nana's tests reveal anything to worry about, I'll stay longer. I want to be here if she has to deal with a serious condition.

Obviously, I'm praying for good news. She seems well, if a little forgetful at times. Nothing out of the ordinary for a woman her age."

"Count on good news. It's a better option than worrying."

"Emmett, I am sorry. I know you'd like me to stay."

"It's okay." He cupped the side of her face. "I'm not going anywhere—unless you tell me to get lost. I'm hoping you won't."

His evenhanded approach quieted the nerves scuttling through her. Then she smiled. "I prefer having you around."

"Good. Because I think we have something special. If you're going back to Pittsburgh soon, we'll deal with it. Take turns with the commute."

"It's not hard. Five hours, give or take." She wound her arms around his waist. Despite her reservations about a long-distance romance, she hoped they'd beat the odds. "I'll look for a nine-to-five job, Monday to Friday. I'm totally done with graveyard shifts."

"Then we'll have weekends together. Most of the time, anyway. I have seniority at Mullaney's—I'll ask for more weekends off. I've put in more than my share because it didn't matter." He pressed his lips to her forehead. "Now it does."

"We'll make this work?" For an instant, Vale allowed herself to believe they would.

"There's one caveat." Emmett rested his chin on the crown of her head. The gesture was sweet, comforting. A surprisingly natural form of endearment for two people in the first stages of dating. "I won't leave the Philadelphia area. I've spent all but the first year of my career at Mullaney's. I like being the neighborhood pharmacist people rely on. If we get serious, I *will* lobby you to move back. I'll do everything in my power to persuade you."

She tightened her hold on his waist. "You have an intimidating side. Who knew?"

"Are you teasing me?"

"Fair play, Emmett. You enjoy teasing me. For the record, I'm not committed to Pittsburgh. I just don't . . ."

"Like the idea of living near your parents," he supplied.

"Right." She rubbed her nose against his neck, delighting when he shivered. "Can we hold off discussing this? You're jumping the gun."

"That's a matter of perspective," he replied, but she felt him relax. He pressed a kiss to her temple. "Vale?"

"Hmm?"

"There's something else on your mind. Something bothering you. Care to fill me in?"

It was unnerving, how well Emmett read her. "My mother and Grant are cutting short their vacation," she explained. "Grant had an accident. Nothing alarming—he fell off a Jet Ski and pulled a muscle in his back. Their flight arrives tomorrow night."

"You were hoping to avoid them, weren't you?"

A jolt of anxiety shot through her. *I'm sure Blythe was too. At least until she gets her marriage sorted out.*

"I'll have to visit on Saturday. Given how long it's been since I've seen Mom and Grant, I'm sure my grandmother will insist." Would Blythe accompany them? Vale hoped she'd bow out. As much as she dreaded seeing them, the visit would be harder on her sister. "On the plus side, Nana will run interference when they start criticizing me. She's an ace."

"Ignore the criticism and keep your cool, for Iris's sake." Emmett released her. "Why don't I take you out somewhere special tomorrow night? There's a new seafood restaurant in Center City."

A bribe, to take her mind off the visit. "Do you care if I wear the red silk again? It's my only nice dress."

Emmett grinned. "I was hoping you would."

Chapter 24

Every unhappy family is unhappy in its own way.

The famous line from *Anna Karenina* wound through Iris's thoughts, like a stray dog hounding her as she burned circles across the foyer carpet. *Her* family was unhappy in myriad and complicated ways. Out of guilt for past indiscretions. Or regret for hasty choices. In Blythe's case, her current slipups were the source of her unhappiness. Even Grant—the most levelheaded of the bunch—wasn't immune. Iris knew his blinding love for Audrey took a toll on his heart.

How would the family's distinctive misery play out this morning? Iris didn't have the strength to guess.

Tired of waiting, she punched out a text.

Both of U—stop stalling. Get your butts in gear.

The command brought Vale down the staircase, her long hair spinning away from her shoulders. All things considered, she looked remarkably serene. She'd paired a simple black skirt with a sweater of pale blue. Cockiness lurked in her eyes. The emotion had often shielded her during adolescence, when Audrey and Grant treated her with chilly reserve.

Good for you, pumpkin. If they were frosty this morning, she'd hold her own.

Vale smoothed down her sweater. "I'm not the one stalling. Blythe is still holed up in the bathroom. I'm just glad she didn't drag Marvin Gaye in there with her. I can respect the Motown greats, but if she doesn't play something from this century soon, I'm jumping out a window. Maybe I'll push Blythe out first."

Plainly Vale was polishing off the sass that had carried her through too many difficult years. Would she get the opportunity to aim some at her mother? *One can hope.*

Iris folded her arms. "Should we leave without Blythe?"

"Totally your call, Nana. I'm not in charge of this circus."

The notion didn't appeal. "I've already told Audrey we're coming together. Can you run back upstairs and check on your sister?"

"No! She's hardly spoken to me since the ball game. I'm not doing anything else to get on her bad side. Dragging Blythe downstairs is *your* problem."

"I don't know why she's stalling—we aren't staying long. I'm sure your mother and Grant are tired. Their flight didn't get in last night until close to midnight. We'll pop in, see how Grant is faring, and leave."

Vale landed a kiss on her cheek. "That's the nicest thing you've said all morning. I can only take Mom and Grant in small doses."

"As if that's a problem. You've been avoiding them for years."

"For good reason."

Iris resumed pacing, caught herself, stopped. It wouldn't do to allow her bad case of nerves to infect Vale. "You'll hardly recognize the house," she said, striving for a cheery tone. "Your mother hired an interior designer to overhaul the decor. Lots of chrome and black furnishings. The new look reminds me of a prison, but who cares about my opinion? Audrey and Grant are delighted with the results."

Iris realized she was babbling. Turning toward the stairs, she cupped her hands around her mouth. "Blythe! Should we leave without you?"

A door slammed. Blythe appeared on the landing with her chin lifted at a haughty angle. She swept down to the foyer.

"I'm driving, Nana." Moving past them, she strode outside. From over her shoulder, she added, "Let's not stay long. We'll see how my dad is and then leave."

Vale climbed into the Audi's back seat. "This is my kind of crowd."

Iris was still buckling herself in when Blythe threw the Audi into reverse. The car flew out of the driveway. Jaw clenched, she hazarded a glance at her granddaughter.

Blythe's normally calm persona was nowhere in evidence. She'd also layered on too much eye shadow and mascara. The bright-pink lipstick she wore nearly made her mouth glow. Silently Iris regretted pouring her a second cup of coffee this morning.

At the stop sign, the Audi came to a jerky halt. Then zoomed forward.

The movement whooshed air from Iris's lungs. "You're driving like a maniac! What's wrong with you?"

Blythe smirked. "Is that a rhetorical question, or just a dumb one?"

"Watch it, missy. I'm your grandmother. Show some respect. And slow down—I'd like to arrive in one piece."

Blythe's shoulders inched up toward her ears. "I'm sorry, Nana. I didn't mean to get snippy. I'm not in a great mood this morning." The Audi slowed to a reasonable speed. "If I don't tell you enough, I love you."

"I love you too, peaches."

From the back seat, Vale said, "Question. Why is Blythe 'peaches' and I'm 'pumpkin'? It feels like I got the short stick in the endearments category."

"*That's* a dumb question," Blythe said.

"How so?"

"Our personalities are nothing alike. A pumpkin has a tough exterior. A peach is tender and sweet."

"Whatever." Vale's cheery face appeared between them. "Here's another question, peaches. What do the 'rents know about your current problems? If I'm participating in a lie, I need details. And time to memorize the script."

"I haven't told them anything. Please don't fill them in."

"How dark are we flying here? Do they know you're staying at Nana's, at least?"

"They do," Iris put in. "When I called Audrey this morning, I told her Blythe planned to stay for several days. I made it sound like she'd just arrived—and that you had too, Vale. Your mother and Grant believe you drove in yesterday on a whim. I left it at that." Needing to embellish for Vale's sake, she added, "They're looking forward to seeing you."

Disappearing from between them, Vale slumped into the Audi's back seat. "You didn't tell them . . . the other thing, did you?"

She meant the fire at the Crafty Cocktail. "I did not," Iris assured her.

Speeding up, Blythe merged with the traffic on Roosevelt Boulevard. "What 'other thing'?"

Iris sighed. "It's a private matter. Vale will tell you when she's ready."

"Are you ready, pumpkin? I'm all ears."

"Forget it, Blythe. Some tragedies I'd rather keep to myself."

"How Greek of you."

"Oh, shut up."

"Girls, stop squabbling." Iris rolled the tension from her shoulders. A tricky move with the seat belt pinning her in. "We're going for a short visit, not an execution. Let's muddle through with dignity. Should we stop for ice cream later? We'll splurge on banana splits."

The lure of dairy had once smoothed over her granddaughters' squabbles, but the brick mansion looming ahead seemed to leak the air from the car. The silence became smothering as the car ascended the curving drive, rolling past the wide swatch of lawn and the dogwoods awash in pink blooms.

The desire to protect her granddaughters propelled Iris from the Audi the moment it came to a halt. When they followed her cue, she threw an encouraging glance. They were unaware of the slick perspiration gathering beneath her armpits.

The front door opened. Audrey waved.

Mouth thinning, Iris studied her daughter. The breeze fluttered a tendril of Audrey's brown coif. Diamonds glittered on her ears. She wore a taupe silk pantsuit that brought out the green in her eyes while artfully hiding the extra weight at her middle. A mishap in Aruba followed by a midnight arrival home couldn't puncture Audrey's composure. She looked supremely at ease as she motioned them inside.

"Daddy's resting," she announced, leading them into the living room.

On the couch, Grant lay prone with a heating pad beneath his back. Unlike his wife, who'd brought home an attractive tan, he was sunburned. Splotches of red covered his receding hairline and prominent nose.

Blythe came forward. The deep lines comprising Grant's face eased into delight.

"Are you in terrible pain, Daddy?" She knelt on the floor beside him.

"It comes and goes. The heating pad helps."

"What were you doing on a Jet Ski? You've never liked water sports. You don't even swim."

Smiling, Grant flicked his daughter's nose. "What's wrong with a little adventure?"

"You could've been seriously injured!"

"Blame your mother. The Jet Skis were her idea. All the sun and sand went to her head."

Audrey released a tittering laugh. "You only live once. Although I suppose we shouldn't have ordered martinis on the beach before we decided to try something new." She blew Grant a kiss. "I'm sorry, darling."

"No worries. It was a great trip."

Blythe glanced from one to the other. "Should we call a doctor?"

"It's just a pulled muscle." Gingerly, Grant lifted himself into a sitting position. "Hello, Iris." His guarded eyes found Vale. "How are you, Vale? It's been a long time."

"I'm great. I'm sorry about your back."

"It's nothing a day's rest won't cure."

Audrey seemed unwilling to acknowledge Vale. To no one in particular, she said, "We're alternating heat and cold therapy, and I promised to give him a massage later. He'll be fine."

Grant winked at her. "I'm holding you to that massage. I'm looking forward to it."

"I know you are, darling."

At last, she regarded Vale. Her expression remained distant. As if Vale were merely a casual acquaintance who'd inconveniently dropped by.

"You look good, Vale."

"You do too."

"How long are you in Philadelphia?" Despite the standoffish pose, hope flickered in Audrey's voice.

Frustration surged through Iris. *Tell Vale how much you've missed her.* Affection held the power to heal the deepest wounds. Audrey had inflicted more than her share of injury, a loathsome tally. This fleeting moment offered her the chance to begin making amends.

But pride took precedence over her heart. Iris doubted she knew she was angry with herself, not Vale.

"I haven't decided," Vale said. "My plans are still loose."

"You're only here for the weekend?"

"I don't know."

"When *will* you decide?"

Blythe, still seated on the floor beside her father, released a nervous laugh. "Stop bugging her, Mom. She's already told you—her plans are up in the air."

The remark lifted eyebrows across the room. Iris pulled in a breath. When did Blythe ever defend her sister? That she'd done so now made Iris giddy. If Blythe had sprouted wings and flown around the room, her parents wouldn't have looked more surprised.

Swiftly Audrey regained her composure. With aplomb, she steered the conversation to safer ground.

"I nearly forgot to tell you, Blythe—the day after we landed in Aruba, I found the most precious store in Oranjestad. I left Daddy lounging at the resort and shopped for hours." Approaching the couch, she helped Blythe to her feet. "I spent too much, but I couldn't resist."

"When *don't* you spend too much?" Blythe shook her head with bemusement. "No wonder I'm a shopping addict. I get the trait from you."

"I wish you'd been with me. We would've had so much fun!"

Grant chuckled. "She went nuts."

"On what? New cocktail dresses?"

"Not even close."

"Jewelry?"

Audrey gave her head a joyful shake. "Guess again."

Watching the interplay, Iris clenched her teeth. As usual, the snappy conversation between the threesome left Vale out.

Blythe gave her father a mischievous glance. "Is there a Saks Fifth Avenue in Aruba? Mom can never resist."

In her exuberance, Audrey burst out laughing. "No, I bought baby clothes! The store is called Peek-A-Boo. Isn't that the most adorable name?"

With dismay, Iris glanced at her granddaughter. Blythe looked stricken with grief.

"I'm sure Booker is pining for a boy—a future Major League pitcher, just like his daddy. Who can blame him? Is it wrong to admit I'm wishing for a girl? I suppose it doesn't matter. I shopped for both sexes."

Grant said, "Don't let her fool you, sweetheart. She's hoping you'll have two kids in a row, a boy and a girl."

"Blythe, would you like to see the outfits now? Or should we wait, until the four of us are together?"

Too excited to await a reply, Audrey launched into a description of the baby clothes she'd purchased, the onesies and rompers and sweet newborn gowns.

Iris watched as her granddaughter seemed to sink into the floor. Blythe wasn't thinking about having a baby—she was considering divorce. A heartbreaking turn of events her parents knew nothing about. *Get her out of here.*

But Iris was helpless to intervene. The tension sweeping the room forbade it. Leave too quickly, and Audrey would take offense. They'd fall into an argument with the others looking on.

Then the unexpected happened. Vale stepped forward. "Mom, that's enough. We get it. You bought the place out."

A mild rebuke, and all eyes turned to Vale. Relief spilled across Blythe's face. Grant wore a look of thunder.

A protest formed on Audrey's lips.

Vale jumped in again. "Since we're sharing news, here's mine. The Crafty Cocktail burned down." She flashed a cocky grin. "The place is toast. Don't worry about sending flowers. There's not enough of the building left for a proper burial."

The news struck Audrey like a blast of wind. She stared, plainly dazed.

Grant palmed his brow. "Let me guess. Bo torched the place to bilk the insurance company. Where's he now? Living a life of luxury in Tahiti?"

"My dad's not that lucky. We didn't have insurance."

"Who opens a bar without insurance?"

"Not me—I saw the policy in black and white when we bought the place. I wouldn't be standing in a shitstorm without an umbrella if Bo hadn't stopped paying the premiums. Basically, I'm screwed."

The foul language brought Audrey from her stupor. She could comfortably treat Vale like an unwanted guest, but she couldn't abide anyone spewing expletives in her well-appointed home. Which, Iris knew, Vale had used on purpose. As good a ploy as any to pull the spotlight off Blythe.

"What did we tell you, Vale?" Audrey's voice rose in pitch. "Going into business with Bo was sure to end in disaster. Did you listen to us? I suppose you're now penniless. Enjoy your poverty. Just don't expect a handout from us . . ."

On normal days, Iris didn't hold much stock in miracles. Life doled out good moments and bad; the trick was to persevere. Yet as Audrey ranted, Iris became aware of the marvel raining down upon the room, the likes of which she'd never witnessed before. A circumstance no less miraculous than if angels had burst through the windows and rendered Audrey mute.

As she railed, Vale and Blythe shared a secret smile.

The affection traveling between them—strong, bright, irrepressible—gave Iris such a lift, she nearly floated out of her sensible shoes.

Blythe put a hand on her mother's arm, silencing her. "Vale, I'm sorry you've lost the Crafty Cocktail. Is there anything I can do to help?"

"Find me a new job?" A jest, and Vale shrugged. "I'll need to polish my résumé when I get home."

"I don't have connections in Pittsburgh. I wish I did."

"It's all right. I'll manage."

Blythe cocked her head. "What caused the fire?"

"We're not sure. The Bureau of Fire hasn't issued a report yet."

"I guess it doesn't matter, if you don't have insurance."

"My dad has already found another job. I'll start looking soon."

The conversation halted as quickly as it had begun. A minor point: the anxiety seeped from Iris's bones. Who needed angels? The camaraderie flowing between her granddaughters was miracle enough.

Taking over, she said, "Grant, take it easy this weekend. You need the rest. Audrey, keep an eye on him. Let me know if you need anything. I'm happy to run to the grocery store."

Audrey took the dismissal with grace. "I will."

To Blythe, Iris said, "Should we go for ice cream? We'll buy your sister a banana split, to mourn the passing of the Crafty Cocktail."

Another rescue, and Blythe swiftly crossed the room.

Chapter 25

They ordered banana splits near Race Street Pier. Finding a bench, they watched boats glide down the river.

Vale kicked off her pumps. "Let's not do that again anytime soon." Wiggling her toes, she tried to relax. "I can't take Mom when she's on a tear. Once she gets going, she's like a steamroller in overdrive. I'm good for another five years."

Iris, seated between them, threw her a puzzled look. "Why are you complaining? You shocked your mother into silence with the announcement about the Crafty Cocktail. You were magnificent."

"You were," Blythe agreed. "Thanks for running interference. I didn't know what to say when Mom started describing the baby clothes."

"I was happy to help."

"It's terrible how you've lost the bar."

"Well, I won't miss the late nights. Wherever I land next, I want nine-to-five hours."

The fleeting smile on Blythe's lips vanished. "You're not the only one who needs to polish her résumé. I do too."

The remark put concern on their grandmother's features. Sighing, she closed her eyes. Plainly she assumed a job hunt meant Blythe was leaning toward divorce. Which wasn't necessarily true.

"What did you do, before you married Booker?" Vale asked her.

"Not much to brag about." Rising, Blythe tossed her ice cream in a trash can. She sat back down. "I worked for less than a year in HR at a law firm. I quit before we married. Between travel for games and living in Florida during the training season, it wasn't possible to keep the job."

"Maybe you need a career to keep you occupied during the season. Something to call your own."

At the suggestion, their grandmother's eyes flew open. She cast Vale a look of pure gratitude.

"Why don't you and Vale take over Green Iris?" she asked Blythe. "You can put together a schedule that works for both of you. I'd love to retire. Detta might decide to stay on, but she's not cut out to run a business singlehandedly. She'll become your employee."

Vale and Blythe exchanged a glance.

Then Blythe frowned. "Nana, we can't take your shop. What would you do all day?"

"I'll learn to knit."

"You aren't into crafts," Blythe protested. "Horticulture is totally your thing."

"I'll expand my horizons. Head to France and look for romance."

"I'm serious, Nana—you can't retire! What do you always tell us? Working with plants keeps you forever young."

They were still debating the topic as the threesome drove back to the house. In the back seat, Vale silently toyed with the idea. Nana wouldn't have to retire—they'd keep her on part-time with Detta. Let them both work whenever they pleased.

Granted, Blythe didn't have a green thumb. To Vale's knowledge, she'd never shown much interest in plants. When they were children, she'd rarely volunteered to go into the shop. By contrast, Vale had never skipped an opportunity to work beside her grandmother amid the greenery.

Who cares if Blythe is a novice? I'll teach her. When she's out of town during the Phillies' training season, I'll bring in extra help. An easy solution.

When they entered the house, second thoughts accosted Vale. After losing the Crafty Cocktail, she was done making snap decisions. Wherever she landed next, she'd get there after thorough, considered thought. Eventually she might move back to Philadelphia—if her relationship with Emmett deepened—but only a fool allowed a new romance to influence a career decision.

Plus, she didn't have the capital to invest in a business.

"Hello? Anyone in there?"

The impatient remark jolted Vale from her reverie. She discovered Blythe waving her hands in front of her face.

"There's no way I'm dragging everything downstairs alone." Blythe tugged her toward the stairs. "Help me carry down the stuff."

"What stuff?"

"I finished sorting the attic. I'm dropping off the donations to Goodwill."

"Should I go with you?"

"There won't be room in the car."

Blythe wasn't exaggerating. By the time they carried everything down, they'd filled the Audi to bursting.

Vale crammed a last bag into the trunk. "What about the toys for Natty? Did you already give them to her?"

Retrieving the keys from her pocket, Blythe opened the driver-side door. "I'm still packing the toys up. I'll finish in the morning." She hesitated. "Why don't we give them to her tomorrow? We'll go over together."

A sweet gesture, totally unexpected. "I'd like that."

Vale waved as her sister pulled out of the drive. She felt suddenly lighter. They *were* mending the breach in their relationship. In fits and starts, but they were heading in the right direction.

On the front porch, her grandmother waited with two cups of green tea. Accepting a cup, Vale sank into a wicker chair.

"It warms my heart to see you and your sister getting along."

"I hope it lasts."

"Give it time."

Time. A commodity in short supply. Vale wanted to get her life back on track. She couldn't hang around her grandmother's house indefinitely. *I need to get my act together.* She'd start by finding a job with good benefits and a chance for advancement.

I also need to help Blythe. Affection—and worry—tangled inside her.

Iris took a sip of her tea. "Blythe assumed I was joking. I wasn't." She eyed Vale appraisingly. "You liked the idea of taking over the plant shop together. You're a natural fit, pumpkin. And you *do* have management experience." When Vale heaved out a sigh, she added, "There's your sister to consider. Owning Green Iris with you will give Blythe her own source of pride when the demands of Booker's career make it impossible for her to see much of him."

"If the idea made sense, I'd love to own the shop with Blythe." Unexpected laughter burst from Vale's throat. "I love the idea of *having* a sister. Blythe and I have been at odds for years. Putting all the bad blood behind us . . . it means the world to me. It doesn't mean your grand plan is realistic."

"Sure, it is. Why don't I run this by Detta? For the record, she owns thirty percent of Green Iris. I'll buy out her share. You and Blythe can pay me back over time."

"Nana, stop! We agreed to work together to keep Blythe in her marriage, that's all. In case you didn't notice, she wasn't on board with the idea of taking over the shop. And we both know you aren't ready to retire."

"Fine. I'll drop the subject for now." Iris paused for effect. "On one condition."

"Which is . . . ?"

"You won't leave until Blythe does. I've waited a long time to have both my granddaughters under my roof. I'm not ready to let it end."

Lifting her cup of tea, Vale blew across the top. *Finally, an easy decision.* Blythe couldn't delay making up her mind forever. With the 'rents back in town, Audrey would eventually ferret out the truth. *And staying longer gives me extra time with Emmett.* A win-win, all around.

"Deal. I'll stay."

"Good. Because there's something I must tell you."

"What?"

Looking away, Iris withdrew a hankie from her pocket. The bright square of linen danced across her brow, swabbing away the subtle gleam of perspiration. Why was she nervous? The hairs on the back of Vale's neck lifted to attention.

"Pumpkin, it's about the tests."

"You got the results? That was fast—it's only Saturday." Fear sprinted down Vale's back. "Please don't tell me it's bad news."

"It's not."

"You got the all-clear?" Relief flooded her.

The emotion morphed into confusion when her grandmother gave her a look of contrition. As if regretting something recent. Nana could be impetuous, a trickster, sneaky—there was no telling what she'd done. *And I wonder where I inherited the traits.*

Iris pulled in a breath. "There weren't any tests." On the exhale, she cast a nervous glance at Vale. "I made it all up."

The comment floated between them. Blinking rapidly, Vale tried to process the news.

"No way," she blurted.

"Oh yes." Mischief replaced the contrition on Iris's features. "If you'd begun to catch on, I'd planned to fake a heart flutter. I would've done anything to keep you in town."

"Nana!"

The shout reached a boy walking by on the sidewalk. He flinched. Picking up his feet, he ran off.

Embarrassed, Iris shushed her. "Don't be angry. It was one of those moments of inspired action. The ends justifying the means, with a little fun added to the mix. I *have* been enjoying myself." She reconsidered. "Except on the days when my granddaughters were at each other's throats."

Vale stared at her, aghast. "You *lied* to me?"

"I did."

"All the days you were supposed to be at the hospital . . . Where were you?"

"Out and about. Visiting with friends, getting a massage. I even booked a facial—my first since Blythe's wedding." Leaning close, Iris batted her lashes theatrically. "Do my pores look clean? The girl spent so much time working on my nose, I nearly fell asleep."

Despite her irritation, Vale grinned. "Your pores look great." She sighed. "Nana, do you have any idea how much I've been worrying? I thought your doctor was checking for Alzheimer's or the big C. *Why* would you lie?"

"It was for your own good! How else could I get you to visit? Blythe called and asked to stay, then Bo told me the Crafty Cocktail was gone—it felt like synchronicity. One of those rare moments when everything falls into place. I couldn't pass up the chance to bring you and your sister back together."

A plan, Vale mused, *that wasn't entirely misguided. Would I have embarked on friendship with Blythe otherwise?*

No.

They would've spent the rest of their lives avoiding each other.

Chapter 26

Early on Sunday, Vale accompanied Iris to church. They returned to find Blythe up and about, thumping around the attic.

Vale glanced toward the stairs. "I'll give her a hand. We're taking the toys over to Natty this morning. Want to tag along? It'll be fun watching her dig through the stuff. I'm totally looking forward to it."

"Do you mind if I skip the festivities?" Iris slipped off her pumps. "I should finish my grocery list. I'd like to run to the store."

Vale started up the stairs. "We'll fill you in on Natty's reaction when we get back."

Sunlight slanted through the attic windows. With so many of Iris's unneeded belongings carted off to Goodwill, the room appeared surprisingly large. Spotting her sister, Vale paused inside the doorway. In the center of the attic, Blythe sat hunched forward on a folding chair, amid boxes and bags, staring absently into space. An unmistakable air of sadness surrounded her.

In her hands, she cradled an American Girl doll. Vale recalled the Christmas when Blythe had received it, in second or third grade. For years the cherished toy held a position of prominence on her bed.

"You don't have to give it to Natty," Vale teased, needing to break through her sister's gloom. "There's no shame in keeping one childhood toy."

The joke went unheard. Apparently, this was another low day. Hopefully the visit next door would take Blythe's mind off her troubles.

Vale softened her voice. "Blythe? You're awfully deep in thought."

"Sorry." The fog cleared from her sister's gaze.

"What are you thinking about?"

"You, actually."

"Really? Why?"

Blythe's attention swept the room. She looked tired, defeated. Yet something new shifted across her features, a more positive emotion.

"Vale, you were right. About a lot of things."

The remark seemed an invitation, and Vale slowly approached. "Like what?"

"If two people love each other, they should fight to stay together." Blythe ran her palm across the doll's curly hair. "Seeing Mom and my dad together yesterday . . . it reminded me how much people must commit to keep a marriage going. Through thick or thin, good years and bad." She cast a sudden, apologetic glance toward her sister. "I don't mean to trash on your dad. You're close to Bo, and I respect that. But he didn't make it easy for Mom or my dad. Though I'm sure they would've had enough problems without the extra drama."

Unease settled in the pit of Vale's stomach. Warding off the instinct to defend Bo, she came a step closer. "I'm glad you're willing to fight for your marriage. Nothing else really matters."

"I just don't know how to tell Booker I'm not the woman he thought he married. How do I explain that I've let him down?"

Blythe cut off abruptly, her throat working. Placing the doll in the box at her feet, she appeared determined not to cry. She needed to talk.

Dragging a folding chair near, Vale joined her. "No one stays the same, Blythe. Time changes all of us. I'm sure Booker understands that. He'll change too."

"I'm scared."

She gently rubbed her sister's back. "Of what?"

"So many things. Of disappointing him. Of dealing with how much our expectations will need to change. But that isn't all of it. I know Booker loves me. Even after I lay everything out, he'll insist he wants to stay in our marriage."

"That's good, right?"

"He's not the sort of man who walks away." A sob broke from Blythe's throat. Fending off the tears, she took a moment to compose herself before adding, "I'm frightened about what happens later. Not tomorrow or next year—what if Booker decides someday that staying with me forced him to give up too much? I'll never forgive myself for keeping him from having everything he deserves."

Vale drew her close. She rocked her slowly, aware that something didn't add up. If Blythe had strayed, why assume Booker would have second thoughts years after the fact? He wouldn't. They'd heal their marriage and move on.

The opportunity to prod further vanished. Iris shouted up to them, "Girls! I'm leaving for the grocery store. If you're curious, there's a little girl next door racing around her front yard like a frenzied terrier. Don't keep Natty waiting too long."

Rising, Blythe gave her shoulders a shake. She wiped the distress from her face.

Vale hurried to the doorway. Iris stood at the bottom of the attic staircase tucking the grocery list into her purse.

"Tell Natty we're on our way."

It took several trips to deliver the toys next door. In a rare occurrence, Ana was home for the day. Together, the three women ferried the boxes and bags into the backyard to give Natty space to spread everything out. Board games and jump ropes and the magician's outfit Blythe had loved in first grade. Vale's neon-green bicycle and two sets of roller skates. Other boxes held soccer balls, baseballs, and bats.

"You guys are the best!"

Natty flung her arms around Vale's waist. Then she sprinted to Blythe to do the same. The affection did its bit to raise Blythe's spirits. She looked thrilled by the child's reaction.

When it seemed she couldn't find her voice, Vale said, "We're glad the toys have a new home. Enjoy them."

A small trampoline snagged Natty's attention. She dragged it onto the grass.

"This is great!" Her eyeglasses joggled as she jumped up and down.

Ana winced. "Don't jump too high."

"I know what I'm doing!"

"I'm sure you do, but this is your first time on a trampoline. Take it easy."

"Aw, Mom. Don't bug me." Leaping higher, Natty chortled.

"Kids. They never listen." Ana turned to Vale and Blythe. "I can't thank you enough. This was incredibly kind."

"Thank Vale." Blythe offered a smile. "This was her idea."

"Not true. We came up with the idea together," Vale said, pleased by her sister's impulse to award her the credit.

"Well, thank you both. You've made my daughter very happy." Ana noticed an unopened box on the picnic table. She glanced at her daughter. "Natty, you missed something."

"I did?" Hopping off the trampoline, the child bounded forward. She rubbed her hands together as her mother wedged off the box's lid. "What's inside?"

"Oh, sweetie. Look at this."

With a sigh, Ana withdrew the American Girl doll. It was in remarkably pristine condition. Like its previous owner—and its new one—the doll sported a tumble of curly brown hair.

"She looks just like me!" Natty sifted through the doll clothes stacked inside the box. "Does she have purple eyeglasses like mine?"

Blythe frowned. "Sorry, she doesn't. We'll buy a pair online. I can't guarantee we'll find purple eyeglasses. There *are* lots of colors to choose from, though."

"That's okay. I shouldn't be greedy. She doesn't need glasses."

"Don't be silly. She'll look just like you once we find her a great pair of specs." Thumbing through her phone, Blythe nodded with satisfaction. "Here you go. There are tons of eyeglasses to choose from on eBay. Pick your favorite—my treat."

"The pink glittery ones are cool."

"They're yours."

Vale gave Ana a knowing glance. "Can you tell the doll was Blythe's? She took great care of her toys."

"And you didn't?"

"Not usually. In fact, most of the stuff we brought over belonged to you-know-who."

Overhearing, Blythe looked up from her phone. "It's not a contest." She motioned to the bicycle, propped against a tree. "You took great care of your bike. I would've been afraid to give Natty mine. I crashed it so many times, the wheels were ready to fall off. Hopefully someone at Goodwill will give it the once-over before they put it on the sales floor."

With curiosity, Ana regarded them both. "Why were so many of your toys stored at your grandmother's house?"

"Call it a rescue operation." Wincing, Vale recalled how often she'd been forced to hide toys from Audrey growing up. "Our mother can't tolerate disorder of any kind, and Nana's a pack rat. How they sprang from the same gene pool, I'll never understand. Whenever Mom went on one of her cleaning sprees, Nana let us haul our favorite toys to her place. The safer option than risking Mom tossing something out while she deep cleaned. She could go overboard, and I mean fast."

Natty placed the doll on the picnic table. "I'm glad you're not a crazy cleaner," she informed her mother. "I'd rather live in our dirty house and keep my toys safe."

Ana took the semi-insult in stride, and a smile crooked the side of her mouth. "Don't mention it, sweetie."

Natty returned to the boxes. "How do you play?" She held up a soccer ball. "I don't know the rules."

"I'll show you the basics," Blythe offered.

"I'll help." Ana ruffled her daughter's hair. "I loved soccer when I was young."

They were kicking the soccer ball around the yard when Emmett stopped by, on his way to run errands. He'd conveniently texted Vale his agenda. Lately, he texted every morning. She'd begun looking forward to beginning each day with his sweet messages.

He took a gander at the toys spread across the picnic table and the grass beyond. "What is this—Christmas in May? There's enough stuff here to keep Natty occupied indefinitely."

Vale gave him an odd look. "You mean Christmas in April. Today's the thirtieth."

"No, it's not. It's Sunday, May second."

"Are you sure?" Withdrawing her phone, she scanned the display. "You're right."

Steering her into his arms, he stole a kiss. "Are you losing track of time?"

"It's been a busy couple of weeks. Take me out of my normal routine and I'm lost." She made a mental note to call her landlord in Pittsburgh. Better still, she'd call her father. Bo would drop off the late rent on Monday.

Problem solved.

The soccer ball flew past, hitting the fence between her grandmother's property and Ana's. Natty grabbed it and prepared to throw.

Remembering the rules, she dropped the ball to the ground. With a mighty kick, she sent it whipping past Blythe and Ana.

Vale glanced at Emmett. "Would you like company tonight?" she asked. "Nana's making dinner for me and Blythe, but I'm free afterward."

Emmett took her hand in his. "I'd love for you to come over. Unfortunately, there's a thing tonight." He looked genuinely disappointed.

"What sort of thing?"

"We're celebrating my nephew's birthday at my parents' house. One of those big family gatherings with too many cupcakes and nearly as many presents as you've given Natty today. I thought about inviting you, then ditched the idea."

Emmett's voice drifted into an awkward silence. He knew she wasn't ready to meet his family. He wasn't enthusiastic about her wait-and-see attitude, but he respected it. Soon they'd begin dating long-distance. Vale refused to fall hard for him until they were sure the commute didn't pose a problem.

A reasonable concern. Yet she felt . . . deflated. It occurred to her that she *would* like to meet his family. That her growing attraction to Emmett might trump her natural wariness.

Reading her face, he rocked back on his heels. "Did I err on the side of caution? Do you want to go?"

"No! I'll meet your family some other time."

"Vale, it's not an imposition. My parents will make an insane amount of food, and you'll get a kick out of watching a four-year-old tear through his presents. Everyone is dying to meet you."

They are? A case of the jitters invaded her belly. *When did Emmett discuss me with his family?*

"No, I'm good," she said, beating a hasty retreat. "It's too soon." This seemed harsh, and she quickly added, "Are you free tomorrow night? If you aren't tired of stir-fry, I'll make dinner again."

"I work until seven o'clock. Can you come over then? Don't worry about cooking. I'm never allowed to leave a family party without leftovers."

"Sounds perfect."

Emmett stole another kiss. "I'll see you tomorrow."

"Have fun tonight."

"I will."

He left, and Vale perched atop the picnic table. The impromptu soccer match was winding down. She hooted as Natty kicked the ball past Blythe. Panting, Blythe sank against a tree. Ana looked equally spent, her cheeks red from exertion. When it became clear they'd given up, Natty scooped up the ball and ran a victory lap.

What she did next stalled Vale's heart.

Racing forward, Natty dived into a cartwheel. When her hands met the grass, Vale's palms burned as if she were performing the gymnastic feat. Natty's legs spun high into the air, and a memory from childhood caught Vale unawares.

The memory of a bright autumn day reeled through her mind like a series of snapshots.

Bo, appearing for one of his unexpected visits. Vale, darting past Audrey to wrap her slender arms around him. Grant in his weekend khakis, his expression thunderous, zipping Blythe into a puffy jacket and hoisting her into his arms.

When the door banged shut behind them, Vale made a beeline for the backyard. Certain her parents were following, she bolted outside.

She'd been younger than Natty that day, propelling herself into a cartwheel as perfectly executed. No older than six or seven, her pulse beating in her ears as she whirled through the air, showing off for Audrey and Bo. The morning chill bit her nose as she landed back on her feet, drawing their applause—drawing their attention for one, rare moment before they turned back to each other.

The image froze in Vale's thoughts, jolting her. The intimacy of Bo's fingers resting on Audrey's neck. The longing in their gazes as they leaned close. How they'd quickly drawn apart when she ran toward them.

The human mind is a selective instrument. Much of our childhood goes unrecorded. Our memories are fragile and diffuse during our formative years.

Yet as Vale returned to her grandmother's house, other fragments rose to the surface. Moments from other days previously hidden in the recesses of her mind. A passionate glance shared between her parents. Audrey's hand lingering on Bo's arm. His voice turning husky when he bent toward her ear.

Confused and sick-hearted, Vale threw clothing into the washing machine. Her mind working overtime, she vacuumed Iris's living room. Stitching the memories into chronological order proved impossible. They were fragmented. The only certainty: whenever she'd glimpsed fleeting moments of intimacy between her parents, Grant wasn't nearby. His absence led Vale to a conclusion she dreaded facing.

Pulling clothes from the dryer, she recalled Blythe's admission at the Phillies–Brewers game.

I hated your father, Vale. I hated the way he upended our lives. Whenever he came around, it caused so much pain for Mom. For my dad too.

Clearly Blythe had sensed just how much Bo upended their lives. Did he carry on with Audrey for years? Were his unannounced visits more about picking up with her than seeing his child? The possibility didn't render Audrey blameless. Why put her marriage at risk by sleeping with her ex-husband?

Dumping clean laundry on her bed, Vale stiffened beneath a sense of betrayal. The past was quicksand; it was impossible to regain her balance. If an affair went on for years between her parents, had her stepfather known? What had it cost Grant to overlook the behavior of his unfaithful wife?

Vale grimaced. What had it cost *her*—and Blythe? They'd spent their formative years with a silent rot festering beneath the veneer of a normal homelife. Vale wondered suddenly if her grandmother assumed Blythe was running around on Booker because she'd witnessed similar behavior in the past. Between Audrey and Bo.

Did I grow up in a family built on lies?

There was only one way to get to the bottom of this. Only one way to know for sure. *I have to go back to Pittsburgh.* She needed to confront Bo. Force him to have a conversation she knew would be devastating.

Trembling, Vale came to a decision. She grabbed an overnight bag and tossed clothes and toiletries inside.

In the kitchen, Iris was chopping fresh sprigs of rosemary. The sharp scent blended with the savory aroma of pot roast wafting from the oven. Hovering in the doorway, Vale worked to calm her nerves. There was no reason to worry her grandmother. Or provoke questions about a sudden trip she wasn't prepared to answer.

Noticing her, Iris lifted the knife from the cutting board. "Is your sister back?"

"She's not here?" In her daze, Vale wasn't aware of Blythe's absence.

"She went to the dry cleaner's to pick up some outfits. I hope it doesn't mean she's back to prowling the bars. There's a limit to how much bad behavior I'll tolerate under my roof."

"Hang on to your patience for a while longer. Blythe has good days and bad. Her roller coaster emotions won't end soon."

"Unless she patches things up with Booker. I can't tell from one day to the next if she's any closer to making a decision."

"She'll get there, Nana. I have the impression she's willing to make the effort to fix her marriage."

Iris set the chopped rosemary aside. "You do? Why?" When Vale rubbed her lips together, she chuckled. "Fine. Don't tell me. If your sister is confiding in you, that's wonderful." Iris reached for a handful of fresh parsley. "Did Natty like the toys? I spotted her outside, hopping around on a pogo stick."

"She was thrilled. She's set with enough toys for three lifetimes."

"Are you hungry? Dinner is almost ready."

Prepared for the question, Vale neared. "I'm sorry, Nana—I'm skipping dinner. I'm driving back to Pittsburgh."

"Wait. What? It's past six o'clock. It'll be late when you arrive!"

"I promised to stay as long as Blythe does, remember? I didn't pack enough clothing for an extended stay." The explanation *was* truthful, if not fully accurate. "I also need to see my super. I forgot to pay May's rent."

The explanation mollified her grandmother. "I suppose driving back on a Sunday night makes sense. There won't be much traffic." Iris stopped mincing parsley long enough to flash a mischievous glance. "Pack more dresses. You can't wear the red silk every time Emmett takes you out to eat."

"I will."

"Speaking of Emmett, why don't we invite him over for dinner this week?"

Despite her gloom, the offer warmed Vale. "That would be nice. I'll let you know which night he's available."

She gave her grandmother a quick kiss and hurried out.

Chapter 27

Vale barely slept.

She'd reached Pittsburgh at eleven o'clock, steeped with exhaustion, her muscles stiff from the drive. She'd quickly fallen into bed only to spend hours chasing shadows across the walls. The apartment felt cold and unwelcoming. The bare furnishings seemed like the castoffs from another life. She felt like an intruder stumbling into the pathetically meager world left behind by another.

Nor could she halt the sordid, newfound memories of her parents from dominating her thoughts.

On Monday morning, like clockwork, Emmett sent a text on his way to Mullaney's. Vale responded with cheery emoticons and a short note. She chose not to mention the trip. Better to share the unpleasant details tonight, once she returned to Philadelphia.

After she showered and dressed, she packed up the best pickings from her wardrobe. She caught the super downstairs and took care of the late rent. She did not call Bo. Why give him time to prepare a mountain of lies?

A cool determination accompanied Vale on the drive to her father's apartment complex. Or was it resignation? She couldn't get a fix on her emotions as she took the elevator to the sixth floor.

A series of polite knocks on Bo's door brought no response. Biting her lip, Vale resorted to pounding. Down the hallway, a woman peered out of her apartment. Embarrassed, Vale sent her an apologetic glance.

The woman shut her door as Vale's father opened his.

"Hey, blue eyes! When did you get back?"

"Last night, but I'm not staying. I'm heading back to Philadelphia."

The good cheer melted from Bo's features. "You look upset."

You think?

With irritation, she appraised his sleep-softened features and bare chest. Jersey knit pants hugged Bo's lean hips. For a man in his early fifties, he was incredibly fit. Too much so, given his ability to charm women.

It didn't escape her notice that he hadn't invited her inside.

"Tell her to go home, whoever she is." Vale brushed past him. "We need to talk."

For a moment Bo remained frozen in place. He wasn't used to receiving commands from his normally agreeable daughter. At last, he shut the door. He padded across the living room.

Vale went into the kitchen. From the bedroom, a rapid-fire conversation ensued—Bo's voice lowered and tense, the woman responding with a burst of laughter. Plainly Bo's mystery guest found the situation amusing.

Opening the fridge, Vale grabbed a yogurt. Last night she'd driven nonstop, too upset to stomach a meal. She'd finished the yogurt by the time the woman left the apartment.

Vale walked into the living room to find her father dressed in jeans and a wrinkled button-down shirt. His golden locks were hastily combed. His feet, however, were bare—a telltale sign that Bo knew he was in the wrong.

He managed to keep himself from pacing. "What's this about?"

"You and my mother. I need answers, Dad. For once, I'd appreciate it if you'd ditch the charm and play straight with me."

"I always play straight with you, don't I?"

"Not always."

"That hurts." A muscle tensed in Bo's jaw. He looked ready to bolt, but he held himself in place. "What do you want to know?"

Doubt surged through Vale. Did she want Bo to verify her suspicions? To spell out the details of his worst choices—and her mother's? She suddenly feared what the truth would cost her.

"Vale? I'm waiting."

Steeling herself, she blurted, "How long were you messing around with my mother? For years, right?"

The query tensed his shoulders—but only for a moment. The familiar mask of congeniality fell across his features. As if he'd talk himself out of a corner with ease. As if he viewed her as simply another woman he'd wronged. Not as the daughter he should love and cherish.

Bo scraped the hair from his brow. "I don't get this, Vale. What do you hope to gain by digging up the past? Here's everything you need to know." He paused for emphasis before adding, "I'm not seeing your mother."

"But you *were* seeing her—for years."

A false sense of dignity put insult on his face. "I don't chase married women. Why should I? The world is full of single women happy to keep me company."

"I'm sick of your evasions. Was my mother the one exception?" Her voice rose in pitch, but Vale didn't care. For once, she wouldn't allow her father to dance past the truth. "Was Mom the *only* married woman you pursued? Gosh, Dad. That makes me feel so much better."

"Slow down. What did Audrey tell you?"

"Answer the question!"

Anger flashed in Bo's eyes. "It was a long time ago."

The admission hung between them. Sickened, Vale pressed a hand to her forehead. She felt clammy, off balance.

Her father slid his hands into his pockets. "There. Are you happy?"

"Not even a little. I feel betrayed."

"What *did* your mother say?"

The question was incomprehensible. Did he believe she'd engaged in a heart-to-heart with Audrey? That they enjoyed anything resembling a normal mother-daughter relationship? Clearly Bo was blind to the ramifications of his behavior.

With disgust, Vale stared at him. She'd overlooked his worst qualities for too long.

"Why do you assume I spoke to Mom?" she snapped. "We're not close."

"Then how . . . ?"

"I remembered some things from my childhood. Moments between you and Mom that didn't add up. It didn't take long to reach the obvious conclusion."

"Don't feel betrayed. What happened between me and Audrey . . . it has nothing to do with you. When she decided we should stop, we did. No harm done."

The callous defense blistered Vale with sorrow. "Are you joking? What about the harm done to *me*? To Blythe, and to Grant—did you ever stop to consider how your choices affected the rest of us? I grew up believing I was somehow deficient. That Mom treated me like a hindrance and Grant treated me with contempt because I wasn't good enough. That I wasn't worthy of their love. But it was never about me. It was about *you*, taking liberties with my mother."

Bo's temper snapped. "Stop attacking me! I'm no different than anyone else."

She stared at him with confusion. "What are you talking about?"

"C'mon, Vale. We all use the cards we're dealt." He swept a hand down his body. "I got this. Good looks and more charm than I need. You want to know what I *didn't* get? Enough smarts to give me options. I barely squeaked by in high school. I'll be tending bar until I drop. I blew my one chance to get ahead when I let the insurance lapse on the

Crafty Cocktail. So I sleep around. I like women, and women like me. So what?"

"*That's* your excuse?"

"It's the only one I've got. Take it or leave it."

Heartache crashed through her. What choice was he giving her?

"We're done here." She flashed him a look of pure hatred. "And by the way, you also blew *my* chance to get ahead when you canceled our business insurance. Do me a favor—stay out of my life."

"Vale, wait." Her father suddenly paled. "Let's both cool down. We'll talk this out."

The charm offensive came too late. Pivoting away, she marched out.

Chapter 28

From Emmett's living room, Vale heard the soft purr of the Volvo's engine die away. The front door clicked shut.

Emmett came into the living room.

By way of greeting, she said, "Ever wonder why the people you know best are the most prone to shock the crap out of you?"

He quirked a brow. "It's nice to see you too, dear. Tough day at work?"

"Tough day in Pittsburgh."

"You were in Pittsburgh? Why didn't you tell me?"

Vale closed her laptop. "It made more sense to fill you in when I got back."

"Which was . . . ?"

"Late this afternoon. I hope you don't mind—I've been hanging around your house since then." Weary, Vale rubbed her face. "I'd rather not see my grandmother until I pull myself together."

"*Mi casa es su casa.*" Emmett noticed the glass before her on the coffee table. Retrieving it, he took a sniff of the amber liquid. "You got into my brandy? You don't drink."

"Thanks for the reminder. I didn't expect a few sips to kick me like a mule." Waving off the glass, Vale pinched her stuffy nose. "Got any allergy meds in the house? The booze was *not* an inspired choice."

In short order, Emmett returned with a bottle of Allegra and a glass of water. "What happened in Pittsburgh?" He seated himself beside her.

She told him about the confrontation with Bo. Discussing her parents' long-standing affair made her jumpy and embarrassed. From the encounter with her father this morning, it seemed clear he felt no guilt about the affair. Did her mother? Vale doubted it.

Summing up, she added, "I'm the spawn of evil."

"Hardly." Emmett smiled. "Is that the brandy talking?"

"Nope. Me, definitely." Reconsidering, she swallowed down an Allegra tablet. "Maybe 'evil' is too strong a word. I'm the spawn of stupid, selfish people."

Emmett slung a protective arm around her. "I hate to agree, but I do. What your parents did is inexcusable. I'm sorry you had to learn about their affair."

"I couldn't get my father to admit how long it went on." She rested her head against Emmett's shoulder. He felt warm, solid, and she was grateful for the chance to talk this out. "I have a bad feeling they messed around for years. Maybe until I finished high school and moved out."

"You must feel betrayed."

"I do. And hurt, angry—"

"Let it go. What your parents did is in the past. It only has bearing on your life now if you allow it."

The remark came from hard-won experience. Vale recalled their first date at Rue de Jean, when he mentioned his broken engagement.

Their gazes caught, and he nodded grimly. "I'm not saying it's easy to let go of your sense of betrayal," he admitted. "We assume the people we love won't break our trust. In the case of my broken engagement, I spent months questioning why my fiancée would choose her ex over me. A real blow to my ego."

"I'm sorry, Emmett. You deserved better."

"It's all right. The experience made me a better man. It gave me a clearer idea of what I want in a wife. Besides, I'm not sure the comparison is a good fit to your situation. What you've learned about Audrey and Bo is a greater shock."

The softly issued words put a lump in Vale's throat. "They never made me feel safe and whole. At least I know why now—they never put me first. They cared about each other more than they cared about me." She inhaled a tremulous breath. "I've spent most of my life doubting myself. Believing I make too many mistakes because I'm somehow lacking. Inadequate."

She flinched when Emmett lifted her hand. With the gentlest touch, he traced her fingernails, which were bitten to the quick. A nervous habit she was unable to break—one first taken up during her tumultuous childhood.

Emmett placed her hand in his lap. The compassion filling his eyes was so deep, she wanted to swim in its depths.

"You *are* enough, Vale. Have more faith in yourself. If your parents gave you the wrong messages, it's their problem—not yours."

"It's hard to see it that way."

"Make the effort. That's all I'm asking." He brushed a kiss across her lips. "I'll let you in on a secret."

"I'm all ears."

"I've watched how my family has changed over time, with me and my sisters taking the lead. My parents are older than yours, but the same lessons apply. One generation steps aside to make room for the next. Your family no longer revolves around your parents, Vale. It's now more about you and Blythe. About the relationship you're forging as sisters, and the children you both may have one day. *You* are the future. The bad stuff from the past doesn't matter. You aren't responsible for your parents' mistakes."

"I'd like children someday," she admitted.

Emmett's hold on her fingers tightened. "How many?"

The interest gathering on his features lifted her heart. "Two or three, I suppose. I wouldn't space them too far apart. It would be nice if they were close enough in age to go through the developmental stages together. Maybe even share the same friends."

Blinking away the tears, she declined to add the rest. *I'll give them a better childhood than mine, with enough love and encouragement to carry them through their lives.*

The pleasant silence wound out. After a moment, Emmett came to his feet.

"Are you hungry? I have tons of leftovers from my nephew's birthday party."

"I suppose."

"I was hoping for more enthusiasm. There's also a large chunk of double chocolate cake. Enough for seconds."

"Is the cake good?" Indulging in something sweet after the day's bitter events appealed.

"You bet." Emmett's brows furrowed as he watched her slide her laptop near. "What are you doing?"

"Oh, I've been searching job sites since I got here." She nodded at the notepad on the coffee table. Her choppy cursive ran down the page. "I'm making a list of target companies in Philadelphia. I've found some good leads."

This random bit of news stilled the air.

"I can't sponge paychecks off my grandmother and Detta forever," she added. "The shop needs the extra help now, but sales will slow down in the summer. I need to move on. Especially since Nana has cooked up this silly idea about selling Green Iris to me and Blythe. Even if my sister was interested—and she's not—I don't have the cash for a buyout."

Retracing his steps, Emmett sat back down.

At the expectation on his face, she laughed. "Did I bury the lede?"

"Apparently." A grin rose on his lips. "You're staying in Philadelphia?"

"Going back to Pittsburgh doesn't make sense. How can I live near my father after everything I've learned?" Sadness darted through Vale, marring the moment's sudden joy. "Living near Mom and Grant isn't my first choice either. But I have you, Blythe, and Nana. It's more than enough."

"We should break out the champagne."

"Don't you dare." Vale wiggled her nose like a rabbit. "I'm already stuffy from the brandy."

"How about a bubbly mix of Pellegrino and mango juice? A celebratory drink minus the alcohol."

"Sounds perfect."

Emmett thought of something else. "Have you told Iris about your decision? She'll be thrilled."

"I'll tell her in the morning." The delight on Emmett's face made Vale feel marginally better and she asked, "Here's an idea on how we can celebrate—why don't we start dinner with the chocolate cake? I'm game if you are."

Emmett surged to his feet. "Coming right up."

Chapter 29

Tamping down her anxiety, Blythe turned on the darkened street. The Audi glided to a halt in the building's valet zone. Through the windshield, she peered at the lobby. Like the streets surrounding Rittenhouse Square, it appeared deserted.

Several part-time college students worked the graveyard shift at the luxury apartments where she lived with Booker. Given the late hour, the valet on shift had presumably dozed off or was hitting the books. Normally the building's occupants didn't arrive in the middle of the night.

Blythe usually didn't either, but she was tired of allowing fear to steal her confidence. Or of delaying a conversation long overdue. She'd used Booker's unrelenting schedule as an easy excuse and hidden out at her grandmother's place for too long. The hardest discussions didn't wait for a convenient time or when you'd finally located the courage to speak up. You had them when they were needed. Which meant she couldn't fight to keep her marriage without revealing the source of her troubles to Booker.

Impatient to get upstairs, she tapped on the horn. The sound alerted Sanaa. A student of applied engineering at the Community College of Philadelphia, Sanaa was a heavyset girl with a timid smile. Groggy-eyed, she sprinted from the lobby.

"Good morning, Mrs. Banks." She came around the Audi's hood. "Sorry to keep you waiting."

Blythe stepped from the car. "Sanaa, it's nowhere near morning." She smiled. "How's school?"

"So-so. I have two exams next week. I'm not ready."

"Don't let me keep you from your studies." She handed over the keys. "And thank you."

Blythe rode the elevator to the top floor with her anxiety returning. Letting herself into the apartment, she frowned at the bluish light spilling from the bedroom. Apparently, the muted TV had been running for hours. Booker liked to channel surf before dozing off. All couples have their habits; Blythe would pry the remote from his grasp to turn off the TV once he fell asleep.

On the wall opposite the bed, sport highlights flashed across the seventy-inch screen. Blythe swung her attention to the tangle of sheets where Booker lay sprawled on his back. A sweet ache tightened her throat.

Nothing woke her husband after a game. The rigors of the long day preparing to play. The unnerving focus he marshaled while pitching one inning after another. The demands took his body to the limits of physical endurance.

We'll talk in the morning. Before the day's unrelenting schedule pulled Booker away. *I'll tell him everything and let him decide.* Before the fear stalking Blythe silenced her again. She was asking Booker to give up too much. But the decision on whether to bail on their marriage should rest with him. She'd deny him the choice no longer.

And if he chose to leave? The thought seized Blythe with despair so deep, she knew she could drown in it. Turning off the TV, she undressed slowly, aware that she needed to rally the courage to trust in their love. Was it strong enough to overcome a crushing setback neither of them had anticipated? She clung to the fragile belief that Booker wouldn't blame her. Not now, or in the future. That they'd move past the disappointment together.

As she climbed into bed, she let a moment's hope drive away the darker emotions. The broad plane of Booker's chest rose and fell in a soothing rhythm. Fitting her body against his, Blythe savored the warmth of his skin. Evading the heaviness overtaking her limbs, she watched his eyelids flutter. His right arm involuntarily twitched. Was he going into the windup in his dreams, readying a pitch for his adoring fans? She loved watching him sleep.

Near dawn, exhaustion took her. She fell into a deep sleep.

She awoke to a husky moan—Booker's. Rolling sideways, he latched his drowsy hazel eyes on her. As he drank her in, his gaze roving every inch of her face, Blythe felt the hunger swell inside her like an ungovernable force. When her breathing hitched, a smile spread across Booker's mouth. He steered her hips beneath his.

They made love quickly, urgently. Afterward, Booker lifted her onto his chest.

He cupped a handful of curls spilling past her cheek. "Good morning, beautiful."

"Hi, baby."

His eyes drifted shut. "What time is it?"

"You really don't want to know."

"Then don't tell me." His body relaxing, he flopped his hands to his sides.

Gingerly, she slid off him. "I wasn't planning to."

As he dozed, a fissure of tension creased his brow. Blythe sensed there was something on his mind. Concern over his pitching strategy? The next series of away games? Booker was especially superstitious when the Phillies were on the road. And he'd blame himself whenever the team's current winning streak ended.

He burrowed his head deeper into the pillow. "I thought you were staying longer with Iris. No problem if you do." Opening his eyes briefly, he yawned. "I'm back on the road soon. Man, I can't wait for some R & R on the tenth."

May 10—his first day off since mid-April. After a full month of playing, he'd sleep in. Sometimes they made love until the early afternoon, then went out for a long walk. He'd take her out to dinner. During the season, they always dined somewhere nice on his rare days off.

Wait until then to talk? Blythe resisted the urge. She'd been stalling for weeks. Wait any longer, and she'd just delay again.

Her thoughts tumbled one into the next. *Booker, you're everything to me.* There wasn't a simple way to begin, and her heart knocked around in her rib cage. *I hope you can bear what I must tell you.*

"Booker?"

"Hmm?"

"We need to talk about our expectations," she rasped out. *Totally not the right starter.*

The remark prodded his eyes open.

"Like having kids, for example."

He tensed.

"What if we never have a family?"

I'm botching this. Blythe tried to start again. Discovered her tongue glued to the roof of her mouth.

She was still grappling for the right words when Booker swung his legs over the side of the bed. He rubbed at his scalp as if dislodging a wave of frustration.

From over his shoulder, he threw her a glance. "Babe, I know you haven't been happy. And I *do* want a family. If I've given you the wrong impression . . ." His voice faded into silence. He looked away.

He clapped his hands on his knees so quickly, she flinched.

"I guess telling you now is as good a time as any," he muttered, dropping his attention to his feet. "Miles and Kiki split up."

The news took her aback. "When?"

"Last week."

Miles Waddell played center field; he was Booker's closest friend on the team. He'd signed with the Phillies the same year.

"Can't they . . . I don't know. Try counseling?"

"It's done, Blythe. Kiki served him with papers."

Miles and Kiki had three children, all under the age of seven. The two couples used to meet up, before the demands of parenting took Kiki off the wives' circuit. Blythe guiltily realized she'd made no effort to stay in touch.

The Waddells' son, Toby, had been diagnosed with autism recently. The psychologist was still assessing where the three-year-old fell on the spectrum.

Booker scrubbed his palms across his face. "If we weren't having our own problems, I would've asked if you cared if Miles stayed with us for a couple of weeks. He's taking Kiki's decision hard. Man, I can't believe I almost brought it up."

"I don't mind. Tell Miles to stay here as long as he'd like." Blythe felt helpless, selfish. Sitting down beside her husband, she failed to catch his gaze. "Booker, it's fine."

"No, it's not. We have our own issues to sort out."

"They can wait."

At last, he looked at her. "No debates, okay? I shouldn't have told you about their divorce. It could've waited." Booker rarely lost his temper, but he was angry now. At himself, or her—it was impossible to tell. His voice tight, he added, "Babe, I can't do this right now. Can you just hold off until the tenth? We'll talk about everything. What you need, how to get back on track—whatever you want."

Swallowing, she bobbed her head in agreement. "Sure."

On the nightstand, Booker's alarm went off.

Chapter 30

Vale groaned as Detta pushed the box of chocolate croissants toward her.

"What is this—bribery by chocolate?" After consuming one of the gooey confections, Vale didn't have room for another. Not after *two* slices of chocolate cake at Emmett's house last night. "Make her stop, Nana. If I get more sugared up, how will I wait on customers? I'm already jitterier than a jackrabbit."

"Detta, stop. Tempting Vale with pastries won't make her change her mind." Flipping the box shut, Iris shelved it beneath the checkout counter. "We can't force her to make the right decision."

"Why not? It's two against one."

"The more you push, the more Vale digs in her heels. Or haven't you noticed?"

"I'm not blind—I'm persistent. Frankly, I'm surprised you're giving up so easily."

Iris shot her a look of irritation. "I'm not giving up!"

As they squabbled, Vale finished stacking bills in the cash register. She hadn't expected her grandmother and Detta to take the news well. Of course they were disappointed. What she hadn't bargained on was a full-out lobbying effort to keep her employed at Green Iris.

On the other hand, her grandmother wasn't peppering her for the reason behind the decision to stay in Philadelphia. Nor did she inquire if Vale saw Bo while in Pittsburgh.

A relief.

Snapping the cash register shut, Vale cut into their bickering. "I'll keep working here for at least a few more weeks," she promised. "I've only begun researching jobs. Best guess, you have me until June. But I *do* need tomorrow off to polish my résumé."

Detta pouted. "Don't you enjoy working with us?"

"Oh, Detta—I love working with you and Nana. I love spending the day in a jungle of plants, and Green Iris has the nicest customers. It just doesn't make sense, long-term."

"But you won't be an employee forever. We'll groom you to take over. If Blythe doesn't want to share ownership, so what? When the time is right, you'll—"

Halting in midsentence, Detta clamped a hand over her mouth.

With irritation, Vale appraised her grandmother. She'd expressly asked her *not* to discuss a change of ownership with Detta.

Iris lifted her palms. "I blabbed. I couldn't resist."

"Nana!"

"Listen to me. Green Iris is a family business. It should stay in the family. You know Detta's son is a podiatrist, and he doesn't care about the shop. Your sister's life is more up in the air than yours, and besides, she's never shown much interest. You, however, should take over one day. You've inherited my green thumb, and you said it yourself—you love working in a jungle of plants."

"Which is beside the point. I'm not a charity case."

Iris settled her hands on her hips. "Are we back to that?"

"Yes, we are. I don't have the money to buy you out. How many handouts can I take in good conscience? In case you've forgotten, you pitched in when I bought the Crafty Cocktail. Your donation went up in smoke."

"It wasn't a donation. It was a gift, believe me. That's how I had to enter it into my taxes," her grandmother teased.

"Either way, I lost your money."

"Here's an idea—forget about finding an apartment. Continue living with me. Bank the cash you would've used on rent for the eventual buyout. And here's something else you should consider. Your boyfriend lives down the street."

Detta's hand slid from her mouth. "Vale has a boyfriend? Since when?"

Iris shushed her. "Think about it, Vale. Emmett will do a happy dance if you continue living at my house."

There was no denying the assessment. Emmett *would* do a happy dance. *I would too.* Living a few doors away made it easy to see each other.

Sensing her indecision, Iris sweetened the deal. "Take tomorrow off to consider the offer. If you still want to work somewhere else, fine. We won't stand in your way."

Torn, Vale rubbed her lips together. "What if I can't save enough to buy you out?"

"If you decide to quit Green Iris at a later date, Detta and I will understand."

"*I* won't understand," Detta muttered. "Vale belongs here."

"Detta, hush. Give her a moment to ponder."

Vale didn't need a moment. The offer was incredibly generous. If she couldn't pony up a suitable amount of cash whenever they *were* ready to retire, it would be her loss. She wouldn't take advantage—she'd find a job somewhere else. Let Iris and Detta sell their profitable business to a buyer with the funds to assume control.

"Are you sure, Nana?" Vale asked, her voice catching.

"We only want what's best for you, pumpkin."

"Do you mind if I still take off tomorrow? I should call several moving companies, check into rates. I'd like to keep the bedroom furniture in my apartment if it's not too expensive."

"Go right ahead. Take Thursday off too if you'd like. We'll manage." Sobering, Iris rested her palm on Vale's cheek. "When were you planning to tell your mother you're here to stay?"

"I haven't decided."

"Never" sounds good. After Bo's revelations about their long-standing affair, Vale wasn't opposed to avoiding her mother indefinitely.

"She'll also do a happy dance, Vale. I'll bet she drops by the house soon to surprise you with an offer to go shopping. In fact, I'm sure she will."

Nothing gave Audrey joy like maxing out her credit cards on shopping sprees with Blythe. Her largesse never extended to Vale. *Which suits me just fine.*

"I'm not interested in roaming department stores with Mom." She looked up suddenly. "Hold on. Have you told her about my plans?"

"This morning, while you were in the shower."

A stealthy ploy. Iris had waited until Vale was out of earshot to share the news.

"I wish you hadn't called Mom. Where I live is none of her business."

"Your plans aren't a state secret." Iris lightly swatted her. "Am I supposed to keep her in the dark? She *is* delighted. Give her a call sometime. You'll see."

Letting it go, Iris strode down the shop's center aisle. She flipped the **OPEN** sign.

The remainder of the day zipped by. The shop bell rang constantly as customers came and went. With May's warming temperatures, many of the flowering baskets and bedding plants quickly sold out. With the help of their part-time employees, the youthful Miranda and Teddy, Vale replenished the stock on the second floor. By late afternoon, it seemed she'd run enough miles for a marathon.

Near closing time, the traffic fell off. Vale had driven in with her grandmother, and they were both grateful when Detta flicked off the shop's lights.

When they reached the house, her grandmother asked, "Do you have plans tonight?" Iris steered the van into the driveway.

Vale nodded. "I'm meeting Emmett for cheesesteaks at the diner near Mullaney's Pharmacy."

"Sounds fun."

"I won't be late. Emmett has an early day tomorrow. Something about a busload of seniors coming in for shingles vaccines."

"Probably from one of the retirement centers. Emmett will have a busy morning." They started up the walk, and Iris sent her a sideways glance. "May I ask the other question, or will you assume I'm prying?"

"You *are* prying." Vale drew her to a halt. "I know you mean well. I don't want to see Mom right now. Can we leave it at that?"

Her grandmother studied her closely. A trace of disappointment sifted across her features. Extinguishing it, she resumed walking. "I'm here to talk it out, whenever you change your mind."

"*If* I change my mind. Don't hold your breath."

"Fine. I won't. If you want the truth, I'd rather soak in a hot bath. My feet are on fire. I'll pry your secrets loose when I have more energy."

Vale chuckled. "Good luck with that."

In the foyer, it became clear something was wrong. A Motown oldie blasted through the house. The Temptations' "I Wish It Would Rain."

Not a good sign.

Her shoulders sagging, Iris glanced up the stairs. "What are your thoughts on drawing straws?"

"Take your bath, Nana. I'll check on Blythe." Tapping out a text, Vale canceled her dinner with Emmett.

The sound level rattled Vale's molars as she ascended the staircase. The door to Blythe's room was ajar. A subtle invitation to enter? Vale hoped so.

Spotting her in the doorway, Blythe scrambled from the bed. Crumpled tissues bounced off the bedspread. They fell to the floor like a smattering of snowflakes. Lifting the tonearm from the LP, she turned off the music.

She swallowed, frowned, then flapped her arms at her sides. "I saw Booker."

Pity carried Vale into the room. Her sister's eyes were swollen from crying. Her nose looked inflamed, the nostrils rimmed in a throbbing red. Her dark hair sported tangles, the hapless curls sticking up in places. Most heartbreaking of all, she wore a large Phillies jersey over her bare legs. No doubt the jersey belonged to her husband.

The normally meticulous room was in equal disarray. Clothing trailed across the floor. On the end table, a circle of confectioner's sugar surrounded a half-eaten box of doughnuts. A scented candle bled wax across the dresser.

Vale shut the door. "I thought I heard your car leave last night, really late." Sometime in the wee hours—Vale hadn't been sure if she was dreaming and had promptly fallen back to sleep. Blythe must've returned at first daylight. "What happened?"

"We didn't get a chance to hash everything out. Booker wants me to wait until May 10 to have a serious sit-down. He'll have the day off."

"That's good, isn't it?"

Blythe sank onto the side of the bed. "You'd think, right? But I know how the conversation will go. Booker is such a great guy, he'll take responsibility for all our problems. How the demands of his career make it hard to have a private life." Her expression crumbled. "I'll let him foist all the blame on himself because it's easier—because I'll lose the nerve to be honest with him. Like I always do."

Vale blew out the candle. Wisps of smoke curled up from the wick, making her irrepressibly sad.

"You have to stay strong, Blythe," she said. "Wait until Booker's day off. If you love him, lay everything out then. Even if it kills you. You owe it to him."

"But I won't. We'll start talking, and I'll lose the nerve because I'm a coward." She pressed the heels of her hands into her eyes so hard, Vale feared she'd maim herself. "What's wrong with me? He's the best person I know, and I'm stringing him along. Letting him believe there's a way to fix the mess I've made of our marriage. Why can't I just let him go?

213

Tell him straight-out the agreements we made when we tied the knot don't matter. They don't because I can't hold up my end of the bargain."

For an awful moment, a dark thought rooted Vale by the dresser. Did the absence of fidelity run in families?

Like their mother, Blythe was married to a good man. Like Audrey, it seemed she'd chosen to cheat on her husband without considering the damage it would do. Which left Vale with a depressing conclusion: some women were prone to stray. Just like some men did.

The sound of ragged sobs broke through her musings. She hurried forward.

Climbing onto the bed, she steered Blythe into her arms. Reclining fully, she rested Blythe's head on her breast as if she were a child in need of soothing. As if a moment's affection might heal her sister's self-inflicted heartache. Blythe clung tight.

"*Shhh*, it's all right." Tears spilled across Vale's shirt, chilling her skin. "You'll get through this."

"No, I won't." Her voice muffled, Blythe hid her face against Vale's shoulder. "I'm a coward. All I've done is delay the inevitable."

The statement's grim truth shook Vale. If Blythe couldn't be faithful to Booker, their divorce *was* inevitable.

"Blythe, you won't solve anything by drowning in sorrow. Think about something positive."

"Like what?"

A difficult question, given the situation.

At length, Vale said, "If Booker can't hash everything out until the tenth, we'll hang out. Want to enroll in a class together?"

"What sort of class?"

"I loved my Orangetheory workouts in Pittsburgh. We can find a class here, sign up together."

Blythe sat up too quickly. "You really *are* staying." A hiccup popped from her mouth.

"I am."

"I thought you'd never move back to Philadelphia."

Vale handed over the box of tissues. "That makes two of us."

"I'm glad you changed your mind. It's nice having you around. You've been a real help."

"Thanks." She flicked her sister's damp nose. "I like having you around too—even when you're on a crying jag."

"Lately, it's my special talent." Wiping her eyes, Blythe flopped back down beside her.

Together they stared at the ceiling.

"I don't know how to start over." Blythe's voice was ragged, but she managed to keep the tears at bay. "How do you do it? Get back up when life knocks you down? You've had your share of screwups, Vale. Got any advice? I'm all ears."

A compliment wrapped in an insult. Vale shrugged it off.

"I'm no expert," she admitted. "Whenever I mess up, I try not to hurt others. I've launched into free fall too many times to count, but I always hit the ground solo. It's a good place to start."

"I've already hurt Booker. I've kept too much from him."

"Treat him with kindness, even if you can't patch things up. If it comes to divorce . . . well, it can bring out the worst in people. Don't let it. Ask his forgiveness. Don't let him go on with his life believing he's to blame. Take responsibility, Blythe."

"How? I'm a coward."

"Yeah? Well, find your backbone. If you don't, I'll read you the riot act in ten different languages."

New tears glossed Blythe's eyes, but she managed a smile.

"I'll try," she agreed.

Chapter 31

Drumming her fingers on the kitchen table, Vale navigated to yet another website. Who knew moving her furniture would be so expensive?

The three quotes sitting in her inbox were all shockingly out of range. She doubted a fourth company would offer a more affordable quote. Which didn't stop her from filling out the online form and hitting "Send."

Setting her laptop aside, Vale poured another cup of coffee. Her grandmother had left for Green Iris two hours ago, at nine o'clock. Blythe was also gone; she'd left earlier than Iris without explanation.

Concern for her sister pricked Vale. Hopefully Blythe planned to meet with friends this morning. A brunch date, or a few hours shopping with girlfriends. Blythe needed the cheering up. When she'd left the house this morning, she'd looked downcast and gloomy.

Pushing the worry aside, Vale returned to the table. She slid a notepad close. Should she forget about a moving company and ask Emmett to help? They could rent a truck and take care of the task together. The other option: run an ad online and sell the bedroom set to a buyer in Pittsburgh.

She was mulling over the decision when the doorbell rang. When she swung open the door, her stomach clenched. Disbelief followed. Her father stopped pacing across the front porch, drawing to a standstill as their eyes locked.

Incredibly, Bo gave a hearty wave.

"I heard from the fire department," he announced, as if they'd been chatting for long minutes and he was glad to fill her in. "Want to guess what started the fire?" When she merely folded her arms, dumbfounded by his appearance, he cheerfully continued. "It was the stove. An electrical fire, can you believe it? I guess I should've taken your advice—remember when you suggested we get rid of the old workhorse and buy a new stove? Man, was I stupid not to listen."

Vale snapped out of her stupor. "You make a lot of stupid choices. What else is new?"

Bo winced. But she had to give him credit: he didn't attempt to defend himself.

"What are you doing here?" she demanded. Apparently, he'd risen early to make the long drive. A surprising gesture. *And a waste of time.* Given the late nights tending bar, Bo usually slept in.

"Will you cut me some slack? You know why I'm here. I wanted to see you to clear the air. You aren't taking my calls."

"Why should I? There's nothing to discuss."

Her father glanced at the street. "Can I come inside?" His nervous gaze slid back to her. "We need to talk."

Another decision, this one more upsetting than whether to ship or sell furniture. What did Bo hope to gain? Anger surged through her. *He can't charm his way out of this.* Despite her reservations, Vale waved him into the living room.

"If you're planning to apologize, don't bother," she snapped. "You can't undo the past. You've already hurt me in more ways than you can imagine."

"I know. I don't deserve your forgiveness."

"You got that right."

"I don't want to lose you either." Remorse deepened the lines framing his mouth. "You're the most important person in my life. Don't you know that? What have I got without you? You're the only person who gives a—"

"I'm not coming back to Pittsburgh," she cut in, needing to injure Bo as much as he'd injured her. A foolish desire, and sadness wove through her.

"You're staying here?"

"There's nothing left for me in Pittsburgh."

"Yes, there is. We're a team, Vale. We'll regroup, pull together the cash to buy a new place."

Dumbfounded, she stared at him. He understood nothing about her motives. Was it any wonder? Bo had never viewed her as a daughter. Only as a pal, and a business partner.

"Don't you get it?" she said, needing to set him straight. "I didn't move to Pittsburgh to own a bar with you. I never wanted to own a business that forced me to work nights and skip anything resembling a social life. Did you actually believe that I did?"

The question took him aback. "We were both excited about the Crafty Cocktail."

"No, Dad. I never cared about the bar. I took you up on the offer because I craved a real father-daughter relationship. Something I never had growing up. Mom and Grant had Blythe, and I spent years feeling like second-best. I moved to Pittsburgh because I wanted something special with you."

"Hold on. We *do* have a special relationship."

"It was all illusion. You were never worth it. And now I'm angry because I passed up a close relationship with my sister for too many years. And for what? The philanderer who happens to be my father."

"I didn't mean to disappoint you."

She gave a watery laugh. "Well, you did."

Bo took a hesitant step closer. He suddenly looked older, the web-work of lines framing his eyes deepening with regret.

"I *am* your father, Vale. Having you around the last four years has taught me how special you are. Can't we get past this?"

"Not unless I can find a way to forgive you. Seeing that I'm not feeling very charitable, it won't happen anytime soon."

The tears came too quickly. Burning a trail down her cheeks. Unleashing the question Vale had never dared to ask.

"Did you care about me?" Backing away, she watched Bo pale as she regarded him with loathing. "When I was growing up, when you were messing around with my mother, did I cross your mind? The random visits, the months you'd go without even calling me . . . Did I matter to you at all?"

"No, you didn't matter to me." Bo cleared his throat. "Not then."

A brutally honest remark. It gripped Vale's heart like a vise.

"When you were growing up, I didn't understand what it means to be a father. I didn't see it as a gift."

"You didn't love me. I was just a . . . convenience. A way for you to stay in touch with Mom."

"Your mom and I knew we weren't good together, but we couldn't break it off. I'd stay away, then I'd begin to miss her, or she'd call . . . We never meant to hurt anyone." The weight of his folly took something vital from Bo's face. He looked crushed when he added, "I love you now, Vale. I should've loved you when you were a kid. I'm sorry I didn't."

The admission placed a heaviness in the room. Like a suffocating layer of snow freezing Vale in place. From the corner of her eye, she caught a flash of blue streaming past the window. A Mercedes sedan. The car pulled into the driveway.

Numb from emotional overload, Vale watched her mother get out of the car.

Chapter 32

Audrey let herself into the house before Vale could react.

"Hello! Vale, where are you?"

Her pearls bouncing, Audrey strode toward the staircase and called out again. Plainly she'd dropped by on her lunch hour at Stern-Belkins. She wore a double-breasted taupe blazer over a matching skirt. Her brown tresses were pulled into a loose chignon.

Swinging around, Audrey glanced into the living room. Her startled gaze leaped past her daughter to land on her ex-husband.

"Bo." A quiver of panic raced across her features. "I didn't expect to see you here."

Something tragic passed between them. The scent it left in the air reminded Vale of the embers from a dying fire. Against her will, she sensed the passion that once flared between her parents, the reckless, ungovernable desire that had burned like a wildfire through their lives. Were they permanently blighted from the damage? Sympathy, unbidden, rose in her chest.

"I'm not staying, Audrey. I'll let you hash this out with our daughter alone."

The color fled Audrey's cheeks.

Vale stiffened as her father approached. Bo waited silently until her eyes lifted to his.

"I'm ashamed of myself, Vale. I hope you'll forgive me eventually."

Without awaiting a reply, he went out.

Vale sank onto the couch. In the center of the room, Audrey wavered. She seemed incapable of deciding if she should sit or remain on her feet.

Lowering her elbows to her knees, Vale said, "I couldn't pry the details from Dad. How long did the affair go on?"

"Until you were in high school."

The quick reply would've been laudable if the topic weren't so painful. Or if they enjoyed anything resembling a healthy mother-daughter relationship. They didn't possess the tools to navigate difficult subjects. To find their way through.

"Did it end when I was fifteen?" Vale guessed.

Flustered, her mother swiped at her chignon. A tendril came loose.

"Yes—when you were fifteen." Audrey's lips quivered. She brushed the tendril from her cheek. "How did you know?"

The terrible pieces clicked into place. "I overheard an argument between you and Grant."

"What argument?"

"The night you were debating about having Bo take custody of me." Recalling her mother's words, Vale clasped her hands in a painful hold.

Don't you think I'd like to ship Vale off? I would, in a heartbeat. I'd pack her bags myself if I thought Bo could take care of her. He can't handle a teenage girl. What choice do I have but to keep Vale with us?

"You said you'd ship me off in a heartbeat if you thought Bo could handle me."

Recognition flashed through her mother's eyes. Then pain. Clearly she remembered that night.

"Vale, I was upset. With myself, and your father."

"I was an inconvenience. You wanted me out of the way."

"Oh, sweetheart. You're my daughter. You mean the world to me. I never would've transferred custody."

"I don't believe you."

Audrey flinched. Recovering, she came forward and sat on the couch. "The argument you overheard . . . I'd broken off the affair with your father. Just a few days before you overheard me and Grant. It was something I should've done years earlier."

"You were married to Grant! What were you doing sleeping around at all?"

Swallowing, her mother bobbed her head in agreement. "You're right. Of course you're right. What I did with your father was rash, selfish. I never should've allowed it to happen. Not once, not ever. The night you remember . . . I was arguing with Grant because he'd caught me on the phone with Bo."

The disclosure took Vale aback. "If you'd broken it off, why were you talking to my father?"

"Bo wanted to continue the affair. I refused. Grant had been suspicious for years, but he never had proof. He overheard snatches of my conversation with your father. Naturally, Grant thought . . ."

Audrey's voice drifted into a muddy silence. A sob escaped her throat. She appeared unable to continue.

"Grant misunderstood the conversation," Vale supplied. "He assumed you were still seeing Bo." Sadness ballooned inside her as she made another connection. "Grant assumed that if you sent me away, the affair would end. Bo wouldn't have an excuse to come around."

"But I'd already ended it."

Did the timing matter? Vale pressed a hand to her brow. A clammy sickness clung to her skin.

The damage was already done.

Heartache swamped her. "Every time you strayed, you took your guilt out on me," she said. "You acted as if I was an extension of the affair. As if I shared in the guilt."

Audrey looked pained, too distraught to respond.

"I was a child, Mom. The product of two irresponsible adults who never should've married in the first place."

Audrey took her by the hand. "Don't ask me to regret my short marriage to your father. I got you in the bargain." When Vale tried to pull free, her mother refused to let go. "I didn't know how to repair my relationship with you, Vale. How to get past your anger. There wasn't enough time. Then you graduated from high school and announced you were moving out."

"You wanted me to leave."

"Do you have any idea how much I regret our last argument? How much I wish I could take it all back? I lashed out because I let my pride override my instincts as your mother. I was tired of every conversation devolving into a battle. When you left, I was frantic. I couldn't reach you."

A futile effort, Vale mused. Soon after, she got a new phone number. For nearly a year she refused to share the number with her grandmother. It was the simplest way to push Audrey out of her life.

By the time Vale *did* get in touch with her mother, in her early twenties, their conversations were short, stilted. The breach in their relationship too deep.

As it still was, now. A dismal truth her mother appeared to sense.

Eyes lowered, she released Vale's hand. The gesture melted away the anger Vale used to shield her deeper emotions. Especially since they'd covered too much ground. More than Vale could easily digest. She suddenly felt vulnerable.

She came to her feet. "Mom, I have a really long to-do list. Lots to deal with."

"Is there anything I can do to help?"

An oddly normal query. Vale couldn't grasp why it made her feel worse.

"I've got everything covered," she said.

Audrey hesitated. "Can you ever forgive me?"

Unable to reply, Vale looked away. She was still trying to process everything she'd discovered. How could she even think about forgiveness?

"Vale, there's nothing I'd like more than a fresh start. One I haven't earned but that I hope you'll give me." With false cheer, her mother added, "I'm so very glad you're staying in Philadelphia. I've missed you."

She pressed a kiss to Vale's forehead.

Without a backward glance, she strode out.

Chapter 33

Natty twirled a forkful of noodles. "Vale, this is the best spaghetti *ever*. I mean, it's really supremo."

Vale motioned to the jumbo-size bowl of spaghetti she'd prepared. "Do you want more? I made enough for an army."

Iris looked up from her plate. "Let her finish her first helping *and* her salad. Natty, you like salad."

Emmett grinned. "She does," he agreed, "but she likes spaghetti more."

They were seated at the table on Iris's patio enjoying the warm spring evening. Everyone seemed in good spirits except Blythe. Although she'd attempted small talk when they'd carried the food outside, she appeared preoccupied and exhausted. Head bowed, she took small bites of her salad while ignoring the plate of spaghetti Vale had served her.

Emmett said, "I guess you found the right website, Vale. And here you thought stir-fry was the only recipe you could master."

"What website?" her grandmother asked.

"Mama Mia's Perfect Pasta. Their recipe for homemade sauce looked good. So I thought I'd give it a whirl."

"You made the sauce from scratch?"

"It took hours."

Time well spent, in Vale's opinion. After the morning's confrontation with her parents, she'd allowed herself to fall apart for exactly twenty minutes. Then she'd pulled herself together and traded a flurry of text messages with Emmett to fill him in. Afterward, a burst of nervous energy stopped her from completing her to-do list. Stumbling across the Mama Mia website, she decided to try her hand at Italian cuisine.

Crunching loudly, Natty made a point of eating half of her salad. With a huff, she set the bowl aside. She inched her dinner plate toward the center of the table.

Blythe placed her untouched meal before the child. "You can have my dinner, Natty. I'm not hungry. I have a three-alarm headache that won't quit."

Iris cast her a worried glance. "Blythe, if you aren't feeling well, go and lie down."

"You don't mind?"

"Not at all. If you're hungry later, we'll bring something up. Try to sleep."

Blythe pushed back her chair. "Thanks, Nana." With a nod to Vale and Emmett, she left.

Natty slurped up a mouthful of noodles. Swallowing, she gave Iris a curious glance. "Shouldn't she go home to Booker?"

"She's staying tonight."

"But why is Blythe sleeping here?"

Dodging the query, Iris regarded Emmett. He'd finished his plate. "Emmett, would you like another serving?"

"No, thank you."

Natty clinked her fork against her glass in a none-too-subtle ploy to draw Iris's attention. "Aren't married people supposed to stay in the same house?"

"Mostly, they do."

"Is Blythe mad at Booker? She's been at your house an awful lot. Has she been sleeping here too?"

Iris tapped the side of Natty's plate. "Eat your dinner. When you're finished, we'll make a plate for your mother." Ana was at her second job.

"She'll be starving when she gets home. Can we make her two plates?"

Vale chuckled. "No worries, Natty. We'll send you home with lots of food."

By dinner's end, the child had managed to devour a second plate of spaghetti. Vale made a mental note to cook the recipe again soon. Given Ana's busy work schedule, she'd appreciate a ready-made dinner to enjoy with her daughter.

Emmett began clearing plates.

Iris shooed him away. "Why don't you and Vale go for a walk?" She placed salad bowls into a stack. "It's a beautiful evening. Natty will help me clear the table."

"I will?" Natty hopped off her chair. "Can't I go with Vale and Emmett?" Her awareness of the adult need for alone time was nonexistent.

Iris handed her the salad bowls. "Carry them inside, dear," she instructed. "Your mother is picking you up soon. I can't have you wandering the earth when she arrives."

Taking the cue, Vale led Emmett through the garden gate. The sun dipped behind the trees. They walked along in the golden light holding hands.

Emmett sent her a swift glance. "How did you leave it with your parents this morning?"

"They both sensed my need for space. Honestly, my emotions are all over the place."

"Long term?"

"I'm not sure. I'm nowhere near the forgiveness stage. I doubt either of my parents will get in touch. They'll wait for me to reach out."

"There's no hurry, Vale. You have every right to need some distance."

A maple tree's low-lying branch curved over the sidewalk. Absently, Vale trailed her hands through the leaves.

"I haven't mentioned this morning to Nana. There wasn't time when she got home from the shop." Slowing her pace, Vale plucked a leaf from the branch. "Not that it matters. I'm sure my mother will fill her in soon. As if my grandmother needs more to worry about."

"Meaning Blythe? I got the impression Natty was onto something." Releasing the leaf, Vale watched it flutter to the ground.

When she remained silent, Emmett slowed his gait. "Did I ask the wrong question?" He brushed a lock of hair from her cheek. "If Blythe is having problems on the home front, it's none of my business. I didn't mean to make you uncomfortable."

"No. It's all right." Taking his hand, Vale resumed walking. There seemed no point in denying the obvious. "Blythe's marriage is a little rocky at the moment."

"So Natty was right. Blythe hasn't been visiting—she's also staying at your grandmother's house."

Vale nodded. "I wish I knew how to comfort her."

"Just be there for her, whenever she needs to talk."

They reached the corner of the street. A car drove past. Tugging her gently forward, Emmett turned left, away from the glare of the setting sun.

Drawing her closer, he draped an arm across her shoulder. "What's the final decision on your bedroom furniture?" he asked. "Are you selling it online, or should we rent a truck?"

Affection warmed Vale. A more welcome emotion than the pain and confusion she'd struggled with all day. Emmett was steering the conversation to lighter topics, no doubt to lift her mood.

"Listing online doesn't make sense. How will I show the furniture to potential buyers?"

"It *would* involve lots of driving back and forth."

Five hours each way, she mused. *What if it takes weeks to find a buyer?* There was also the issue of packing up the rest of her apartment. Clothing, the best pickings from her kitchenware—a tall order.

"Emmett, do you mind if we rent a truck? Tackle the job together?"

"I thought you'd never ask." He smiled, clearly pleased. "Should we make the drive next weekend? I'm off on Saturday."

"Unfortunately, I'm not. Detta and Nana are having a sale at Green Iris. I'll be working until closing."

"What about the following weekend? We can pack up the rest of your apartment, then stay at Grand Regency on Saturday night. Have you ever been there? They have a great Sunday brunch."

Vale's pulse jumped. Aside from lingering kisses while they watched movies in his living room, Emmett had been the perfect gentleman.

For long enough.

She drew him to a standstill. "Are you propositioning me?" A fizzy delight swam in her blood.

It deepened to longing when fire banked in his gaze. "I'm asking if you're ready to take our relationship to the next level. I'm ready. I've been ready since our first date at Rue de Jean."

Pausing, he coasted his thumb across the sensitive skin of her lower lip, and she trembled. Vale looked up at him with an exquisite blend of expectation and wonder. She was suddenly breathless.

"I *am* certain I'm in love with you, Vale. I fell for you the very first night—when I brought your sister home, and you defended her honor in your bare feet and old bathrobe. You're brave, and you never give yourself enough credit. You're more steadfast than anyone I know, although I doubt you see the trait in yourself. Which is why I'm completely, no holds barred, in love with you."

Pulling in a breath, Emmett reined himself in. He scraped a hand through his hair.

"Hey, if I'm going overboard, just say the word." A question settled in his eyes.

One she readily answered. "I love you too, Emmett."

"You do?"

"Totally."

"Should I make that reservation at the Grand Regency? I want our first night together to be special."

"I do too." On tiptoes, Vale pressed a kiss to his mouth.

It was all the encouragement he needed to take her into his arms.

Chapter 34

"Nice walk?" Her grandmother dunked another pot into the sudsy water. Pausing, she regarded Vale closely. "The expression on your face—why, I can almost see bluebirds fluttering around your head. Like something out of a Disney movie."

Vale released a dreamy breath. "That's about right."

"You're in love." Iris gave a knowing look. "Don't attempt to deny it."

"All right. I won't."

"Where's Emmett?"

"He went home."

"You just missed Ana. She picked up Natty five minutes ago."

"How's Blythe?" Her euphoria melting away, Vale glanced at the ceiling.

Iris rinsed the pot. "Out for the count."

She's asleep at nine o'clock? "Are you sure?" Normally Blythe stayed up late.

"Well, the lights are off in her room. Either she's holding a séance, or she's dozed off." Setting the pot aside, Iris released a weary breath. "I hope the conversation goes well when she talks to Booker next week. They'll have the entire day together, and enough time to discuss everything they need to do to fix their marriage. I just wish I could shake this feeling."

"A feeling about what?"

"I can't pin it down. It's not good. My intuition is firing on all cylinders."

Iris held great stock in her feminine intuition, as if she possessed the ability to glimpse the future and forestall any possible calamity. A silly notion, in Vale's estimation. Sometimes life knocked you down when you weren't prepared. The trick was learning to roll with the punches.

"Nana, relax. Blythe is having one of her bad days, that's all. Don't read more into it."

The remark did nothing to allay the concern darkening her grandmother's eyes. "I can't help but wonder if I'll celebrate one granddaughter's wedding the same year the other gets divorced," she admitted. "All I've ever wanted is for both of you to be happy."

"Don't get ahead of yourself. I'm not ready to mail out wedding invitations, and Blythe *is* still married. Stay positive. There's every chance she'll work out her problems with Booker on the tenth."

"It's strange, hearing you take the optimistic view. You've always been my glass-half-empty grandchild." With bemusement, Iris shook her head. "Emmett has been good for you. I'm glad he came into your life."

"Me too." Vale approached the sink. "Nana, I'll finish cleaning the kitchen. Why don't you put your feet up and watch TV?"

"Actually, I'd rather soak in a hot bath." Iris started toward the foyer. "Have a good night, pumpkin."

"You too."

Taking her time, Vale cleaned the last of the pots. She finished stacking the dishwasher. Leaning against the counter, she pulled her phone from her pocket.

With excitement she navigated to the Grand Regency's website. A lavish array of photos popped onto the screen. The bedroom suites were plush, inviting. She imagined spending hours making love with Emmett in one of the king-size beds.

Anxiety darted through her. *I have exactly* no *alluring lingerie.*

They'd waited this long for intimacy. No way would she pack old bras and panties for the trip. Or her ratty bathrobe. Wasn't there a lingerie store in Queen Village? A quick search provided the answer. Yoni's Intimates was located a mere block from Green Iris. Next week she'd find time to stop by.

Nor did she have a current scrip for the pill. When had she last *needed* the little pink pill? Her relationship with Emmett was the first one in years. No doubt he'd take care of protection, but what about the long term? She needed to make an appointment with a gynecologist soon.

When is my period due? After waiting for intimacy, she didn't want to ruin the big moment. Or be forced to reschedule their night at the Grand Regency because she hadn't been keeping up with her calendar.

Vale's pulse thumped in her throat. The last weeks had been so busy—

Dry-mouthed, she thumbed open the calendar app. Her menstrual cycle was dependably regular. As predictable as the seasons. Except now, it wasn't.

Her period was late.

Seriously late.

Chapter 35

Water gurgled as it swirled down the drain.

Wiping the moisture from the mirror, Iris gave herself a mental pat on the back. Of all the renovations she'd made to the house she'd owned for nearly forty years, the whirlpool tub in her private bathroom was the smartest. Nothing set her mood right like a long soak with the tub's jets kneading the tension from her muscles.

Steering a nightgown over her head, Iris walked into her bedroom. Reaching for her robe, she considered her options. Climb into bed and read for an hour? Or return downstairs? Vale might enjoy sharing a cup of chamomile tea. After all the ups and downs in the girl's life, she'd finally met the perfect man. Discussing Emmett until they readied for bed seemed the perfect way to end the day.

She went into the hallway.

A puddle of light seeped from beneath Blythe's door. A low murmur came from the room.

Rapping lightly, Iris poked her head inside. She was surprised to find her granddaughter running a brush through her hair, her phone glued to her ear.

"Hold on." Covering the phone, Blythe told her, "It's Rihanna. We're meeting for a late dinner. You remember her, don't you?"

Who could forget the effervescent sales rep? Her friendship with Blythe dated back to high school.

"Blythe, it's after nine o'clock." With dismay, she assessed her granddaughter's sallow complexion. Dark traces from exhaustion gave her eyes a puffy appearance. "If you're hungry, why not have something here? I was just going downstairs to ask Vale if she'd like a cup of tea. We'll join you while you raid the fridge."

Her granddaughter waved off the suggestion. "Nana, I haven't seen Rihanna in weeks. We need to catch up."

"What about your headache?"

The dresser drawer rattled as Blythe pulled it open. "I took a nap, which did the trick. I feel loads better." She pulled out mascara, eye shadow, and a tube of lip gloss.

Iris hid her disappointment. "Well, all right. Don't stay out too late."

"I won't."

Downstairs, all the lights were doused. Another surprise, and Iris paused in the darkened foyer. She knew Vale wasn't in her bedroom. Where was she?

Moonlight streamed through the living room. In the cold light draping the couch, Iris caught sight of her. Vale's legs were drawn up to her chest, her gaze unfocused. An unmistakable air of distress surrounded her.

Iris flicked on a lamp. "What's wrong, pumpkin?"

"Everything." Vale waited until she joined her before adding, "Why can't I ever catch a break? Every time I start to pull my life together, something gets in the way. My stupidity, mostly."

A harsh judgment, given all her granddaughter had been through. "You're not stupid. Far from it. Whatever has convinced you that you are?"

For a tense moment, Vale refused to answer. Her attention slid to the window, as if searching the night for answers. Searching for a reprieve. The persistent intuition bothering Iris for hours put a heaviness on her heart. Was her intuition off the mark? Worry over Blythe often dominated her thoughts—was Vale the one in trouble?

A spasm racked Vale's face. "I'm pregnant."

The declaration hung between them. Speechless, Iris tried to process the shocking announcement.

Her silence went unnoticed.

"It's not Emmett's child—we haven't been together. I got pregnant in Pittsburgh. I told you all about it, Nana—the night I came into your bedroom and woke you up. When I asked you to stop giving Blythe a hard time."

"We had quite a wide-ranging conversation that night." She recalled Vale's embarrassment when she'd mentioned sleeping with the man in Pittsburgh.

"One stupid night of tequila and stranger-sex, and here I am. Paying for another reckless mistake." Self-loathing glazed her granddaughter's features. "What's wrong with me? I feel like I'm carrying a curse. And I love Emmett."

"I know you do."

"How am I supposed to tell him? Or should I just break it off? With single parenting on the horizon, I can't expect him to stay with me."

"Slow down, pumpkin. You're certain you're late?"

Grimly, Vale nodded.

"You're not jumping to conclusions?" Iris feared she was grasping at straws. "No woman's menstrual cycle is exact."

"Well, mine is pretty darn close. It's never off by more than a day or two."

An objection rose inside Iris. Stifling it, she pressed her lips together. Prior to menopause, her cycle had also been impressively reliable. A trait plainly inherited by her granddaughter.

"The night in Pittsburgh . . . did you count back?"

"It was the first thing I did. I'm sure I was ovulating. The one time in my life I slept with a stranger—the *only* time I've ever had unprotected sex." With a hollow laugh, Vale swiped at her watery eyes. "I must be cursed. Nana, you have no idea how little sex I've had for a woman my age. I'm practically a monk. Now Emmett has come into my life, and I've ruined everything."

"Let's not get ahead of ourselves. I'll get dressed, and we'll run out for a home pregnancy test. It's the only way to know for sure."

At the suggestion, Vale slumped against the couch's soft cushions. "Let's wait until morning. Right now, I want to go upstairs. Pull the covers over my head and—"

Cutting off, Vale looked past her. Embarrassment bled across her cheeks.

When she straightened, as if preparing to ward off a blow, Iris's keen intuition—the dependable sixth sense that had been bothering her all day—sent alarm bells ringing through her. With dismay, she followed Vale's line of sight.

To Blythe, standing in the foyer's shadows, her shoulders trembling with shock or outrage or both.

Chapter 36

Blythe—dressed for a night out in pencil-thin jeans and heels—came into the living room. Her eyes locked on Vale.

"You're *pregnant?*"

Vale looked away. How much of the conversation had her sister overheard? Too much, apparently.

She lowered her elbows to her knees. "It appears so."

"Well, that's just perfect."

"Blythe, I don't need the piling on. I feel bad enough as it is."

"She's right," Iris put in. "Don't pile on. If it's true, Vale has a lot to sort out."

The warnings swept past her sister. Like skipping stones racing across water.

"Let me get this straight. You're pregnant from a one-night stand? What are the odds?"

"Drop it, okay?"

"You slept with a random guy in Pittsburgh? Who does that?"

Condemnation rimmed her sister's voice. On her face, Vale saw only revulsion.

The goodwill they'd forged during the last weeks—the affection and the love, the small overtures that marked the beginning of their burgeoning trust—it all fell away. For a split second, Vale felt nothing.

Then anger vibrated through her. Where did Blythe get off, casting judgment?

Her attention narrowing, Blythe halted on the opposite side of the coffee table. "Haven't you ever heard of contraception?" She didn't seem to trust herself to come nearer. "This is perfect. My sister gets laid *once*, and she'll have a baby bump by summer. Are you ready for a child? This is one time you can't run away, Vale. Not with a child depending on you."

"Stop judging me!" Vale felt sick then, and horrified. She was twenty-nine, old enough to raise a child. Why did Blythe assume she wasn't up to the task?

Because my reputation precedes me.

Not this time. Even if the news removed Emmett from her life. Even if he walked away.

The possibility shook Vale as she rose. "Why don't you get your own life in order before you start criticizing mine?" She rounded on her sister. "You've screwed up your marriage, but you're not interested in fixing it. You ought to spend less time going out and more time dealing with your own problems."

"I'm not criticizing you!" Blythe's voice rose in pitch. "I'm asking if you're ready to raise a child."

"Get away from me, Blythe. You have no right to stand there grilling me."

"It's a simple question. You don't even have a good job. Helping out at Green Iris doesn't count."

Their grandmother leaped to her feet. "Girls—stop shouting at each other!"

The command threw the room into silence. Then Blythe choked out a sob. The pitiful sound brought Vale closer, an apology forming on her lips. Blythe wasn't grilling her. The news had surprised her, that's all. In her clumsy way, she was only trying to help.

Blythe's phone buzzed.

"Rihanna, hi." She turned away. "Yeah, I'm coming—just running late. See you in ten."

Vale watched helplessly as she left the house. The sharp glare of headlights cut through the living room windows. The car sped down the street.

Vale swallowed down her shame. Why had she allowed Blythe to bait her?

She glanced at her grandmother. "I didn't handle that well."

"Don't heap all the blame on yourself. Your sister *was* out of line."

A distinction of no consequence. Blythe wasn't herself. Her life was in shambles. Vale knew this. Why allow the argument to escalate? Doing so put their newfound relationship in jeopardy.

A concern Iris plainly sensed. "You and your sister have a history of animosity," she pointed out. "Those habits are hard to break. It's easier to fall into an argument than to hear each other calmly. In time, you'll get there. Just have patience."

"Who's Rihanna?"

"An old friend. Blythe is meeting her for a late dinner."

Would they roam the bars afterward? Vale hoped not. Allowing the bad feelings to fester until morning wasn't a great option.

Better to patch things up tonight when Blythe returned.

Chapter 37

The sound of running water shook Vale awake.

A hard object pressed against her cheek. With a groan, she wedged it out. A mystery novel she'd borrowed from Emmett. Placing it on the nightstand, she listened to Blythe knocking around the guest bathroom, readying for bed.

The door to her sister's room clicked shut. Vale swung her feet to the floor.

There's no time like the present.

A bout of nerves accompanied her across the hallway.

"Blythe?" She leaned against the doorjamb. "Can I come in?"

The light beneath the door vanished.

"Blythe, c'mon. I only need a minute."

"Go away."

A slurred command, and Vale's heart sank. Clearly Blythe was back to her old tricks. Reasoning with her would have to wait until morning.

Returning to her room, Vale fell back onto the bed. Fully clothed, too exhausted to pull off her jeans and climb under the sheets. Too worried about her sister. Dousing the lamp, she fell into a deep, dreamless sleep.

Past midnight, Vale woke again. Anxiety pulled her into a sitting position. Outside an owl hooted, the sound lonely and fierce.

It seemed a warning. And although Vale didn't share her grandmother's belief in female intuition, she couldn't shake the feeling that something was terribly wrong.

Blythe.

An urgency carried her into the hallway. She turned on the lights. The glare snapping her awake, she strode into her sister's room.

A knife's edge of light followed her inside, illuminating the clothes flung on the floor. Black pumps and chunky gold earrings, partially hidden beneath the bed. Her sister lay beneath the covers, her face pressed into a pillow.

Vale's frantic attention halted on the nightstand. A small orange bottle spilled white tablets across the surface.

Sleeping pills.

Frantic, she checked Blythe's pulse. It was weak, barely discernible.

"Blythe, wake up."

She didn't respond. Fear threatened to immobilize Vale. Blythe had mixed alcohol and sleeping medication—a deadly combination.

The prospect of losing her sister galvanized Vale. Yanking down the bedspread, she rolled her over. The strong stench of whiskey accosted her. Blythe's breathing was shallow.

"Wake up, Blythe! Please, sweetie—wake up!"

The bedroom light snapped on. Iris rushed to the bed.

In a panic, Vale shouted, "Nana, call 911!"

Chapter 38

In the corridor, a gurney clattered past. Voices rose and fell as the hospital's night shift handed over the reins to the morning staff.

Vale dragged her eyes open. Her grandmother continued to sleep in the chair pressed up beside hers. They'd both dozed off in the middle of the night after the ER staff transferred Blythe to the semiprivate room.

On Iris's shoulder, her rolled-up jacket served as a makeshift pillow. An uncomfortable solution at best. With a yawn, Vale appraised the hospital room's second empty bed. She'd suggested Iris stretch out there to catch a few winks. Who would be the wiser? Iris had refused. No doubt she'd awaken soon with a stiff neck.

A nurse with gray eyes and a purposeful gait came into the room. She strode past the empty bed. "Good morning."

Vale rubbed the sleep from her eyes. "Is it morning?" Outside the window, clouds scuttled across the grayish sky.

"Just about." The nurse checked the IV and Blythe's pulse.

Vale shifted anxiously, clasped her hands together. "How's she doing?"

"Her vitals are good." The nurse glanced at the monitors, then back at Vale. "Is she a relative?"

"Blythe is my younger sister."

With a satisfied nod, the nurse said, "Once Blythe wakes up, she'll feel lethargic and will need to take it easy until tomorrow. Make sure she drinks plenty of fluids after she's discharged." The nurse arched a brow. "You might also want to remind her *not* to take sleeping medication if she's consumed alcohol."

"Believe me, it's the first thing on my agenda."

A wisp of last night's panic skated through Vale's blood. Then gratitude warmed her. In their wisdom, the paramedics had collected up Blythe's sleep meds when they'd arrived at the house. According to the ER staff, it appeared Blythe had taken two pills—double the normal dosage but nowhere near the lethal amount. A misjudgment, not a suicide attempt.

Beside her, Iris stirred. The jacket rolled off her shoulder and into her lap. Wincing, she rubbed her neck. "What time is it?"

Vale checked her phone. "It's half past seven."

The nurse chuckled. "You both look like you could use some coffee." She started for the corridor, hesitated. "The cafeteria is open downstairs. Would you like directions?"

Iris shook her head. "Thank you, nurse. I know where the cafeteria is located."

Together they approached the bed. Blythe slept soundly. Vale detected a heartening tint of color returning to her sister's cheeks.

It didn't stop a jolt of fear from pitching through her. "Last night, before the ambulance arrived, I really believed . . ."

When her voice broke, Iris hugged her. "Put it out of mind, pumpkin. We didn't lose your sister."

"We might have, Nana. I can't bear the thought." Goose bumps sprouted on Vale's arms. "I don't want to lose Blythe ever. She's maddening and precious and impossible to understand, and I love her."

"She'll come out of this with flying colors. You'll see." Iris cast Vale an inquisitive glance. "Last night . . . how *did* you know she was in trouble?"

Vale wished she could offer a logical explanation. "I heard an owl hooting outside. It sounds crazy, but it gave me the strongest feeling that Blythe was in trouble. Like it was a signal. The next thing I knew, I was rushing to her bedroom to see if she was all right."

"And here, you've never held much credence in female intuition."

"I may need to reassess my opinion." Silently, Vale resolved to never again tease Iris about her trusty sixth sense.

"Well, I'm glad you're beginning to trust it. I'll wager it means you're beginning to trust yourself too."

And believe in myself. The last weeks had been marked by so many changes. Somehow, Vale had managed them all. Not necessarily in the best way in each instance—she *still* wasn't sure if she wanted to repair her relationship with Bo or Audrey. But she hadn't stumbled beneath any of the challenges she'd faced. She'd kept her footing.

Pulling from the reverie, she brushed a curl from Blythe's forehead. "Why doesn't she wake up?" Impatience mixed with the worry nesting inside Vale as she readjusted the blanket. "I won't feel better until she does."

"Stop pestering her. She needs the rest." Turning away, Iris retrieved her purse from where she'd wedged it behind the chairs. She snapped open a compact. With a gasp, she recoiled from the face staring back at her in the mirror. "I look like death warmed over!"

Vale chuckled. "You look fine." The moment's levity made her feel slightly better. "We both need a hot shower and a day with less excitement. After last night, we've both had our fill."

"Well, there's more to come—for me, at least." From her purse, Iris fished out a hairbrush. She ran it through her hair. "How am I supposed to tell your mother and Grant that Blythe is in the hospital? The news will send them right around the bend."

"Don't tell them. Odds are, Blythe will be released today. Let them trot off to their busy workday at Stern-Belkins none the wiser."

At the suggestion, Iris withered her with a look. "Give your new-found intuition a whirl," she tossed back. "What is your gut telling you?"

That it's not a great idea. "Okay, you're right. They should know." Vale hesitated. "What about Booker? Shouldn't you call him too?"

"Good heavens . . . should I?"

"If I were Booker, I'd want to know if my wife was in the hospital. I'd be angry if I *didn't* know."

"I would too," Iris murmured, the indecision thick in her voice.

"Just give him the basics, Nana. In fact, you should call him first."

"I don't want to upset Blythe by overstepping. I doubt she'll be thrilled that I've told Audrey and Grant. She'll be embarrassed."

"Then call Booker too." Vale nodded toward the bed. "It's not like we can ask her opinion. She's asleep."

"And she's been through enough," Iris said firmly. "Let's wait until she wakes up and weighs in. She might want to call Booker herself. For now, it's enough to notify Audrey and Grant."

Leaving Blythe's husband in the dark felt wrong on so many levels. But Vale knew she'd lost the debate. "Should I go on the caffeine run while you call them?" she offered, although she didn't want to leave Blythe.

Iris dismissed the suggestion. "I'll walk down to the cafeteria. I need to stretch my legs. Do you mind waiting for a cup of coffee? I'd like to have a cup downstairs before calling your mother. I should be alert and peppy before ruining her day."

"Take your time, Nana."

Vale returned to her station by the bed. The first glimmers of daylight spread across Blythe's slumbering form. She looked peaceful, her breathing slow and steady. With affection Vale swiped another stray curl from her brow. Then she twined her fingers through the thick strands tumbling across the pillow.

Wake up, sleepyhead. Vale tugged gently, hoping to rouse her.

No reaction.

Growing impatient, she flicked a sharp finger against Blythe's cheek. A childish maneuver, like she'd done when they were children. As simple a way as any to steer her sister from sleep.

Blythe's eyelids fluttered.

A sign of progress, and Vale bent toward her ear. "Earth to Blythe. Are you picking up signals?"

"Hmm?"

"I know you're in there. C'mon. Open your eyes."

She flicked Blythe's nose. A bit of mischief to drive off the worry.

"Hey!" At last, Blythe's bleary gaze found hers. "What are you doing?" she demanded.

"Waking you up, dimwit." For good measure Vale flicked her cheek. She couldn't bring herself to resist. "Is it working?"

"Stop it!" Blythe's eyes rolled around like marbles before steadying. "Where am I?"

"In the hospital."

"My throat hurts."

Vale winced. *What do you expect when you've had your stomach pumped?* The news could wait until later.

"Would you like to sit up?" She handed over the adjustable control.

A soft whirring, and Blythe lifted into a sitting position. The last remnants of sleep ebbed from her features. On a sharp breath, she noticed the IV winding from her arm.

"I'm in the hospital? How long have I been here?"

"Since last night."

"I don't remember."

"It's all right—you're fine."

Recognition broke across Blythe's face. "I took a sleeping pill." Panicked, she lifted her head from the pillow. "When it didn't work, I took a second one."

Pressing a hand to her shoulder, Vale kept her in place. "Why didn't you read the directions?" Blythe relaxed beneath her touch, and she gentled her tone. "Never mix sleeping meds with booze. Promise you'll never do that again."

"I won't, I swear."

"Good. That's all I needed to hear."

"I didn't mean to harm myself . . . I only wanted to sleep."

"I know, baby. It's all right. You're safe now."

Baby, a term of endearment Vale used long ago. When they were very young, before circumstance built a wall between them.

Hurry up, baby. The school bus is here. The scent of her sister's childhood bedroom suddenly flooded Vale's senses, sweet like fruit on a hot summer day. She recalled Blythe zigzagging past a stuffed bear nearly her size, propped at the base of her bed. Hoisting a book bag onto her back, then hurrying forward to take Vale's hand.

Baby. The word formed a bridge between their hearts. As their eyes locked, Blythe steered her hand past the snaking IV line. She rested her palm on Vale's wrist.

Her expression crumpled.

Tears spilled down her face. "Vale, I'm so sorry. Last night, before I went out—I shouldn't have reacted so badly. You didn't expect to get pregnant. I'm sure you're in shock. You have a lot to sort out, and I should've been supportive."

"It's all right. Stop beating yourself up." Anxiety vibrated through Vale. She'd given her late period exactly zero thought. Not since finding Blythe unconscious last night. If she was pregnant, she *did* have a lot to sort out.

"I'll make it up to you. Help in any way I can. You'll be a great mother. The best."

"*If* I'm pregnant. I'll pick up a test later."

"Either way, I shouldn't have lashed out. Totally the worst reaction when your sister is dealing with a major issue. I should've been there for you." The apology made Blythe's mouth quiver. She attempted a smile but failed miserably. "Can you forgive me? I promise whenever you do have a child, I'll feel only joy. I'll host a spectacular baby shower. Under no circumstances will I allow myself to feel jealousy."

Jealousy? Vale reared back with surprise. *Why would Blythe be jealous?* The heartfelt admission made no sense. If Blythe wanted a baby, all she needed to do was patch things up with Booker and—

Vale blinked. Was Blythe implying Booker was against the idea? Many couples disagreed on when—or if—to become parents. Marriage didn't guarantee a future with children running about.

At the questions rising on her features, Blythe said, "I can't carry a child to term."

The air stretched tight.

"Of course you can." Vale tensed beneath the heaviness raining down between them. Against the sorrow building underneath her rib cage. "You're young, healthy—have as many children as you want."

"I can't. I've had four miscarriages." Blythe's voice was ragged. Sudden resolve broke past the pain hardening her features. "All the miscarriages happened at the beginning of the second trimester. If I tried again, I'd have the same result. Vale, I'm sure about this. I can't have children."

Four miscarriages?

Vale resisted the news. "Does Mom know?" she asked helplessly.

A ridiculous question. As if the practical and goal-driven Audrey could fix the situation.

"No one in the family knows, except Booker. I told him about the first miscarriage. It happened just a few months after our wedding. I thought it was a fluke. Something I'd put behind me once I got pregnant again. I was so excited about having his baby."

"He doesn't know about the other miscarriages?"

"He was in the middle of the season each time. He assumes I've been waiting to try again. I couldn't bring myself to explain that I've been trying all along."

A chill ran down Vale's spine. "I don't understand."

"It's a problem with my uterus—something went wrong, early in Mom's pregnancy with me. The condition is rare . . . I pulled the losing card from the deck." Pausing, Blythe inhaled a deep breath. Then she asked, "Do you know much about embryonic development?"

"I don't," Vale admitted.

"In a female embryo, two ducts are supposed to fuse together. They're called paramesonephric ducts. They look like tiny wings. Once they fuse, they form the female uterus. Mine didn't fuse completely, but I didn't have any way of knowing. My periods have never been very regular, but that's true for lots of women. I didn't have a clue anything was wrong until after the fourth miscarriage."

"What happened then?"

"I finally relented and let Dr. Golovan run tests. I was afraid to get a workup earlier. Deep down, I suppose I knew the results would be devastating."

"Dr. Golovan is your gynecologist?"

"She's wonderful. She never pushed me to have a workup until I was ready."

"Can't anything be done?"

"In some cases, surgery works. My condition is too severe."

Pity swept through Vale. And anger. At life, at the random cards drawn in the genetic shuffle that left her sister—who clearly *wanted* a baby—without the option. Without the ability to bring a child into the world.

Nana had it all wrong—Blythe never cheated on Booker. It all suddenly made sense. *She's been thinking about leaving him because she's unable to carry his child.* Blythe—a perfectionist who demanded achievement in every aspect of her life—couldn't perform a basic function some women took for granted. *She's endured four miscarriages.* She'd bravely tried repeatedly to carry a baby to term, only to watch each attempt disappear in sad rivulets of blood.

"Blythe, there *are* alternatives."

Her sister held up a hand. "I know. We could adopt." Sorrow nearly took her voice. "I just don't know how I'm supposed to ask Booker to give up the chance to have his own child. I don't want to ask him. I don't think I can bear to. Every time I'm convinced that I have the courage to broach the subject, I bail."

"Discuss this with him. Please don't make a unilateral decision about ending your marriage without letting him weigh in. It's not fair to your husband. I know you're scared—I get why you've delayed telling him." Blythe wanted a guarantee he wouldn't regret the decision later, to stay with her.

The remark struck too close to home. "Stop pushing me." Her sister's eyes turned blank as slates.

"Oh, Blythe. I love you. I can't imagine what you've gone through. I just want you to consider if the losses you've endured are driving you toward a bad decision. One that'll break your heart, and Booker's too."

"Stop playing devil's advocate! Do you honestly believe you'll come up with anything I haven't already thought of? I need to make this decision alone." Blythe was suddenly angry, a vivid, animated presence. "Booker is a gifted athlete. Maybe it's better if I let him go. Maybe *that's* why I can't bring myself to tell him about the miscarriages. Because I'm supposed to let him find someone else, a woman who can give him everything—"

As her sister railed, Vale imagined Booker on the pitcher's mound. Planting his feet and then going into his windup. The roar from the stands and the smell of the stadium. The impossible, perfect movement of his body as he executed the throw, the ball leaving his fingers and rocketing through the air.

Blythe is wrong. In her gut, Vale knew Booker would choose her over genetics. Yet she couldn't fault Blythe's logic. It was flawed and tragic, but understandable.

Would she sacrifice their marriage without ever telling Booker why?

Chapter 39

Iris returned juggling a Styrofoam cup and her purse.

"Peaches—you're awake!" Oddly, she followed the remark with a look of consternation. She came to a standstill. "Oh dear."

Vale pried the coffee loose from her fingers. "Now what's the matter?" After the distressing conversation with Blythe, she needed the caffeine boost. *And a good cry,* she mused. She felt heartsick for Blythe.

Iris clapped a hand to her brow. "I spent so much time talking Audrey and Grant out of a tree, I forgot to call Detta. She assumes we're coming in. There's a shipment arriving at noon. The part-time staff won't get in until one o'clock."

From the bed, Blythe huffed out a breath. "Oh, Nana. Why did you tell Mom and Dad about my . . . episode? I'm an adult, not a five-year-old."

"Don't give me that look. You've kept too many secrets from them as it is."

"Because I'm an adult! It's my prerogative."

"Blythe, save your sass for your parents. They'll be here soon enough."

"*What?* Why didn't you tell them not to come?"

"Because they don't listen to me!"

As they fell into a debate, Vale fetched her purse. She effectively brought the bickering to a halt by withdrawing her keys and jingling them loudly.

To her grandmother, she said, "Do you want my wheels? I'll take Lyft home."

"No, I'll stay until Audrey and Grant arrive. I'll call for a ride when I'm ready to leave."

"Okay." Vale pressed a kiss to her sister's brow. Blythe still appeared prickly after their tense conversation. "Behave until Nana breaks you out of this prison."

"I will."

"Hopefully they'll discharge you this afternoon. Oh, and drink plenty of fluids—doctor's orders."

"Got it." Sudden emotion made Blythe's eyes glisten. "Vale . . . thanks for everything. I love you."

"I love you too."

A small gasp escaped their grandmother. Iris dabbed at her eyes.

"No crying," Vale teased, "and don't worry about Detta. I'll run home, grab a shower, and go in. We'll handle the delivery together."

"You're a lifesaver, pumpkin."

Vale strode into the bustling corridor. A doctor in scrubs hurried past; three orderlies talked loudly as they hurried behind him. Nearing the nurses' station, Vale slowed her gait. Pain darted through her lower back. She pressed a hand to her spine, and droplets of coffee leaped from the cup.

As they splattered across the floor, cramps spread through her abdomen in a burning, familiar trail. Her monthly. She was starting her period.

I'm not pregnant.

She nearly whooped with joy.

Behind the nurses' station, a woman with a harried expression shuffled through paperwork. Blue scrubs, with a pencil balanced precariously behind her ear. Vale scanned her badge: Dr. Emily Bolton.

Vale cleared her throat.

"May I help you?"

"Dr. Bolton, hello. I hate to bother you." With a twinge of embarrassment, she dropped her voice to a whisper. "Can I get a pad or a tampon? My, uh, monthly bill came due."

"Of course. Wait here."

After Vale finished up in the restroom, she tapped out a text to Iris:

Got my period. NOT pregnant!

Her phone pinged. A string of happy-face emoticons flashed across the screen.

Chuckling, Vale left the hospital with a bounce to her step.

Elation accompanied her as she drove through the morning traffic. The sky appeared faultlessly blue. Even the bumper-to-bumper traffic of Philadelphians wending their way to work couldn't dent her mood. Because there was no startling news to drop on Emmett's head. She wouldn't have to reveal the foolish mistake she'd made in Pittsburgh the week the Crafty Cocktail burned down.

Her relationship with Emmett wasn't in danger. Perhaps, in time, their love would lead to marriage.

Vale's past relationships were too short-lived and infrequent to make her a romantic. Yet she couldn't stop the notion of coasting down an aisle in an old-fashioned gown of white lace from overtaking her thoughts. Emmett, waiting at the altar in a dashing black tux. The church festooned with flowers.

Whispering promises and exchanging rings. A long honeymoon in Hawaii or the Bahamas. They'd stroll down the beach in the morning before spending the day in their hotel room making love.

The reverie made her grin. When had she ever spun sugar-sweet notions about marriage?

Never.

The reason was obvious. She was waiting for Emmett to come into her life. *And I'm so glad he did.*

Her grandmother's Victorian came into view. Spotting a car at the curb, her elation vanished.

Diamond-bright glints of light scattered across the hood of the red Porsche Carrera GT. Instinctively she knew the sports car belonged to the Phillies' star pitcher—the brother-in-law she'd never met.

A hunch quickly verified. Vale watched Booker climb the front steps with something in his arms. A box. Like the other boxes already stacked on the porch.

In slow motion, she got out of the car. The intrusion went unnoticed.

"Hey, Booker," she called out, feeling the need to alert him to her presence.

He glanced over his shoulder.

"Do you need help?" Vale ascended the steps.

"That's the last one." Straightening, he rubbed his hands down his jeans.

Staring was impolite, but she couldn't help herself. How often did the average fan meet one of the MLB's top players? *Even one married to my sister.* Booker was all muscle and taller than expected. Lean, without an ounce of body fat. His eyes seemed a bit too small for his broad, square face. Yet they were bright, alert, with a hint of self-effacing charm. She sensed kindness in their depths.

Snapping out of her stupor, she stuck out her hand. "I'm Vale."

The moment's awkwardness wasn't lost on Booker. "Yeah, I know who you are. It's nice to meet you." After they shook hands, he frowned. "Man, I wish we were meeting under better circumstances."

"You and me both."

He tipped his head to the side. "You don't look anything like your pics."

"What pics?"

"The ones of you and Blythe as kids."

A surprised breath escaped her mouth. "My sister has photos of us together?" Until recently, it would've made more sense for Blythe to burn her in effigy.

"Are you kidding? She loaded a ton of them onto her phone. Right before we got married."

She did? They hadn't been on speaking terms the year Blythe tied the knot.

Flabbergasted, Vale asked, "How am I different from the pics?"

"Cleaner, definitely." Despite the sorrow in his eyes, Booker flashed a grin. "There's one shot in particular that's priceless. You're seven or eight and covered in mud. And I mean, head to toe. You must've been some tomboy."

"You have no idea."

"Not Blythe, though. She's a total clean freak."

"Actually, she *was* a sporty kid. And she always had a million friends. She just wasn't into tromping through the woods. I was more of a loner."

"Me too," Booker said. "At big functions, I still get tongue-tied. Except when Blythe's with me. She can talk up a storm with anyone. Never feels bashful at all."

"Thank our mother. She gets the trait from Audrey. Nothing ruffles Mom's composure."

"True."

The conversation dwindled. Vale considered wishing him good luck at tonight's game. The idea was promptly dismissed. She couldn't recall who the Phillies were playing, and Booker wasn't here in his sports-hero persona.

She toed the closest box. "Blythe's stuff?"

"Just some extras things she wants to keep at Iris's place, long-term."

Or permanently. "Like what?"

"Blow dryers, brushes, nail polish, a massage gun—man, don't make me go through the list."

"The glam-queen habits . . . also from our mother." Vale bobbed a thumb at herself. "Want to guess who didn't inherit the trait?"

The remark seemed to relax Booker the slightest degree. "You should see how much stuff your sister brings on a trip. If I didn't know how to pack light, we'd spend more on baggage fees than tickets." Brow furrowing, he shoved his hands into his pockets. The tension returned to his features. "She was supposed to stop by this morning to pick everything up. When she didn't show, I figured I'd save her the trip. I'd give anything to know why she's . . ."

His attention fell to his feet.

"So unhappy?" Vale prodded. "Between you and me, I'm sorry she is."

The remark lifted Booker's head. "If it's not out of line to ask, would you talk to her? I don't want to lose Blythe. She's the best part of my life. I've told her it won't always be this hard—I'm nearing retirement. Just a year or two to go. Then we'll have a normal life. No more away games or long seasons when we're hardly together. Half of the guys in pro ball lose their wives before their career ends. I don't want to lose mine."

The plea in his eyes touched Vale deeply. The guy was killing it on the field, but all he really cared about was her sister. On impulse, she hugged him. The gesture startled him, and he began to draw away.

"I'll do my best," she promised, squeezing him back into the hug.

Booker patted her lightly on the back. "Thanks." Smiling, he eased away and started down the steps.

"Booker?"

He glanced back up at her. "Yeah?"

"There's something else. Blythe is okay, but, well . . . she's in the hospital." Before second thoughts could intrude, Vale rattled out the rest.

The news put alarm on his face. With a hasty farewell, he jumped into his car. Vale watched the Porsche zoom off toward the hospital.

The first bright sparks of inspiration caught Vale unawares. Darting around the edges of her mind like a mischievous child waving a Fourth of July sparkler. Begging her to follow.

There was a way to help her sister and Booker.

Chapter 40

When he entered the hospital room, Blythe's heart overturned.

In a hoodie to avoid detection, Booker swept in like a stallion at full gallop. His attention missed Iris, thumbing aimlessly through a paperback beside her granddaughter's bed. He made it halfway across the room before losing all forward momentum, his eyes frantic and his mouth slack as he came to a halt. He was clearly spooked by the beeping machines and the IV tethered to Blythe's arm.

The paperback dropped to the floor. Iris leaped to her feet. "Booker!" He didn't respond.

Taking his face in her hands, Iris steered his gaze to hers. She promptly launched into a ramble. "Blythe is fine. It's just a little mishap. Nothing to worry about. She'll be released later today, after the attending physician makes her rounds. There's a delay, something about a surgery that's been bumped up . . . I'm sorry I didn't call you. I couldn't decide if I should. After Blythe woke up, she felt we shouldn't bother you." Iris released him. "How *did* you—"

Blythe looked away from the accusation rising on her husband's face. "Vale told him, Nana," she said.

"Ah. I see." Masking her confusion, her grandmother inched toward the corridor. "Why don't I wait outside for Audrey and Grant? I'm sure they'll be here any minute."

Iris left an uneasy silence in her wake.

Breaking it, Booker approached the bed. "You *weren't* going to tell me?"

"You had a game last night. Another one today."

"What's that got to do with it?"

Blythe didn't like how he was putting her on the defensive. "You're back on the road tomorrow," she countered, stiffening against the sorrow building inside her. Churning past her ability to hold herself together. "You don't handle changes to your routine well. It messes up your pitching."

"This isn't an inconvenience. You're my wife. Screw my routine."

"I didn't want to wake you!" Couldn't pull herself past the shame to call him.

"So if I'm ever rushed to the hospital and you're not around, just keep it to myself? Don't let you know? Thanks, babe. I'm glad we got that straightened out. I sure as hell wouldn't want to inconvenience you." Booker scraped a hand through his hair. "Our marriage is in worse shape than I thought."

"Stop putting words in my mouth. That isn't what I meant."

"What *do* you mean, Blythe? I feel like we've been shadow-boxing for months."

A surge of adrenaline flooded her. She welcomed the sensation, how it made her alert. How it vaulted past the reservations that had kept her silent for too long.

"Our marriage *is* in trouble, Booker." She let the statement sink in for an awful moment. "Not because of you. This is all on me."

She gave him the basics. The diagnosis from Dr. Golovan. A series of miscarriages beyond the one he knew about. By the time she finished, she'd taken all the color from his face.

He rocked from one foot to the other, the way he did before jogging to the pitcher's mound. Before he steeled himself to face the thunder from the stands and the jostling reporters and the cameras recording his every movement—aspects of his fame that Booker tolerated as the price of glory.

He folded his arms, clearly resisting the news. "We can't have children."

"Not biological children, no."

"Should we get a second opinion?"

"It won't make a difference. I'm unable to carry a baby to term."

"And you've known this for . . . ?"

"Months. Longer, really. I guess I suspected the worst even before I let Dr. Golovan do a workup." Blythe looked away. "Booker, if you want a divorce, it's okay."

His glazed eyes found hers. *"What?"*

"It's okay if you want out." A sob tightened her throat. She swallowed it down. "I get it. You're an incredible man with rare gifts—why wouldn't you want to pass them on to your own child? Totally understandable, and I won't stand in your way. We'll both find someone else," she added, knowing she never would.

Booker stilled. Washed the last traces of anger and disbelief from his features. He wasn't a man comfortable with allowing his emotions to override his self-control. She knew he was trying to rein himself in, regain the focus that made him such a fearsome opponent on the ball field.

Abandoning her, he pivoted toward the corridor.

"Where are you going?" Blythe demanded.

He looked at her as if she were mad. "To call the coach. I'm not playing tonight. I have to take care of you."

Have to. She couldn't tell if he *wanted* to.

"Don't put that on me! I have my family. This isn't on you," she said, as if he didn't matter. Booker *was* her family—the center of it.

The remark grazed his composure like a fast punch. Then his expression changed. It gained the fierce determination that made him nearly invincible the instant he wrapped his fingers around a baseball. Pocketing the phone, he retraced his steps.

"I love you, Blythe. I don't want a divorce." He sat on the side of the bed. "How many miscarriages?"

The sadness in his voice hurt more than his anger. "Why does it matter? I can't have your children."

Taking care to avoid the IV line, Booker leaned close. "It matters because you went through it alone. I wasn't there for you." He brushed his lips across hers. Through the blur of tears, she realized he was crying too. "When you came by in the middle of the night . . . you meant to tell me all of this. Am I right? I didn't give you a chance."

Blythe nodded. "I tried to tell you that night. Then you brought up Miles and Kiki getting divorced. You said you didn't want to talk about us until—"

Booker winced. "I got a day off, on the tenth," he supplied.

She nodded.

"Babe, I'm so sorry. I'll make it up to you." Booker kissed her deeply, pressing her head into the pillow, nearly climbing in beside her when she began kissing him back urgently.

The bed squeaked. The sound drew them apart.

Blythe offered a watery smile. "Go to work." Sitting up, she gave him a gentle push.

"Not yet."

"It's almost noon. You're already late."

"Babe, I don't care."

In the corridor, voices rose. Her mother's, then her grandmother's. A scuffle broke out, and something thumped to the floor. Knowing Iris, she'd formed a one-woman blockade to halt Audrey and Grant from entering.

With dismay, Blythe lowered her head to the pillow. "I won't be released for hours," she muttered. "Why don't they go to the office, and come back later? We can talk tonight."

Booker shot her a knowing glance. "They've earned a doctorate in helicopter parenting." He chuckled. "They've got to stop coddling you."

Blythe adored her parents, but they went overboard with the 24-7 surveillance. "You think? *You* tell them." They needed another trip to Aruba, like yesterday.

Her husband got to his feet. "Are you giving me permission?" Normally he treated Audrey and Grant with respect as they vacillated between acceptable behavior and hero worship of their son-in-law. "Because if you are, I'm going. I'll tell them to get lost, but I'll do it nicely."

Blythe rubbed her wet nose. "Are you serious?" When Booker started rolling his shoulders, like he was readying for a pitch, she said, "Promise Mom and Dad I'll call the minute I'm released. They can pick me up then."

"Got it." Limber and steely-eyed, he started for the door.

"Booker?"

"Yeah?"

"How long can you stay?"

He grinned. "As long as you want."

Chapter 41

After a quick shower, Vale changed into clean clothes. She grabbed her laptop and went into Green Iris.

The shipment of hanging baskets—petunias, million bells, and impatiens—arrived promptly at noon. Detta gladly allowed her to ferry all the baskets to the second floor for display. Vale was finishing up when part-time staffers Miranda and Teddy came into the shop. They immediately set about helping customers.

During a lull in the afternoon, Vale slipped into the stockroom. At a table in the back, she flipped open her laptop.

Am I really considering this? In the search bar, she typed: surrogate parenting.

Her fingers flew across the keyboard. Navigating to a national site, Vale carefully read the information. Searching closer to home, she found another site located right here in Philadelphia. Then she compared the information. She was a good age to become a surrogate. Healthy, without preexisting medical issues. She didn't have children of her own, a prerequisite on *both* sites for women—*gestational carriers* in the parlance—who weren't related to the baby's parents. Undeterred, she found three blogs written by surrogate mothers. Each woman had carried a baby in a private adoption agreement for a close family member. For a sister, in two instances; for a younger brother and his wife, in another.

There was a work-around. A solution *if* Vale chose to take the leap. *Assuming Blythe and Booker are willing to jump with me.*

A more thorough search brought up a blog written seven years ago by a woman living in Harrisburg. She'd carried a baby for her older sister, a cancer survivor. Which led Vale to a family law site, helpfully written by a Philadelphia firm.

Excitement and reluctance vied for prominence in her heart. Excitement at the possibility of helping Blythe and Booker by carrying their baby. Reluctance over what the process would entail. A year or more from her life, depending on how quickly IVF worked. Discomfort during pregnancy, at least in the final months. The emotional turmoil it would entail to carry a baby that wasn't her own. A child she would bring into the world, then hand over to her sister. On the upside, Blythe and Booker would have interesting stories to share with Vale's niece or nephew when their bundle of joy was old enough to learn the details.

A dose of reality put a damper on her mood. Go through with this, and she'd put off any plans she and Emmett might wish to make regarding *their* future.

A sensible bolt of anxiety shot through her as she fell back in the chair. This would be asking a lot of Emmett. *I'm crazy about you, Emmett, but can we dial back the romance for a year or so? Just until I have my sister's baby and get my body back in shape.*

Ditching the thought, Vale drummed her fingers on the table. Considering, she pulled the laptop closer. Emmett wouldn't stand in her way. Sure, the decision might throw him at the outset. But Vale trusted in his devotion. He wouldn't object, not if she was sure she wanted to go through with this.

Which left the big question: Was she willing to make the sacrifice for her sister? For once, she didn't allow self-doubt to override her best instincts.

Yes, I am.

How many chances do any of us get to make a real difference? To alter a loved one's life—to mark our hope in the future by bringing a child into the world?

With newfound determination, Vale navigated from one site to the next. The wealth of information kept her reading for long minutes.

Chapter 42

At a booth near the back of Asian Fusion, Emmett waved.

The long, narrow restaurant bustled with activity. Located two storefronts down from Mullaney's Pharmacy, the place was a favorite among locals.

Vale wended past the line of patrons in the take-out line. Emmett gave her a kiss before she slid into the booth across from him.

He handed over a menu. "How are you holding up?"

"I could use eight hours of uninterrupted sleep. Last night with my sister, being unable to wake her up . . . it was frightening. Thankfully the paramedics arrived fast. She's fine now, but I'm still jittery."

Emmett placed his hand on hers. "You must be exhausted."

And excited or nervous—or both. Pinning down her emotions proved impossible, and the urge to share the plan nearly spilled out. Vale rubbed her lips together. It was best to discuss the surrogacy option with Blythe first. Tomorrow morning, when they were both fresh.

Why worry Emmett unnecessarily?

He asked, "How's she doing?"

"She sounded okay the last time I called. She'll be released soon. Mom and Grant will drive her back to Nana's."

"Where's Iris?"

"At the shop. Nana made an appearance right before I left. Something about catching up on bookkeeping, but I suspect she's giving Mom and Grant alone time with Blythe." Vale ran a finger down the menu. "I met Booker today. He brought some of Blythe's things over to Nana's."

Emmett set his menu aside. "What's he like?"

"I don't know what I expected . . . a sports jock with a big ego, I suppose. Who could blame him? But he's sweet. Down-to-earth and totally in love with my sister. Booker asked me to talk to Blythe, see if I can help patch things up between them. They're supposed to have a big talk on May 10, when he finally gets a day off. But I got the impression he's looking for insurance."

"That's a big ask."

"You never know." She couldn't resist giving a jaunty shrug. "Blythe may come around. I didn't make any promises, but I did send him off to the hospital. I hope it went well."

The waitress came to take their order. When Vale couldn't decide what she'd like, Emmett selected pineapple chicken and Mongolian beef. Within minutes, the food arrived. A comfortable silence enveloped them as they shared the entrees.

When had they become so relaxed together? Spearing a chunk of pineapple, Vale tried to recall. From the very beginning? Emmett gave her a sense of wholeness. Of well-being.

He was also generous with his time. With silent amusement, she toyed with her meal as people stopped by their booth to say hello to the local pharmacist. An older couple, a boy with a smattering of freckles, a heavyset man—at each interruption, Emmett set down his fork and shared pleasantries.

At last, he resumed eating. Beneath the table, Vale slipped off her pumps.

"Emmett?"

"Hmm?"

"You're close to your sisters."

"I am."

"What would you do for them?" She brushed her toes against his ankles, drawing a grin. "I'm talking about major stuff. The things that really matter."

"As in a life-or-death situation?"

"Basically."

He steered a bite of Mongolian beef to his mouth, hesitated. "Like, would I give one of my sisters a kidney?"

"You would, right?"

"I'd talk to you first."

The response lifted her brows. "You would?"

"You love me."

The confidence in his voice didn't stop Vale from bobbing her head in the affirmative. "I do," she murmured.

"The inference being, you might feel territorial about my kidneys. If you're in a serious relationship, you shouldn't dole out body parts. Not without your partner's go-ahead." Popping the beef into his mouth, he chewed thoughtfully. Eyes sparkling, he added, "If you're seeking the go-ahead, I won't stop you from giving Blythe a kidney. I draw the line at your heart. That particular organ belongs to me."

The witty side to Emmett's personality was a new discovery. As was his ability to surprise her.

Chapter 43

That night, Vale managed to sleep in snatches.

The cramps from her period were a nuisance. The discomfort, however, seemed a minor inconvenience. Every few hours, a fresh bolt of enthusiasm snapped her eyes open and made her reach for her laptop. Snuggling against the pillows, she reread her favorite testimonials. All were from sisters who'd embarked together on the journey she'd soon propose to Blythe.

Despite the lack of sleep, Vale felt energized. Even more so when, near dawn, Blythe's door creaked open.

Footfalls padded down the stairs. Vale leaped off the bed.

She found her sister on the front porch, surveying the retreating night. The air held a stillness that seemed magical. That perfect, silent moment before daybreak.

"Hey." Vale joined her at the railing. "You're up early."

"Look who's talking." Blythe arched a brow. "You look positively cheerful."

"I do feel good." She gave her sister an appraising glance. "You look better. How are you feeling?"

"Like a woman in need of a serious do-over. No more drinking or sleeping meds. I might take a run this morning. Want to join me if I do?"

"Sure."

Vale was about to add something else. The boxes snagged her attention. Still pressed up against the house where Booker had left them. With a start, she realized she'd forgotten to carry them inside. In the rush to get ready for work yesterday, the task had slipped her mind.

Following her gaze, Blythe said, "It's all right. When Booker came to the hospital, he mentioned bringing them over."

"Do you need help carrying them upstairs?"

"Don't waste your time. I can't bring myself to unpack them."

"I'm glad. They don't belong here. You don't either, little sister."

"I know." Blythe lowered her elbows to the railing. "I've been thinking about everything you said yesterday. Wondering if the losses I've been through are driving me to a bad decision. All I've dreamed about since Booker proposed was having his baby. Watching our child grow and thrive. Doing the rounds of Little League, joining the PTA. Is it wrong to want something so much?"

"Of course not. Especially since I have a solution."

Disbelief glossed her sister's features. "Like what?"

In response, she guided Blythe to a chair. Once they were both seated, Vale clasped her hands together. A bird darted across the yard as she collected her thoughts.

After a beat, she said, "Are you familiar with surrogate parenting?"

"I've heard of it." Blythe paused for a long moment. Then she said, "To be honest, I wouldn't feel comfortable hiring a woman to carry our child. Booker's career makes him too high-profile . . . What if the surrogate changed her mind? Or went to the media? Or wrote a tell-all book after we took custody of our child? Celebrity has its drawbacks, Vale. I'd never take the chance."

"The surrogate *won't* change her mind or publicize the pregnancy."

"You don't know that."

"Yes, I do. *I'm* the surrogate. I'll carry your baby."

Blythe stared at her.

"We aren't blazing new trails here. I've found lots of instances of a woman carrying a baby for her sister. It's not uncommon. There are cases across the US dating back to the 1980s. In fact, many of the original surrogacy contracts were made between family members. You and Booker can *make* a baby—you just need a pod to grow the pea." When her sister continued to stare at her, clearly dazed, Vale added, "There are no laws in Pennsylvania prohibiting gestational surrogacy. Our case will be treated like a private adoption. We'll need an attorney to submit a prebirth order, but that's simple."

At last, Blythe found her voice. "What's a prebirth order?"

"A document listing you and Booker as the baby's legal parents. We'll have an attorney file the request with the court when I'm five months pregnant. When I deliver your baby, the prebirth order will transfer to the birth certificate."

A glimmer of hope crested in her sister's eyes. "You've really done your research."

"I have."

"I don't know what to say."

"Say yes! Let's do this."

Stunned, Blythe fell back in her chair. A wave of emotion shook through her. Covering her mouth, she muffled a sob.

There was no missing the gratitude brimming on her features.

Chapter 44

Emmett planned a Friday night out. A new French restaurant and a stroll on Race Street Pier afterward to listen to a live band.

Vale asked him to cancel. She didn't explain why she preferred to stay in.

They met at his house at precisely six o'clock. They were both carrying bags from the grocery store.

"I'll cook," he volunteered, leading her inside. "Do you like fish tacos?"

"Who doesn't?" She declined to add that it was a healthier option than the fried chicken and macaroni salad she'd grabbed in the deli department. "Should I help with the prep?"

"No need. Put your feet up, relax."

He went upstairs to change. With jittery movements, Vale unpacked the groceries. She nearly dropped the fried chicken on the way to the fridge. She took a deep breath. It didn't still the anxiety leaping through her.

In a flash, Emmett reappeared in soft jeans and a Phillies T-shirt.

Well, if that isn't appropriate. She couldn't stop the grin from spreading across her lips.

Today—in between dropping plants at Green Iris and drawing withering looks from her grandmother and Detta—she'd received a flurry of calls from her sister. Blythe had driven over to see Booker.

While he'd been dumbfounded at first, he *was* on board with the surrogacy plan. Ecstatically so. After helping Blythe move her belongings back into their apartment on Rittenhouse Square, he'd shared the news with team member Enrico Gonzales. Enrico's cousin through marriage, Philadelphia attorney Lia Nobles, had agreed to draw up the surrogacy contract and submit the prebirth order to the court when the time came.

"What's so funny?" Emmett peeled the T-shirt away from his chest. "You've got something against the Phillies? Better watch it—I'll tell Booker."

Nervous laughter popped from her throat. "I love the Phillies. You have no idea how much." She got hold of herself as he walked to the sink and washed his hands. Then she added, "Blythe is back with Booker."

"That's great! What turned it around?"

"The boxes, at first. The ones Booker left at the house yesterday. Blythe couldn't bring herself to unpack them."

"Makes sense. Sometimes it's the little things that make you stop and question what you're doing. If you're making the wrong decision." Emmett found a skillet and placed it on the stove. "Did you ever get to the bottom of why she was considering divorce?"

Shame bit at Vale. "At first, I thought she was running around on Booker. I didn't feel right, telling you."

"Don't worry about it. Your loyalty is one of the reasons why I love you." On the way to the spice rack, he gave her a peck on the cheek. "What was the problem?"

"Blythe can't carry a baby to term. She's had four miscarriages."

The disclosure brought him to a standstill. Then he closed the spice rack. In slow motion, he retraced his steps to her side.

She had to give Emmett credit. He was a quick study.

"Vale, last night at Asian Fusion—what you asked, about my sisters. What I'd do for them." With the gentlest movement, he steered a lock of her hair behind her shoulder. Rested his palm at the base of her neck. "It wasn't a theoretical question."

"No."

"So you want to . . . ?"

"Carry their baby. Give my sister and Booker the child they've dreamed of having."

"Every pregnancy is a risk."

"I understand the risks."

"You're talking about a year out of your life. It's a big sacrifice."

"One I'm willing to make."

Emmett blew out a breath. "You're certain about this?"

"I've spent the last day researching gestational surrogacy and pregnancy in general. I'm in great shape. I want to do this for my sister. I'm positively sure."

Emmett folded her into his arms. Rested his chin on the crown of her head. "Assuming you pass a physical, which I expect you will . . . once you begin treatments at the fertility clinic, we'll have to abstain. For months, possibly. You know that, right? No intimacy until the gynecologist is sure you're pregnant."

She pressed her cheek against his chest. Listened to the steady thump of his heart.

Then she laughed. "It's strange, hearing you talk about sex when we haven't yet—"

"There's no time like the present." Lifting her chin, he kissed her. "If you want to skip the fish tacos, we can go upstairs."

Vale sighed. She'd gladly skip dinner. *If only.*

"Sorry to disappoint. I'm menstruating."

"Some guys have all the luck."

Smiling, she rubbed her nose across his. "We still have Pittsburgh. Did you book the hotel?" Doubt crested inside her. "Unless you'd rather wait."

Emmett's hold around her waist tightened. "Not on your life."

Chapter 45

"Cold hands!"

Vale warded Natty off before she trailed snow all the way to the couch in her quest to check on Mr. Mysterious. As usual, the child had forgotten to put her mittens on before leaving the elementary school. Under no circumstance was Vale allowing those cold fingers anywhere near her belly.

Outside, the school bus trundled off into the February snowfall.

"Okay, okay." Natty backed up. "I'll warm them up."

With ill-concealed excitement, Natty kicked off her boots. She flung down her book bag, peeled off her coat, and briskly rubbed her hands together.

In a new habit, she now hopped off the school bus and ran next door to check if Vale was home. Weekends too. The journey usually ended in disappointment since Vale was determined to continue working at Green Iris full-time. At least until swollen ankles and her pea-size bladder stopped her.

Given the choice, she'd gladly skip the third trimester. Backaches, heartburn, the strange cravings for cheese omelets at three a.m.—twice, when Blythe stayed over at their grandmother's house, Vale had sent her on late-night food runs. Being able to give her sister the ultimate gift made it all worthwhile, but the process left a lot to be desired. At this rate, Vale would lose sight of her feet soon. She no longer walked; she waddled.

Natty, however, found the third trimester fascinating.

She'd nicknamed Blythe and Booker's happily gestating son *Mr. Mysterious*. More than anything, Natty wanted to learn the name they'd chosen for him.

Vale was curious too. Even so, she didn't mind waiting until the baby's due date in April to find out.

Approaching, Natty wiggled her fingers. "They're toasty warm, honest."

"Hold out your hands. Let me check."

"Jeez, you're picky."

Vale found the temperature of the kid's fingertips acceptable. Relenting, she rolled up her sweater. She eyed her baby bump; she was beginning to resemble Buddha.

"You could save us both a lot of trouble by wearing mittens," she said. "Why don't you put them on before you get on the bus?"

"I forgot."

"Well, go on. You can say hello."

Lowering her hand, Natty made small circles across Vale's tummy. Predictably, the movement started a flutter. Mr. Mysterious was an active baby, especially in the afternoons.

"He's kicking!"

"He likes you."

"I can't wait to meet him." Natty sighed. "Does it hurt when he kicks?"

Only when I need to pee. "Not really," Vale assured her. "He feels more like a tiny fish swimming around inside me."

"Who do you suppose he'll be more like—Booker or Blythe?"

The question warmed Vale. Secretly she hoped he was a perfect mix, taking after them both.

"Babies inherit traits from both parents. Some of those traits are obvious right away, but others take time to develop. Don't expect to be able to tell immediately, Natty. Babies change and grow quickly. Sometimes they resemble one parent at first, then later, the other."

"Do you care who Mr. Mysterious takes after?"

"Not even a little. I'll adore my nephew's chubby cheeks and every one of his tiny toes whether he resembles Booker or my sister."

"Emmett hopes the baby takes after Booker. He's rooting for a future starting pitcher for the Phillies." Natty wrinkled her nose. "I'm not supposed to tell you. Don't let Emmett know I blabbed."

Vale grinned. "I won't."

The news didn't surprise her. Emmett's love of the Phillies ran deep. During the last months, he'd formed a close friendship with Booker. Whenever they got together as a foursome, Emmett and Booker delved quickly into conversation. Blythe would lob Vale a pleased glance that was easy to decipher. *They get along like brothers-in-law.*

There'd been no talk of marriage—not yet—but Emmett had been incredibly supportive throughout the pregnancy, reminding Vale that she looked beautiful, propping her swollen feet on his lap for massages whenever they caught a movie at his house. Lately, she'd begun spending more nights at his place, aware of the question Emmett seemed ready to ask—but which he was holding off on posing until after her delivery date, when they'd have their lives back to themselves.

The doorbell rang. Three short rings, a pause, then three more. A code established by Natty's new babysitter, a girl from the high school.

"Oops—gotta go." Natty sprinted from the room.

As she dashed out, Audrey came in. Shaking a dusting of snow from her coat, she smiled in greeting.

Unlike Natty, who wasted time daily running between houses, the sensible Audrey checked her daughter's work schedule each week. Without fail, she stopped by on Vale's days off.

Joining Vale on the coach, she rustled open a silvery bag. "This is a dry brush. It helps with circulation. How *are* your legs?"

"Tingly most of the time. I'd love to take more walks."

"Do laps around your grandmother's house. It's too icy outside."

"I know. I'm sticking to indoor laps until the weather breaks."

Murmuring her thanks, Vale accepted the gift. Audrey seemed unable to visit without bringing something along. Comfy no-slip socks, a buttery-soft maternity robe—the peace offerings covered the awkward silences when they weren't sure what to say to each other. Would they ever scrape all the frost off their conversations? Some days they did better than others.

Building a true mother-daughter bond would take time.

Her mother asked, "Are you still having trouble sleeping?"

"On and off. The body pillow helps." Vale now relied on the U-shaped pillow, a Christmas gift from her mother and Grant.

"It's marvelous, isn't it? Why weren't those pillows available during my pregnancies? With both you and Blythe, I spent the last trimester with a mountain of pillows in bed, unable to get comfortable." Audrey paused, her gaze faraway. Then she smiled. "You know, there *are* benefits to having more than one child. After the first pregnancy, your body is primed for the next. Everything seems easier, from staying in shape to managing breastfeeding. At least that was my experience."

A subtle hint, one her mother had made before. *Marry Emmett, and don't wait too long to start your own family.* Becoming a grandmother delighted Audrey. If she could pull the feat off twice, she clearly didn't mind.

Skirting the topic, Vale said, "Would you like a cup of tea?" Mulling over a second pregnancy—and marriage—could wait until after Mr. Mysterious's birth.

"Oh, I can't stay long. I must get back to the office. Grant and I are both working late tonight." Distress puckered her mother's brows. "Do you need help dressing for dinner? I won't dash off if you do."

"Getting ready isn't a problem. I've chosen a nice, stretchy skirt and a blouse." With careful movements, Vale eased herself up from the couch. "I'm done steering anything over my head until *after* the delivery."

"Is Blythe picking you up?"

"At six o'clock." They were meeting Iris and Detta for dinner in Queen Village.

With a quick kiss, her mother left. Vale went upstairs and took her time showering. After she blew her hair dry and donned a robe, she padded into her bedroom. Absently, she glanced at her phone on the nightstand.

Since last year, she'd avoided getting in touch with her father.

Nor did Bo attempt to call. He was plainly aware Vale wasn't ready to speak with him. He didn't know about her relationship with Emmett or that she'd chosen to become a surrogate for Blythe. So many wonderful changes, yet her father knew about none of them.

The now-familiar guilt sifted through Vale. Why keep one parent in the doghouse while forgiving the other? The terrible choices they'd made in their own lives no longer mattered. Sure, both Audrey and Bo had failed in parenting her well, or even adequately—but that was the past, and Vale refused to let it color her experience of the here and now. She didn't have to carry the burden of their guilt like a pack mule. She was happy. Confident in her ability to map out her own future.

She reminded herself that she'd been angry with both of her parents. Yet Audrey, with her short visits and generous gifts, was once again part of Vale's life.

Call Bo? She'd been considering the option for weeks.

Reaching for her phone, Vale quickly dialed.

Bo picked up on the first ring. "Hey, blue eyes!"

She swallowed down her nerves. "Hi, Dad."

"How are you? I'm so glad you called."

"I'm great." The tension melted from her shoulders. "How are you?"

"I'm fine. Slogging through a slow February tending bar. There's not much night life in Pittsburgh when the temps drop into the single digits." A long silence, then: "Remember when we tore out all the drywall ourselves the moment our closing on the Crafty Cocktail ended? I was sure we'd both break our backs."

Vale laughed. "It was dumb, not hiring a contractor at the outset." One of the many ways they'd scrimped to get the place open. "Lucky for us, Nana gave me the cash so we could hire someone reliable. She was worried I'd take an eye out, swinging a hammer."

"You almost did, once or twice. Me too."

They steered the conversation to other topics. With the Steelers out of the running, which team would they root for at the Super Bowl? Would spring come early to Pennsylvania? When they ran out of small talk, Bo cleared his throat before saying, "I miss you, Vale."

"I miss you too, Dad."

"Can I come and see you sometime?"

"Sure. Come whenever you'd like."

"Does next Monday work?"

"Monday's great." Sinking onto the bed, Vale hesitated. A grin broke across her mouth. "There *are* some things I should tell you."

"I'm all ears."

"Well, I've met a really nice man."

"Good for you! What's he like?"

"He's wonderful. I can't wait for you to meet Emmett. And there's something else." Vale rested her hand on her belly. "It's about me and Blythe . . ."

Chapter 46

A buzzy elation ran through Blythe's veins as she scanned the busy restaurant.

"Looks like we beat Nana and Detta here," Vale said, unbuttoning her coat.

"I got a text from Nana. They'll arrive soon. A few stray customers were holding them up."

After she helped Vale peel off her coat, Blythe motioned to the maître d'. She'd reserved the private room at the back of Rosanna's, a seafood restaurant near Rittenhouse Square. During the baseball season, whenever the Phillies athletes and their wives dined out late at Rosanna's, the restaurant's staff would lead them in through the service door to the private room. Come through the main entrance, and Booker and his teammates would spend long minutes signing autographs.

The maître d' led them toward the back of the restaurant. He motioned them to a dimly lit hallway.

Vale arched a brow. "Where's he taking us?"

"You'll see."

Normally the private room featured a long table with seating for twenty. Per Blythe's instructions, the staff had replaced the table with a cozy four-top. The chandelier threw sparkles across the Baccarat glasses and rose-tinted plates.

On a sigh, Vale eased into a deeply cushioned chair. "I'm afraid to ask what you're spending on dinner."

"We're celebrating."

Vale patted her tummy. "We still have two months until your little bruiser makes his grand entrance. Aren't you being hasty?"

Blythe was spared from answering. Their grandmother and Detta bustled in. They'd managed to freshen their makeup and change into dresses—apparently at the shop, after finishing with customers.

Detta shimmied her shoulders. "I'm so excited!" Dropping into a chair, she looked expectantly at Blythe. "Have you told her?"

Iris swatted her. "Don't spoil the surprise."

"What surprise?" Vale asked.

The question went unanswered as three waiters came in. They ferried salads, a crusty loaf of bread, and alcohol-free mango spritzers. Blythe had ordered the starters ahead of time. Lately, Vale needed sustenance every few hours, growing cranky if required to wait too long between meals.

Reaching for the loaf, Vale tore off a chunk. "Nana, would you pass the butter?"

"Here you go, pumpkin. Now, don't eat too much bread. You'll spoil your dinner."

"Trust me, I won't. I'm famished." Vale murmured her thanks as a waiter handed her a menu. "What's good here, Blythe?"

"Everything."

"I can't decide."

"If fish doesn't appeal, the filet mignon is fabulous," Blythe said, pulling a document from her purse. The gesture went unnoticed as Vale buttered her bread.

On cue, Iris handed over two Montblanc pens she'd purchased to commemorate the moment.

One for Blythe, the other for Vale.

Vale caught the interchange. "Okay, what's going on?" She appeared torn between curiosity and hunger.

Blythe took a deep breath. On the exhale, she announced, "We're going into business together. No arguing—it's already done." Pushing Vale's plate aside, she set the document before her. "All you have to do is sign. Right here, at the bottom of the second page."

Taking the contract, Vale read quickly. "This is a buyout for Green Iris."

"Yes."

"Financed by you and Booker . . . and giving me fifty percent ownership."

Reluctance crowded Vale's eyes. In response, Blythe scooted her chair closer.

"Vale, you've refused to let us do anything to thank you, other than cover your medical expenses. Nana and Detta will continue working at the shop part-time, but they're no longer the owners. You and I own Green Iris, fifty-fifty."

Vale pushed the pages away. "Blythe, this is an incredibly sweet gesture. But I can't accept. How can I let you give me half ownership? Use the money to buy a house. This is too much."

It's nowhere near enough.

Love for her sister threatened to steal Blythe's voice. Eyes blurring, she pressed the contract into Vale's hands. "I'll buy a house later," she said. "I want to own Green Iris with you."

"You don't even like plants."

"You'll teach me everything you know."

"We'll help," Detta put in. "Blythe will pick up the ins and outs of horticulture in a snap."

Vale gave her head a resolute shake. "I'm not a charity case!" She stabbed a finger on the contract. "My half is valued well past six figures. No one with a shred of decency sponges that much cold hard cash off her little sister. I'd feel like a thief!"

The objection sent a surge of emotion sweeping through Blythe. Throughout her sister's pregnancy, she'd worried about the green devil of envy getting in the way of their growing affection. Of feeling jealousy as her baby grew inside Vale. Yet she'd felt nothing but awe.

And love, for the gift Vale was selflessly giving her. A child. A family, with Booker.

Blythe threw up her hands. Then she swiped at her watery eyes.

"Oh, Vale—I'm not doing this for you," she blurted, her voice hoarse with gratitude. "I'm doing this for *us*. For you *and* me. If we're in business together, we'll see each other nearly every day. I want to own Green Iris with you. Who cares where the money comes from? Let's do this."

Rising from her chair, Iris went to Vale. "Say yes, pumpkin. Blythe wants to own the shop with you. Don't you see?"

Vale sat in rapt amazement. After a beat, her attention fell upon the contract.

Iris handed over a pen.

It hovered in the air as Vale's expression shifted. "We're young," she murmured, her eyes suddenly bright. Twirling the pen between thumb and forefinger, she regarded Blythe. "We can expand Green Iris. Open a second store in the suburbs. Not right away—we should wait until we're both past the busy-mommy years. Put together an expansion plan we'll implement in our late thirties."

Blythe clapped her hands together. "I love the idea! We'll find ways to give back to the community."

"Like donations to Philadelphia's community gardens."

"Yes! What if we open a nursery in one of the burbs with room for children's gardens? Little vegetable plots in the summer."

"Our kids will work there too."

With amusement, Iris cast Detta a glance. "My granddaughters, taking over the world."

Chapter 47

April and May

On a blustery day in April, Noah Booker Banks was born at 3:20 in the afternoon.

Despite Blythe's lobbying, her self-effacing husband refused to saddle his son with his famous name. There would be no Booker Banks Jr. What if the boy grew up fascinated by science or the arts, without the slightest interest in picking up a baseball?

The debate was quickly put to rest. Noah was a good, strong name. For a strapping ten-pound infant, it suited well. Noah was a placid baby, a trait Vale suspected he'd inherited from his father. Not that Blythe hadn't left her mark too: by her son's first-month birthday, wisps of curly brown hair were sprouting on his scalp like delicate feathers.

"Give Auntie Vale a big kiss." Blythe leaned close with her baby, allowing Vale to run her palm across his incredibly soft curls.

Noah blinked his large butterfly eyes. Chuckling, Vale kissed his rosy cheek.

Then she frowned at her sister. "Why don't you *ever* listen, peaches? I planned to drop the milk at your place this afternoon. FYI, I'm not a slacker." Vale had agreed to supply breast milk until Noah reached the three-month mark. A minor inconvenience to ensure her nephew's continued good health. "You've been coming over to Nana's house seventy percent of the time. We agreed to share the driving, fifty-fifty."

"It's Saturday. I'm saving you the trip." Blythe lowered herself into one of the new rocking chairs their grandmother had installed in Vale's bedroom.

Settling into the other rocking chair, Vale shifted down her bathrobe. She attached the breast pump. Blythe's knees brushed against hers as they both began rocking.

Noah gurgled in Blythe's arms. Brushing her nose across his forehead, she gave Vale an appraising glance. "How's Emmett?" she asked.

"He's got a major case of spring fever."

"What do you mean?"

"He's gutting the guest bathroom in his house. The last time I checked, he was back on YouTube, learning new tricks for setting in tile." He'd also dragged a sawhorse and a stack of lumber upstairs. Vale had no idea what he was up to next. Punching out walls for an addition to the house? She didn't dare ask.

Blythe gave her a look of impatience. "I meant, how are *you* and Emmett? Give me the juicy details."

"Like I have any. Okay, here's one—he's now officially the most patient man on earth. We should give him an award or something." Switching breasts, Vale resumed pumping. "We've gone on several walks together, but that's about it."

"No cozy nights at his place, snuggling on the couch and watching movies?"

"Blythe, I'm conked out most nights. In bed earlier than the average toddler."

"Doing what—sleeping or hiding from Emmett? Honestly, Vale. I've never thought of you as gutless. Don't make me revise my opinion."

Filling the bottle, Vale promptly handed it to her sister. Blythe's son required no prodding; Noah took the bottle and began sucking in earnest. While his pudgy hands waved about, Vale poked at the jelly surrounding her middle.

She released an exasperated breath. "Okay, maybe I'm feeling less than confident," she admitted. "I'm not ready to let Emmett see me in a state of undress. Nursing bras and a jiggly belly are *not* conducive to romance."

"Stop being ridiculous. Emmett is head over heels for you. A little postdelivery flab won't put him off. Take a nap this afternoon and see him tonight. He'll understand if you don't want to stay out late."

Iris breezed into the bedroom. "Emmett *will* understand." She handed Vale a bouquet of tea roses—the third bouquet from Emmett this week. "Pumpkin, he's a mature man. He'll also understand if you don't want him anywhere near your leaky breasts. It's Saturday night. Go out for a nice meal, live a little. He's waited long enough for some alone time."

Relenting, Vale pulled out her phone. After thanking Emmett for the roses, she asked, "Should we go out tonight? I'm game if you are."

"That's a great idea, sweetheart." There was no missing the pleasure in his voice. "The reservation is all set—Rue de Jean, six thirty."

"Wait. You made a reservation *before* I called? Kudos on thinking ahead."

In response, Emmett released a low, throaty laugh that tickled her all the way to her toes. "Vale, I've made a reservation every Saturday night for the last three weeks. I'll pick you up at six."

Per Blythe's advice, Vale took a nap in the afternoon. After a warm, leisurely shower, she donned her forgiving sapphire-blue cocktail dress—another gift from her shopaholic mother. The empire waist hid the extra padding on her tummy while showing off her legs. After a spritz of perfume, Vale ran a brush through her hair one last time. Twirling before the mirror, she felt reasonably attractive.

Throwing a sweater across her shoulders, she decided to wait on the porch. Clouds raced across the sky. The air smelled fresh, with the first hints of spring. It seemed so long ago the Crafty Cocktail had burned down. Her life had taken a 180-degree turn since then.

In a good way. She smiled.

In a *great* way.

Emmett steered his car into the driveway and got out. Her spirits lifted as he tossed the car keys into the air and neatly caught them, his attention latching suddenly on her.

"New dress?" His gaze took a hungry stroll down her frame.

"From my mother." Vale plucked at the silky material. "I can't imagine how she chose a dress that fits me perfectly. She has a sixth sense about fashion."

"You look gorgeous."

"You do too."

Meeting him at the bottom of the steps, she fingered the tie at his throat. Let her hand coast across the coarse skin of his chin. Longing stirred inside her. She *had* missed him. More than she'd realized.

Emmett cleared his throat. "Stop undressing me with your eyes." He grinned. "There's a limit to my endurance."

"Mine too," she admitted.

"Come over after we eat. Or move in permanently. I'd ask the big question, but I'm not sure you're ready to hear it."

She looked up at him with an exquisite blend of love and delight. "What question?" she asked coyly.

He reached for her hand. "Let's talk about it over dinner."

ACKNOWLEDGMENTS

This book grew out of conversations I've been privileged to have with women struggling with infertility. As the adoptive mother of four beautiful, healthy, and now adult children, I find the topic often arises in my personal life, and when chatting with readers. Special thanks to my brilliant editor Christopher Werner, for helping to shape the initial storyline with sensitivity and care, and for taking the time from his busy schedule to read early drafts.

My heartfelt thanks to J. D. for sharing her personal surrogacy journey during the writing of *A Brighter Flame*, and Dr. Elaine Eustis, MD, for providing expertise regarding female infertility. Any errors of fact in the book are solely my own.

The publishing journey is demanding, and I'm grateful to work with so many tireless, dedicated professionals: my agent and trusted friend Pamela Harty of the Knight Agency, Lake Union editorial director Danielle Marshall, author relations manager Gabriella Dumpit, developmental editor Krista Stroever, copyeditor Sarah Engel, production manager Jen Bentham, and proofreader Kellie Osborne. Heartfelt thanks to Caroline Teagle Johnson for the lovely cover design.

For helping my books reach a wider audience, many thanks to Crystal Patriarche and the fantastic team at BookSparks; Suzanne Weinstein Leopold and the fun reviewers at Suzy Approved Book Tours; Pulpwood Queen Kathleen Murphy; and the many generous book bloggers, reviewers, and bookstagrammers who have sent my publishing career aloft.

To professor Dr. Tricia Nolfi—who managed to chase down research during the coronavirus pandemic, often on short notice—I love you, sis. It's a blessing to have a baby sister with your savvy, humor, and expertise.

And to Barry, for reading every review throughout the years and believing even when I entertained doubts. I love you, always.

ABOUT THE AUTHOR

Photo © 2016 Melissa Miley

Christine Nolfi is the author of *The Passing Storm*, which *Publishers Weekly* called "tautly plotted, expertly characterized, and genuinely riveting"; *The Road She Left Behind*, a top book club pick by *Working Mother* and *Parade* magazines; the award-winning Sweet Lake Series: *Sweet Lake, The Comfort of Secrets,* and *The Season of Silver Linings*; and other titles. A native of Ohio, Christine now resides in South Carolina with her husband and their crazy wheaten terrier, Lucy. For more information, visit www.christinenolfi.com.